SCOURGE OF STARS

Book Two of
THE SIGIL TRILOGY

Books by Henry Gee

Fiction

The Sigil Trilogy
1: Siege of Stars
2: Scourge of Stars
3: Rage of Stars

By The Sea
Futures from *Nature* (editor)

Nonfiction

The Beowulf Effect (forthcoming)
The Science of Middle-earth: revised e-book edition (forth-coming)
The Science of Middle-earth
Jacob's Ladder
In Search of Deep Time
Before The Backbone
A Field Guide to Dinosaurs (with Luis V. Rey)
Shaking the Tree (editor)
Rise of the Dragon (editor)

Praise for The Sigil Trilogy

"Great stuff. Touches of Douglas Adams, Barrington Bayley, David Britton and Steve Ayelet only emphasise the splendid originality of this book. Henry Gee is thoughtful, funny, original. And pretty thoroughly mind-expanding in the tradition of Wells, David Lindsay, Stapledon and Clarke. In fact everything you yearn to find in a good contemporary SF novel. Really enjoyed it!"
—SFWA Grandmaster **Michael Moorcock**

"Siege is compelling, grandiose, and breathtaking in its spacetime and its characters are intriguing, personal, and complex....This book of Henry's is going to be high on the charts."
—Greg Laden, scienceblogs.com

"One of the very best books I've ever read."
—Critique.org

"I got so engrossed in it that I could not put it down. Siege of Stars is a very good Sci-Fi novel, in the tradition of Arthur C. Clarke and Ray Bradbury. It spans space and time on a grand scale, but at the same time delves into the questions of what it means to be human. I recommend this book."
—Lee Gimenez, bestselling author of *The Nanotech Murders*

SCOURGE OF STARS

Book Two of
THE SIGIL TRILOGY

Henry Gee

ReAnimus Press

Breathing Life into Great Books

ReAnimus Press
1100 Johnson Road #16-143
Golden, CO 80402
www.ReAnimus.com

Cover art by Clay Hagebusch

ISBN-13: 978-0615696300

First print edition: September, 2012

10 9 8 7 6 5 4 3 2 1

For Karl, who gave his name to a small, destructive and (mercifully) fictional asteroid.

Acknowledgments

The germ of this story — or, rather, two germs — can be found in two SF vignettes I wrote in *Nature*, one pseudonymously. One, called *Et in articulo mortis* (*Nature* **405**, 21; 2000) describes Post-Embryonic Petrosis as an evolutionary response to star-hungry dragons. The other, *Are We Not Men?* (*Nature* **435**, 1286; 2005) reported the emergence of many hitherto-mythical hominids onto the world stage, including Sand Druids and Jive Monkeys. Perhaps ill-advisedly, I thought I'd put the two ideas together in a box and see what came out. The result is as you see.

I offer my thanks to Karl Ziemelis, Andrew Burt, Vonda McIntyre, Ian Watson, Jack Cohen, Brian Clegg, Bruce Goatly, John Gilbey, Richard P. Grant, Heather Corbett Etchevers, Jennifer Rohn, Chris Surridge, Peter Watts and all the residents of the LabLit community forums, and the many others who read various drafts of this book, for their continuing encouragement and comments. David Doughan and Adam Rutherford helped me with my Latin, and Tony Kerstein with my Hebrew.

Chapter 1: Philanthropist

Aspen, Colorado, Earth, January 2033

As I biheeld into the eest an heigh to the sonne,
I seigh a tour on a toft trieliche ymaked,
A deep dale bynethe, a dongeon therinne,
With depe diches and derke and dredfulle of sighte.

(As I looked to the east, towards the sunrise
I saw a tower on a hill, cleverly built
A deep dale beneath, a dungeon inside
With deep ditches, and dark and dreadful to see.)

William Langland — *The Vision of Piers Plowman*

The New Year was ushered in with a gale and accompanying blizzard. Jack, however, had business that was too urgent to be delayed by such things as mere weather. As Director of the nominally Cambridge-based Merlin Technologies Institute for Historical Geomorphology, he needed to fly to the New York offices of Merlin Technologies' philanthropic arm for an urgent meeting with the Board. The reason was — as it so often is — money. The new excavation at Souris Saint-Michel had the potential to be so huge that Jack and Jadis and their small crew would never cope. Jack would propose that the Institute relocate from Cambridge to Saint-Rogatien, where it would devote ninety per cent of its resources to Souris Saint-Michel.

After showing them the data and pictures acquired so far, he'd hit them with detailed plans for the immediate acquisition of plant and expertise, requiring a massive injection of capital and a thirty-fold increase in operating budget. Even though the Institute had been set up with the purpose of

11

supporting Jack and Jadis' work, it was an audacious plan, even reckless, and he knew it. His hopes were not high.

Given the stakes, he'd very much wanted Jadis to come too, as (he'd felt) their chances would have been higher were their presentation backed by them both. She'd made the predictable (and justifiable) excuses about having to stay home to run a new operation that required more oversight with each day that passed, and had yet to find its feet.

But—and this Jack found disconcerting—before she'd had a chance to respond to Jack's plea in words, her eyes had flashed at him an expression of what he could only describe as having caught herself *outside* herself, and, having done so, snapped back with the horror that comes with the revelation that the world we inhabit is far from the cosy and familiar place to which we've become accustomed, but something alien, and infinitely greater.

It lasted just for an instant, but he was convinced that Jadis felt it, too, because she was edgy for the rest of the day. Jack decided not to mention it again. Her parting embrace, as he set off for the airport at Blagnac, was fractionally more urgent than usual.

"It'll be all right," he'd said, and kissed her on the top of her head. But she'd turned on her heel and walked back to the house without a word.

The cool, bland, Fifth-Avenue suite could have been the office of a cheap sting operation rather than the largest private venture capital firm in the world. Ruxton Carr clearly preferred to spend his trillions on his projects, rather than his own surroundings. Jack had never met any of the Board before except by videoconference (which, he thought, was never as good as the real thing). The six men, all of whom he'd have passed without a second glance in the street, betrayed no reaction whatsoever to Jack's performance. He was introduced to none of them, and he had no idea which one of them—if any—was the legendary Mr Carr. His presentation was received politely but in absolute silence. He'd barely got to the end of the final slide when the anonymous man at the head of the table raised his hand to an earpiece, cupping it and exchanging a word.

"Dr Corstorphine," he said, "a limousine is waiting for you in the lobby. Goodbye."

Well, that's that, Jack thought. We'll just have to do what we can with what we have, even though it would be like trying to cut down trees by scraping at them with our fingernails.

The limo took him to JFK, as he'd assumed—but not to a regular passenger terminal. Two suits met him kerbside and escorted him to a small, charcoal-black and very sleek-looking aircraft that looked more like a stealth-winged spaceplane than a business jet. Nobody said a word—he appeared to be quite alone as he boarded and strapped himself into what seemed like a rather excessive five-point harness. The jet taxied through the dark and sleet, took off very gingerly and—when it was airborne—put on the most terrific spurt of acceleration Jack had ever experienced. The harness was there for a reason. Forced back into his chair, Jack felt that he was on a roller coaster rather than a plane.

It seemed like no time at all until the plane slowed, descended and landed at a dark, snowy airstrip just like the one they'd left. The aircraft door opened and a set of steps telescoped down to the snowy ground. The warm fug of the plane was instantly replaced by the thin, bitter chill of high mountains in winter. Jack gasped for breath. The plane didn't appear to have any cabin crew, so Jack unfastened himself and stood up. He saw spots before his eyes and his head swam. They were clearly very high up. The Rockies? Stepping gingerly down the steps he saw that the plane had landed on a short runway in a high mountain valley. Bright stars poured down on every side through the clear air.

Slightly above him, on a ridge, was plainly his destination, a long, low cabin set upon a platform of massive cut stones. A welcoming yellow light poured from a picture window that ran all the way along the valley-facing side of the building. He was expected.

Jack wondered how he was going to climb to the top—he hadn't expected to bring his winter mountaineering gear—and there were no steps, nor any sign of a path up to the cabin through the pristine snowfall. And he was rapidly getting colder. He decided to climb back into the plane to await further instructions, and turned away. He was brought up short by a friendly bleeping noise behind him. He turned again to see a snowmobile, engine running, but no sign of a driver. There was a smiley face painted on the front. A cheery voice chimed from a small speaker above it. "Come on up, Dr Corstorphine," said the voice, "I've been expecting you."

Less than a minute later he was at the front door of the cabin. The door opened without his having to knock: he was met by a tiny man with huge, yellow-green, startlingly cat-like eyes in a face the color of old teak, surmounted by an unruly shock of snow-white hair. The man admitted him to a salon that ran the length of the entire cabin, the picture window at his left. At the far end was a fireplace of monumental size, and two well-worn red leather chesterfields stood, one on each side. Jack had a strong yet fleeting feeling that he'd been there before. The hairs rose on the back of his neck.

His host was wearing the bottom half of an Armani suit, held up over a red-and-white striped Jermyn Street shirt by a pair of novelty suspenders decorated with rubber tyrannosauri. His feet were bare and—Jack couldn't help but notice—remarkably hairy. His accent was straight out of London's East End. And, like an East-End costermonger, he talked non-stop.

"I don't believe we've ever actually met, Jack. May I call you Jack? I'm Ruxton Carr." Mr Carr put out a hand. Jack shook it. The grip was painfully decisive, giving the lie to the almost comedic appearance of the animated little man who stood before him. "We've been very impressed with your work. Very impressed. So naturally we'll give you everything you and Dr Markham need. Pity you didn't both come," he said, "I'd like to have met her. But I can understand why she didn't."

Jack had the impression of a cloud passing behind Carr's eyes, as if the sun had been dimmed, or that the diminutive philanthropist were searching for something buried in his mind, an irritating piece of mental grit that he knew was there but couldn't quite grasp. But it lasted no more than a moment, and Carr resumed his rapid-fire delivery, continuing as if he were really talking to himself.

"Did I say everything? Yes, everything. Don't stint. Just do it and send us the bill. Oh, sorry, Jack, you must be parched after your journey and your presentation—which went very well, I hear. Soda? Beer? Wine? Tea? All here, you know. I rarely get out of this place to... well, *you* know. Ah! Eureka..."

Carr capered off to a drinks cabinet without waiting for Jack to respond, and came back with two tumblers filled to the brim with an Islay single malt so dark and peaty that Jack almost choked, pausing only a moment to wonder how Carr had known that this was his favorite drink, even though he rarely got the opportunity to sample it, as Jadis said she hated the smell and wouldn't allow it in the house, and Jack never liked to drink on his own. How?

"Why will we be so accommodating, I hear you ask," Carr continued, "so, of course, I'll tell you. You can't take it with you, and I'm older than I look. Much older. But apart from that, the Board and I are convinced that the work you and Dr Markham are doing is of the utmost importance — the *utmost* importance. We think it might even save the planet. How will describing a city that's been dead for a gazillion years save the planet, I hear you ask? You do? Great! So of course, I'll tell you — I haven't the faintest idea.

"But I have a hunch, that's all it is, a hunch, and I always follow my hunches, because they've never let me down. Not ever. That's something that you and I have in common, I believe? Trust your hunches, Jack! In the end, they're all we've got. Like my hunch that you're an Islay man, am I right? Of course I'm right!" The little man laughed and slapped his thigh as if he'd cracked the most amazing joke.

"So drink up, Jack, you've got just enough time to meet the next suborbital window. Give my best wishes to Dr Markham. Goodbye — and good luck!"

Hunches, Jack thought, as the sleek stealth-winged private jet wafted him, his good news and several more tumblers of Laphroaig smoothly homewards at Mach 4.7, across the inky black Atlantic, the ocean hurrying backwards beneath him as if actively trying to get out of the way.

His world had been a castle built on gamble after gamble; that MacLennane had backed his own then-unframed, untested hunches about landscape, which had later borne fruit at Saint-Rogatien and now at Souris Saint-Michel. And MacLennane's last and greatest gamble — that Jack's own hunches could be brought to maturity not by some accomplished Professor, or even a rising academic star, but by an undergraduate just twenty years old, unproven and untested. Science is not built from certainties, he thought (inexplicably, in the voice of Ernestine Yanga), for we cannot extend knowledge by forever elaborating on what we already know.

No, we have to take chances. Hunches — that's what it's all about. And when he thought of his wife, his hunch was that the best chances are always those that one knows instinctively are dead certainties. He felt sure that Ruxton Carr would have agreed.

Ruxton Carr, however, had other concerns.

He had known he was ill for some time, but had always made excuses not to see a doctor. Too busy, he had always said, covering up the real reason, which was that he was frightened. Islay alone could no longer dull the ache in his chest and along his left arm. From a pocket in his trousers he drew an ornate pearl-inlaid, boxwood pillbox, flipped open the lid, and swallowed a mouthful of pills. Oxycodone. Ever his friend and ally. He poured another slug of Lagavulin to send the pills on their way, sank onto a chesterfield and closed his eyes. Just before he did so, he was conscious — semiconcious — of a tall, white-faced figure, standing, facing him. She bent down, her hair brushing his hands, his face.

"Jade?"

"It's time to go, Ruxie," she said. "Time for the last big push." She touched his wrist with one long finger, and then, just for the merest split instant, it was '79 again, the rain bucketing down outside

… he was in Khan's shop, selling music centres, when…

She…

… and then he was helpless, surrounded by noise, and blind.

Chapter 2: Infant

Gascony, France, Earth, September, 2040

And he looked up, and said, I see men as trees, walking.
Mark **8**, 24

Tom and Fairbanks were playing in the sun-baked yard outside the kitchen door, chasing the crisped, fallen leaves as they eddied and swirled in the first gusts of autumn. The boy grabbed and grasped at the leaves — missing them every time — while the dog barked encouragement. Fairbanks was now too old to do much active chasing himself. His back legs were arthritic and far too weak to propel his bulk into the air, as they once had. But he enjoyed watching the small boy run round in circles, laughing and hooting.

Which is why the big old dog was perplexed, and then worried, when the boy sat down abruptly on the ground, covered his eyes and screamed at the top of his voice. The little boy was not, (judged the dog) calling for his mistress in particular, but was instead letting out an inchoate cry of pain and terror. It reminded Fairbanks of the sound made by a vixen at bay in the field adjoining the garden, or that made by one of The Horribles' multitudinous small victims just before they'd had their necks broken. Naturally enough, Fairbanks was concerned. He advanced on his friend, whimpering, nosing apart the hands covering the boy's face, sniffing out his fear (he detected that the boy had peed himself) and trying a few consoling licks. The boy calmed down somewhat and threw his arms round the dog's neck, grasping handfuls of his mane. Then, with his face buried in the dog's fur, the boy tried to open his eyes again.

This time the searing, burning sensation wasn't quite as intense as it had been a moment earlier, when he'd opened his eyes and let the world pour in all at once. No, this time, he could smell the dog, feel the fibrous strands of his outer coat, the softer nap of his inner fur, the ripple of his muscles, and hear his steady breath and the beat of his heart.

But there was something else too, a new dimension to the smells and sounds that took the form of a large, blocky patch with indistinct edges. The patch moved slightly, taking the smells and sounds with it. And then the patch made a noise—a kind of conversational growl of encouragement—and he realized in an instant that the patch, sounds and smells went all together, and that they all belonged to Fairbanks, his most bestest friend in the whole world, who always understood, always knew.

The boy screwed his eyes up so tightly that tears began to squeeze out and ran into the house with Fairbanks in lolloping pursuit. Tom's hands and ears and nose guided him up the stairs, where he heard the quick footsteps of his mother hurrying down to greet him, her arms picking him up and hugging him, her smell tinted with anxiety—

"Darling, what's the matter?" she said. "Why are you crying?" It was only a little while later, when she had settled Tom on the sitting-room sofa, that Tom had calmed down enough to speak.

"*Maman*," he said, "my eyes hurt when I open them." but he'd refused to open them when she or Jack had asked. Afraid that Tom's eyes had trapped some irritant, they called the village doctor, who administered some drops as well as he could, and left. Later still, and long after nightfall, Tom had returned to more or less his usual, happy state, except that he kept his eyes tightly shut.

"*Maman*," he asked, "can you hear and smell with your eyes?"

She turned out the light and hugged her son.

"Yes, Darling, you can. Perhaps you'd like to try it now?"

Although he was reluctant, the burning heat on his eyelids seemed to have disappeared, and he opened them — on a dim vision of blank, angular spaces, except for one, a more curving, irregular form that was moving and changing its shape as it did so. He smelled it and knew it was his mother. Around her edges — *edges* — were lots and lots and lots of long thin lines, which he touched and discovered were his mother's hair. His hands flew to her face, which he knew to be in the middle of all the hair, and felt — saw — that it was moving in an odd way and was wet. The wetness was coming from the two large holes in her face that were her eyes.

His mother's shape changed further, as if she were some tentacled hydra, extending two long outgrowths which, rather alarmingly, got larger and larger at the ends. He began to flinch, but just in time he smelled that they were only her hands, her fingers, reaching out to caress him.

"Oh, you sweet boy," she said. "Everything's going to be all right. You'll see." Tom didn't know what she meant, but she was his *Maman* and apart from Fairbanks the centre of his world, so whatever it was, it was probably okay. He turned over and dreamed the dreams that only blind people know: dreams that he would soon leave behind.

Jadis walked very slowly downstairs, making sure she placed each foot carefully on the creaking wooden treads, in case the rich and uneasy mixture of emotions currently assaulting her mind lifted her physically off her feet. Fear, terror, dread, horror, joy — and relief. And hope. Relief that a long and nagging worry had been lifted; hope that her little son would soon be walking out into the light, unafraid.

Jack was waiting for her in the sitting room with a glass of wine, which she accepted gratefully. They both sank into the ever-more-sagging sofa in front of the fire.

"He's fine—just fine," she'd said in response to his un-voiced expression of concern. "You know," she added, "I'm probably being the classic hysterical mother..."

Jack snorted. A mother less hysterical than Jadis would be hard to imagine. The past six years had been difficult, both at work and at home, but somehow Jadis had always managed to hold everything together. As Jadis got older, her airy girlishness had faded as the steel in her had come to the fore. Although she had never, to Jack's knowledge, raised her voice at Souris Saint-Michel, he knew that some of the younger members of the eighty-strong team referred to her as the Wicked Witch. It was no coincidence that these were the team members who never stayed very long.

"What's up with Tom, then?" Jack asked. "You mightn't have been hysterical, but he was. I know he's only six, but Tom's always been unflappable. Even Fairbanks was worried."

Jadis smiled, thinking of how Fairbanks had adopted Tom as soon as he'd seen him, a tiny infant just a year old, and had never let him out of his sight. She'd lost count of the postmen, academic colleagues, friends, relations and stray visitors who'd given Fairbanks a wide berth when the vast, snarling bear of a dog thought that anyone was coming too close to his infant charge. She thought that Fairbanks had got on with Tom so well because of a shared view of the world—and wondered how much Fairbanks had actually taught Tom, perhaps without even knowing that he had. Tom was blind, and Fairbanks wouldn't have done very well on an eyesight test, either. The world of boy and dog had been one of hearing, touch and smell. But things, it seemed, were changing.

"Oh, Jack, where to begin..." sighed Jadis, grasping his right arm like a mast to steady her in a storm: "you know, all those ophthalmic surgeons, those psychologists, those specialists we took him to, one after another—and they all said that yes, he was blind, but they couldn't actually find what was wrong with him?"

"Mmm..."—he stroked her hair, teasing out each strand, spreading them all out as a great scapular around them both.

"And do you remember the one in Toulouse," she went on, "who said that he might even suddenly learn to see, one day?" Jack remembered. Ah yes, that was the one occasion he could remember—the only one—in which Jadis had become incandescently furious. He remembered how her pale skin had turned even paler, her eyes coal-black, and her hair had seemed to take on a life of its own, streaming out in all directions like turbulent seaweed, when she'd turned on the hapless specialist and said words to the effect that she'd hoped that the doctor would have spoken to her like a fellow scientist, and not give her the standard patronizing brush-off treatment; but, sadly, she wished she'd trusted her expectations instead, which were, she'd said, disarmingly, poignantly low. Not that she'd raised her voice—quite the opposite—but her tone was so commanding, her articulation so pitilessly precise, that all the doctor could do was hang his head and shuffle backwards *out of his own office*.

Jadis' constant uneasy shifts in Jack's embrace, as if she weren't entirely comfortable, said it all. She was remorseful, embarrassed, because the doctor had been right after all. But this was no time to press the point, thought Jack. Time to move things forward.

"So what do we do now?" he said.

After a thoughtful pause, Jadis sighed, and said, quite decisively, "I think we should just let things be." Having made up her mind, she relaxed suddenly as if released from some kind of possession, and sank contentedly back into Jack's embrace. "Let Tom work it out on his own. He's always done so before."

"If it ain't broke...," added Jack, but Jadis was already on the margins of sleep, as if she'd shed a heavy load that had long weighed her down, and, having been relieved of it, could now afford to collapse from exhaustion.

Staring into the sinking embers, he thought back to the long, agonized conversations they'd had a few years back, when SSM was well under way, about children. Jack had been reluctant—the memories of her pregnancy were still too painful—but Jadis, who after all (she said) had been the one who'd suffered the pain, was adamant. She kept saying something he didn't quite understand about a lost pulse, and a horrible, bloody recurrent nightmare she'd had about the Nest, and how it was about time she'd done something about it.

And then there was the dismal year or so when they'd been 'trying for a baby'—a phrase that Jack thought quite the dreariest in the English language. Despite the fact that they'd had sex more frequently than they'd ever had, none of it had been very much fun. Jack remembered one night when they were holed up in the caravan at SSM, the rain flooding down outside, and he'd had one of his extremely rare colds. Now, he thought, most men, even when running a temperature of a hundred and one, would find the prospect of opening one's eyes to find oneself being ridden by a nude and sensationally sexy woman at least cheering, if not arousing. But being told in stentorian tones that he was to 'perform' because she was ovulating and that if 'we missed this chance' we'd have to wait 'another whole month'—well, it was a turn-off.

After a while they'd both decided that this mechanically procreative effort was more likely to damage their marriage than produce offspring. Natural reproduction was a complete failure—as they'd known it probably would be. And, as it turned out (after many consultations), although Jadis' uterus had healed, there had been a lot of scarring, making the chances of implantation and placentation very low indeed, even had they managed to conceive, either naturally or *in vitro*. The only chance was some kind of surrogacy — which Jack found too weird, and Jadis flatly refused even to consider. That, or adoption.

This would have been easy but for one thing: a worldwide shortage of spare babies. The European birth-rate had been in long-term decline for decades and was now so low that children under five years old were almost never available for adoption. Babies from other parts of the world were also increasingly rare. Even in what had once been called the Third World, birth rates had been slowing, and the demographics were made more complicated by endemic war, famine and disease. Over the past decade, much of sub-Saharan Africa had been depopulated by chronic drought and famine, exacerbated by malaria, AIDS and a seemingly constant barrage of pestilences nobody had heard of before, each one more horrible than the last. Few had realized it yet, but the populations of every country between South Africa and the Equator had sunk below the level of viability. Many of these states had effectively ceased to exist except as flags of convenience, and were in fact administered by a variety of multinational concerns, some of which used them as game reserves. Elephants, lions, gorillas, cheetahs and zebras were on the increase as the human tide receded.

So, no babies there, then.

Eastern Asia had long been a source of babies for adoption, but even there the market was drying up as the regional economies soared. In fact, the trade had switched in the opposite direction as Korean and Thai would-be-parents competed for the few remaining babies in Russia and Romania.

So, no babies there, either.

Jack and Jadis were becoming reconciled to childlessness until they decided to discuss the issue with Domingo on one of his increasingly rare (and cherished) visits — his talents had been recognized in Rome and he was now, more often than not, at the Vatican. For their part, Jack and Jadis had come to regard him as their confessor, and appreciated his own concession to their agnosticism in that he always visited them in what he termed an 'unofficial' capacity — in baggy shorts and customarily eye-watering 5XL aloha shirt ("I wouldn't want anyone to know it was me," he'd said).

And he was, they thought, a good listener, and most of all a good friend. Domingo knew of Catholic agencies that rescued babies from the burgeoning slums of countries such as Brazil or the Philippines, and he'd gladly make some discreet enquiries.

For his own part, Domingo thought he'd never seen Jack and Jadis look so anxious, and his heart surged out towards them. As he wrote on his private recommendation to the agency concerned, it would not be God's will to deny children to these people. He omitted to mention, however, that these were the same people who had given him his own first taste of family life, even though he'd had to attain his own maturity to get it.

So it was that one snowbound December day in 2035, Tom Markham Corstorphine made his way up the potholed drive, swaddled in a blanket and carried in the arms of Father Domingo Sanchopanza on the last stage of a journey that had started a year earlier in the middle of Borneo, when Islamist rebels fuelled by thoughts of the Khalifa had razed a remote jungle village, massacring all the inhabitants — all except one, who had come into the world just a few hours earlier. There was one thing they should know that might change their mind, Domingo had explained, that he was blind, perhaps from the Khalifa's destruction of his village;

to which Jack and Jadis said then they would love him all the more.

Domingo handed baby Tom over to Jadis in their kitchen, with Jack and Fairbanks in attendance, all looking in wonder at the new arrival. As Jadis cradled him in her arms, cooing softly and searching every wrinkle of her new baby with her intense, slightly cross-eyed gaze, Domingo started to laugh—softly at first, but building into a great, hearty guffaw.

"You know what day it is, of course!" he said, wiping tears from his eyes with his vast, hairy arms. It had occurred to none of them that it was Christmas Day. Fairbanks jumped up at his old friend, eager to share the joke. Domingo patted him—"can you play the ox and the ass both at once, my friend?" he'd asked.

Tom managed well, and Jack and Jadis all but forgot he was blind. It wasn't until Tom was four and attending a day-nursery in a neighbouring village that they felt the real impact of his being blind. No, the teacher said in response to Jadis' evident disbelief, of course, Madame Corstorphine, you're right, he's otherwise well-adjusted and settled, but no, Madame Corstorphine, we can't have him here any more. We haven't got the resources, you know, and then there's safety to think about..."

What utter nonsense, Jadis wanted to say, before bringing him home. The happy child sat in the passenger seat of the jeep, burbling merrily about all the scrapes that he and his friends had gotten into that day, while Jadis tried to think of any cause they might have had for thinking that his lack of sight was any burden. Tom had been exploring the house since he was a toddler, coping with stairs and doors and every other hazard; since the age of two he had known the huge garden as well as she had, and played near the uncovered pond without incident.

They had even taken him to SSM and—this was the only other time she even remembered taking note of his blindness—she now recalled when she and Tom, then aged three, were visiting the long avenue they called the Champs Elysées which, like all the thoroughfares of the ancient city, had now been illuminated with giant-sized LED street lamps, so that it looked no darker nor more threatening than any other cityscape at night, for all the strangeness of the brooding polygonal monoliths and pyramids.

She had been chatting with a group of surveyors who'd just opened a structure called the Hexagon when all the lights suddenly went out, and they had been sucked into that same gut-wrenching blackness that had greeted her when, for the first time, she and Jack and the others on the first exploration crew had switched off their headlights. She heard people scream and whimper as primal darkness swept into every crevice. The blackout lasted less than ten seconds, until the backup generators came online. She had immediately looked down at Tom, holding her hand, who looked no more than slightly confused.

"*Maman*," he asked, "why is everyone scared?" She had been so swept up in her own fear that she had not at first realized that her small son had not noticed the blackout— because he lived his life in such darkness.

As she drove home from the nursery, half-listening to her son's innocent prattle, she pondered that blindness must be, for Tom, a natural state—his other senses reported his world so well that vision would only ever be, at best, a corroboration of more reliable modalities; at worst, a source of confusion and anxiety. Even without sight, he lived so well in the world that they had always felt as if he was as sighted as anyone else. But that, she thought, could have been an assumption dictated by our own narrowness of perception, living as we do in a world in which vision the most dominant sense, the sense we live by, and which has forced our other senses into an undergrowth so deep that we lack the language to describe flavors and textures except by metaphor.

We have no words, Jadis realized, for the colors of smells.

Because of this, Tom would never be able to describe his world to her, and this sudden knowledge hit her with a pang.

Apart from behavior, though, had Tom's eyes themselves ever given the game away? Did they flail anxiously hither and thither, like the eyes of blind people? No, they didn't. Were his eyes closed and sunken, like sightless eyes, long unused? No, they weren't. Indeed, they had given every appearance of being keen and alive. They were very large, fringed with long black lashes, and with yellow-green irises so broad that they left little room for whites. The pupils were not circular, but very slightly elliptical, almost pointed at the top and bottom.

When they were thinking of names for him, Jack had remarked that his eyes were so cat-like that they'd just have to name him 'Tom'. "That," he said, "and the fact that he's got an enormous, well... just *look* at him." Jadis looked down at the nether regions of her new baby (Jack was changing his diaper at the time), saw what Jack was pointing at, and giggled.

Well, Jadis thought, on the very edge of sleep in Jack's arms, Tom had been blind for no apparent reason, and now he could see, equally miraculously. No sense in wondering the whys and wherefores of it: instead, her mind started to reorganize her schedule for the next several weeks so she could spend as much time with Tom as possible, guiding him very gently into what would be a strange and possibly terrifying new world.

By the time that the six-year-old Tom first opened his eyes to see, Jadis' research at Souris Saint-Michel had turned a spectacular enigma into a city. There were no written records, no pictures, no carvings, nothing that a human eye would recognize as art: but the ground was littered with stone artifacts of such sophistication that the Remillardian type proved to be just one of the simpler varieties. There were millions of animal bones of all kinds, many representing species never before recorded from Ice Age Europe. And there were thousands of Neanderthal skeletons, yielding trillions of bases of DNA.

Even in the absence of written records, Jadis' meticulous, methodical approach to the data—the layout of the subterranean city, and the radiometrically established ages for the buildings, skeletons and artifacts—had teased out sufficient patterns for her to be able to sketch the city's history.

For more than half a million years, the Neanderthals and their immediate antecedents had sculpted Europe to their liking. They dammed rivers, changing their courses, shaped mountains, and built immense pyramids whose purpose was obscure, but generally assumed to have been religious.

But when modern humans arrived just before 40,000 years ago, the original Europeans faced a new threat. The invaders bred far faster than the Neanderthals, and swept all before them, despite their clearly inferior culture. It was then that the Neanderthals decided to go into hiding. They abandoned the surface, hiding in Souris Saint-Michel and perhaps other cities that remained undiscovered, though Avi Malkeinu's group had found what seemed to be a smaller version of a Neanderthal-style buried city beneath Mount Carmel. SSM itself ceased to be viable some time after 26,000 years ago, for no reason that Jadis could yet discern. The last inhabitants left, sealing up the wall behind them. Or perhaps they'd sealed themselves in, never more to emerge.

Balthazar had been right when he suspected that Souris Saint-Michel would be a mouse that roared. The world was stunned by all these revelations, and Jack and Jadis had become much-sought academic superstars—rôles they did not much like, although they did their best to accommodate reasonable requests. But they'd had to post round-the-clock security at SSM, and were glad that they did not live close to the site itself or to the new Institute campus at Aurignac. Press interviews always made Jack irritable, and although Jadis usually managed better, she was often withdrawn and silent for hours afterwards.

One concession they made to celebrity was the acquisition of a television—something they'd never had any time for, and found hard to get used to. But when asked to give interviews, they had never heard of the stations that journalists represented, and could rarely understand the references they made to the TV and current-affairs shows in which Jack and Jadis' work now featured. Even though the Institute had furnished them with the very latest Merlin-Tech-equipped computers and scorchingly fast, high-bandwith internet, Jack and Jadis always steered clear of internet news, gossip and blogs. They felt they had better things to do. After all, running SSM was a round-the-clock enterprise that left little time for much else.

Reluctantly, however, they felt that they should be better informed: and so, cautiously, they called their long-standing and long-suffering electrician, Laurent Gaspard, who had occasionally been called in at strange hours when it was found (for example) that a dormouse had gnawed through a cable in the attic, and he'd had to venture into this dark sanctuary for rodents, owls and other wildlife; and perforce do battle with one or more of The Horribles on the way. Gaspard was a brave man, but, Jack thought, his bravery was amply reflected in his call-out fee.

In addition to his electrical services, Gaspard ran a TV sales and rental franchise in Masseube. Jadis called on him one day while on the way back from Seissan market, to see if they might rent something, you know, just to see if they could live with it.

Their first TV was not a success. Jadis felt that she couldn't relax with Jack in the evenings because she felt that the great black monolith was looking at her, intruding. It went back to the shop after a week.

"We can't have that *thing* in here, Laurent," complained Jadis: "Looks like a giant bat, just hanging there. Can we try something less... well, obvious?"

Gaspard then supplied them with a flexi-screen ('latest organic semiconductor technology!') mounted in a gilt picture frame which, he said, could go on the wall above the sitting-room fireplace. It could double as a remote computer monitor if they liked (they didn't) and could even be used for videoconferencing (which they admitted had possibilities). But after five minutes of sales talk, Jack and Jadis felt their eyes glazing over. Jadis said that this was all very well, but how, *mon cher* Laurent, did you switch it on, or, more to the point, off?

The agent, sensing imminent technophobic *ennui*, moved to the main selling point for any reluctant TV owner—that this model would, in standby mode, look indistinguishable from a framed painting or print, indeed, any picture they wanted. And if they got bored, they could change the picture on command or set up a slideshow. He showed them a wide selection of possibilities in his catalog, most of which were either clichéd, pornographic or both. Jack said he rather liked the surprising diversity of exuberantly flesh-toned Titians, and started to recite a rude limerick on this theme in English, which left Gaspard looking nonplussed and Jadis irritated. Interrupting Jack in full flow, she asked the agent how could they have a custom picture?

And so it was that the monitor now looked exactly like the picture it replaced, a now-faded framed reproduction of *Riña de Gatos* ('The Cat Fight') by Goya, something they'd had since their Chesterton days, and which they'd kept as the two furred and be-fanged protagonists looked so much like two of the The Horribles.

Having now finally installed the TV — which Jadis would only ever refer to as the *Thing* — they found themselves extremely averse to switching it on, at least to begin with. Their end-of-day winding-down had become a sacred, special time that nobody had been allowed to disturb, with the exception of Fairbanks, and Tom, when he had been very small and reluctant to go to sleep on his own (and who, being blind, wouldn't have watched TV anyway). Now, however, they felt obliged to watch the *Thing*, to force themselves: which they did, in increasingly horrified fascination.

The TV news was ever varied, but ever much the same, in that every single item seemed colored by the implications of the discoveries at SSM. Politicians were more guarded, more cautious, as if a greater, older power was always looking over their shoulder. Comedians became wild-eyed and edgy: if human existence had been a late coda to a vast, lost civilization, little remained that was sufficiently important to make fun of, so they launched into one of two opposite directions — unspeakably bestial crudity or brittle, knowing surrealism.

Reporters in the increasing number of war zones, or covering the steadily rising tally of death from famine, disease and the more overt manifestations of climate change, seemed to struggle to make their voices heard, as if the immediate tragedy and horror of their subjects paled before the immensity of time that civilization had been known to exist—and that this immensity was, by and large, inhuman. It wasn't long before Sir Raphael Dimbleby, the doyen of the more thoughtful TV pundits, wondered openly whether SSM were the final proof of the ephemeral futility of human existence, quoting Macbeth's lines about life as a tale told by an idiot, full of sound and fury and signifying nothing.

Jadis, watching, pulled Jack's arms around her. "What have we done, dearest Jack," she implored, her voice cracking, "what have we *done*?"

Jack looked more intently at the latest report on the ongoing rebellion in somewhere or other. "I still think we should have gone for the Renoir," he said. "Or the Titian. You know, while Titian was mixing rose madder, his model reclined on a ladder..."

Jadis sat up, suddenly bright-eyed again, and walloped Jack with a cushion. Jack fought back—

"Her position, to Titian," he managed to utter, between whacks "... suggested coition..."

Fairbanks joined in, and the whole melée ended up on the hearthrug, the *Thing*, playing to itself, now quite forgotten. Jadis, wedged on the hearthrug between Jack's embrace and Fairbanks' gently snoring form, laughed to herself.

"... so he leaped up the ladder..." she murmured.

"An' 'ad 'er...," Jack concluded, eyes closed.

The *Thing* burbled to itself into a darkened room.

In times of existential crisis, people by and large turn to the certainties offered by religion. Whether or not these certainties really exist is a secondary question that few choose to confront. And what most gripped the world about Souris Saint-Michel was the definite, indisputable signs of Neanderthal religion, and in particular the sacrifice of modern humans to the nameless gods of their captors. This news, summarized in one of a seemingly never-ending series of reports in *Nature* ('Evidence for Neanderthal funerary and sacrifical custom' by Jadis L. Markham and twenty-seven others) was both denounced and welcomed in editorials and pulpits.

Denunciation was very much in the rule among the more austere Protestants, especially in the United States, who felt that religion in non-humans debased the very idea of religion itself, as well as being a challenge to biblical literalism. Jews were, by turns, fascinated, repelled and awed by the antiquity of it all, even though the more Orthodox rabbis claimed it was a scientific fraud designed to undermine the sanctity of Torah. Avi Malkeinu had written to Jadis of the small ultra-orthodox contingent who'd set up demonstrations outside his own dig at Mount Carmel. "I get most work done on Shabbat," he'd said, "when they've gone home." The Imams of the Khalifa, finding no ready guidance, and indeed more concerned with their own internal schisms, wisely said nothing.

The only positive reaction came from the Catholic church. "His Holiness deplores human sacrifice as barbaric," a black-garbed Papal legate said in a package on the main news bulletin one Friday evening in 2040, a few weeks after Tom received the dubious gift of sight. "However, with the new encyclical, *Undique Humanitas*," the legate continued, "His Holiness proposes that the problem of the non-human origin of the religion from Souris Saint-Michel can be solved very easily — by the simple expedient of widening the definition of humanity."

At this, the legate flashed a twinkling, toothy smile that made Jadis and Jack sit up in wonder: the name at the bottom of the screen, not that they had any need to read it, said 'Mgr. Domingo Sanchopanza, Vatican Science Advisor'.

The Papacy had, it seemed, been well ahead of the game. For not only had the human world to worry about the implications of non-human cultures in the dead past, but those that were still very much alive. The surprise 2032 airlift to Israel of the Tibestian 'Sand Druids'—Gaston de Bonnard's *Prêtres du Sable*, who'd miraculously stepped out of an 18th-century traveler's tale and onto the screens of the world—had been a news item for a week or so. But a longer-lasting and much-debated preoccupation was the revelation the following year that the genome of Sand Druids (they called themselves 'Annakhnu') had evolved along a trajectory utterly foreign to that of the rest of humanity.

The implications of this were hard to unravel: either the Sand Druids really were humans, but had undergone a series of unusually harsh population crashes over many thousands of years of life in the middle of the Sahara, sculpting their DNA into strange, inhuman forms—or that their lineage had been distinct from that of modern humans for tens of millions of years, well before the modern human lineage had emerged.

Whatever the answer, a number of other strange, lost peoples now started to emerge from long obscurity in remote regions of the world, taking their cue from the Sand Druids to claim their share of the limelight.

It was a common human conceit to imagine that by the start of the twenty-first century, people would have rustled every bush and looked behind every tree in search of undiscovered species. But the world is far greater than humanity, even scientists, can imagine, and undiscovered species, if they are sentient, often have a knack of being discovered only on their own terms.

In 2033, a tribe of very peculiar pygmy 'hominids' (that had become the convenient and media-friendly if strictly inaccurate catch-all term for human-like but non-human creatures) emerged from the jungle in northern Sulawesi to give a press conference. With their all-over pelage of thick black fur and enormous, circular, completely red eyes, these people looked even less human than the Sand Druids. From their point of view, however, it might have been better had the Sulawesians chosen to remain in hiding, because their press conference—aired on live global webcast—was disrupted by a band of equally unknown but much larger hominids who decapitated the pygmies (and a few reporters who came too close) and ran into the bush, taking the A/V equipment with them.

No trace of either species had been seen since, and people were beginning to wonder if it had all been an elaborate stunt, until the emergence in 2035 of the Menehune. These hominids had been living for millennia, completely unsuspected, in the remote Alaka'i Swamp in the highlands of Kaua'i, Hawai'i. That, and the incident the following year in which a brigandish band of sasquatches burst into a bar in Dawson's Creek, British Columbia, demanding whiskey and human sacrifice.

After that they started popping up all over the place.

Looking at Domingo, on sparkling form, as ever, Jack and Jadis felt that whatever their own views on religion, the Papal stance was the only civilized course. Good for Domingo, they both thought, and now that the *Thing* had had their attention, it showed them news that turned their expressions from vicarious glory to outright horror. It was news—of a sort—of what had happened to Faye and Primrose.

The Saint-Rogatien Dream Team of 2031 had always occupied a special place in Jadis' heart—especially as it was very largely this same team that had broken ground at Souris Saint-Michel. She tried to keep up with them all, as far as she could.

Eric Onoye and Mathilde Reynard had got married and had taken over Ernestine Yanga's office in an increasingly beleaguered Nairobi.

Primrose Tsien and Faye Callaghan—respectively Jadis' former technician and graduate student—had also become partners at home and at work, having established Callaghan-Tsien (or 'CATS') Adventures, a very successful expeditions business, taking all-female teams of explorers up the many still-unconquered peaks of Tibet. Although the Chinese government had loosened access to the region, much of it remained wild and hardly visited by human beings, let alone westerners.

In the globally harsh winter of 2038, Faye and Primrose and their party had been trekking up a peak so obscure that it was known only by its GPS coordinates, when they lost contact with their base camp in the unseasonably heavy weather, and were not heard from again. Jack and Jadis were perhaps some of the more anxious among the worldwide TV audience following the long but ultimately futile attempts to trace them.

So news of Faye and Primrose guttered and petered out. Two years on, news watchers were now fascinated by the furor that inevitably greeted *Undique Humanitas*, and the strangely compelling personality of the Science Advisor at the Court of Saint Peter.

After the news, came *Zenge*.

Michael Zenge, a one-time White House press secretary and political journalist, hosted the most widely syndicated chat show in the world. His success was attributed to a perfectly judged understatement. Polite but warm; mild and self-deprecating to a degree; conservatively-suited, silver-haired Zenge would just sit next to his guest, posing what seemed the most innocuous questions, and then just let them talk. In so doing, guests often let slip the kind of revelations that more up-front interviewers could never manage to prize from their victims.

Another Zenge hallmark was that he never went for the obvious roster of celebrities eager to plug a movie or a book, but sought genuinely interesting and varied voices, many of whom would be unfamiliar to most people, and sometimes even downright eccentric — but all of whom had interesting stories to tell, and whom he presented as sympathetically as possible. Jack and Jadis had been guests themselves about five years earlier, in the only live TV interview they'd ever consented to give since their Cambridge days. *Zenge* was almost the only thing on the *Thing* that they enjoyed watching.

"Who's he dug up this time?" asked Jadis, remembering the captain of the trans-sexual trans-Antarctic cycling team of the previous week.

"Not sure," said Jack, who'd risen to refill their wine glasses. "I don't recognize him. Too much hair."

"More hair than last time, anyway," said Jadis. She took the wine, her own cloud of hair swaying. She drew close to Jack as he sat down again, trying not to spill the wine. And so in static fascination they watched the emergence of yet another new species of hominid onto the world stage.

"Freddy, can you tell us why you like Tolkien?" asked Michael Zenge.

"Freddy who?" asked Jadis.

"I don't know, I missed the credits," replied Jack.

"Yes, of course, Michael, of course I can," replied the guest known only as Freddy.

"And….?" Zenge prompted.

"Oh, I see, you actually want me to tell you?" The studio audience laughed.

"Yes, please, if you would…"

The guest scratched his left nostril with the index finger on his right hand and adjusted himself awkwardly in his seat. "But of course, Michael. It's like this. When I first looked into *The Lord of the Rings*, I was struck at how all the different peoples of Tolkien's Middle-earth are happily living together, with harmony and cooperation in place of strife and discord."

"The Elves, Dwarves, and so on? What we used to call a 'multicultural' society'?"

"Yes. But don't forget, Michael, the stone giants in the mountains. Not to mention those glorious tree giants, the Ents, so sadly declining to extinction — with, I have to say it, such British fortitude. I found it most admirable. And affecting. A model for our times."

Jadis tensed, her lips pressed together in a hard line. "Jack, I don't like this one at all. He's... he's.... creepy." She had now sat up, perched on the edge of the sofa, her front now illuminated by the wash from the screen.

Jack saw her eyes burning like coals, the tautness in her neck muscles. Jack tensed up too: she was right — there was something very, very odd indeed about this guest. He braced himself for what his instinct told him was a nasty surprise around the corner. Part of his mind replayed another occasion when Raphael Dimbleby had quoted Macbeth: by the pricking of my thumbs, something wicked this way comes.

"How did you come across *The Lord of the Rings*, Freddy?" asked Zenge. "If I might say so, it is a very popular work in many countries, but it's a surprise to hear its praises sung from the Tibetan Plateau."

"Tibet," said Jadis, "oh no, it can't be... and Faye was always going on about hobbits..." Her eyes got wider with each new revelation, and she started to bite her nails.

"Great literature transcends cultures and geography, Michael, as I am sure you're aware," the guest continued. "But I admit it, foreign literature is somewhat hard to come by in my... er... neck of the woods. Ha ha ha!" Freddy's laughter was like the sound of concrete blocks being dragged over corrugated iron: Jadis winced as if physically slapped. The guest, a thousand miles away in a studio in England, was seen quite obviously scratching his groin. The camera panned rapidly to his face, or what could be seen of it. The guest's eyes were completely covered with aviator shades, the rest furred with long off-white hair.

"Is this guy for real?" asked Jack. "Isn't this another hoax?"

Once more, the guest tried to adjust himself in his seat. The problem was that he seemed far too big for it. The audience, once sympathetic and warm, had now become edgy and nervous. Zenge, affecting not to notice, sat forward in expectation. As if on cue, the guest leaned slightly forward as if to share a confidence.

"It's a very interesting tale, how we acquired Tolkien's masterpiece, Michael," he said. "Most interesting indeed."

"That's the tale everyone knows? About the all-woman expedition to Tibet and what happened to it? Can you dispel the myths?"

"Oh, Jack," gasped Jadis.

"Ha ha ha!" Freddy screeched. The sound of a dinosaur being dismembered by a chorus of blunt chainsaws. "Yes, oh yes, Michael, we made them feel most welcome at our humble mountain fastnesses, or, to be poetic, our Caves of Ice, whence flows our Sacred River Alph. Ha ha ha!" A roaring shriek like a battery chicken farm being hit by a rocket-propelled grenade. "So nice to have a visit from others in Middle-earth, if you will. I am pleased to say we gave them a very warm welcome. Anyway, one of those nice ladies had *The Lord of the Rings* in her baggage. A big read, one supposes, for those long days when blizzards confine one to base and one cannot find a good film on the television. Ha ha ha!" Plate steel attacked by ill-tuned combine harvesters at full throttle.

"Fuck me," said Jack under his breath, holding Jadis tightly. She had begun to shake.

"Could you read it, though? Straight off the bat?"

"Naturally, Michael. To be sure we see very few others at our home—which is why any visit from outside is to be treasured. But we are not completely ignorant, you know. Some of us have even scaled the heights of Henry James. No, no, we could hack our way around Tolkien very passably, thank you." The guest now idly picked at his left nostril, teasing out a long, lime-green skein of mucus, which he ate, chewing appreciatively for some seconds, wiping his fingers on large handkerchief from the breast pocket of an expensive-looking blazer.

"You say that visits from the outside are to be—in your words—treasured…?" Zenge asked.

"As the old *koan* from the lamasery has it," replied Freddy, "'you can check out any time like, but you can never leave'. Ha ha ha!" The guest now sat back expansively. This had the effect of thrusting his pelvis forward, spreading out the lower limbs, and making the guest's gender shockingly, vastly apparent even beneath heavy corduroy trousers. The guest smiled, baring huge yellowing canines.

Jadis sprang up, struggling free from Jack's constraining embrace, and threw the wine bottle at the screen.

"You bastard!" she yelled at the top of her lungs. The bottle bounced, splashing bloody gouts of Bergerac on the carpet and into the fire, creating fizzing bolts of hot liquid that shot out over the hearth. One hit Fairbanks on the nose. He'd been distressed by the obvious, rising anxiety of his mistress, but this was just too much. He yelped and ran for it, padding up the stairs to shelter underneath Tom's bed. Jadis's screams continued: "you evil bastard!" She punched a hole through the screen: sparks arced across the gap and died, but the picture, being formed in a distributed network of organic semiconductors, continued regardless: "You... you... *filth*!"

The studio audience was tittering like a lunatic on the verge of running amok as Zenge and Freddy skirted around the delicate topic of how Faye and Primrose and their colleagues had met their grisly end at the hand of this — *Thing*. Jadis now turned on Jack, fists pummeling his chest — "turn the fucking *Thing* off, Jack! Turn. It. *Off*!"

And so he did, but when he'd tried to take her in his arms and still the incandescent eyes, the flailing arms and ragged masses of hair, she fought him back.

"Look what we've done, Jack," she screamed, "look what we've *done*!"

Tom had now got up, roused by the racket, and was standing at the sitting room door, in pyjamas and dark shades, Fairbanks peeping out nervously from between the boy's knees.

"*Maman*? *Papa*?"

Jack's first instinct was a strong urge to flee, but a second later knew that this would be unhelpful at best. So he simply held her, and held her again, until she could flail no more, and crumpled into his arms, wracked with sobs. He laid her carefully on the sofa.

"*Maman* is fine, Tom" said Jack. "Just tired. You two go up to bed, I'll come and tuck you up in a minute." He sat by his wife, calmer now, stroking her hair. She pulled herself into his lap as if she was a cat, her arms thrown around his waist.

He wanted to say so many things, but he was not a man given to long speeches, and everything he could think of seemed either pat or trite. Shared horror for Faye and Primrose? Yes, he'd loved them both, too, but they were grown women in the high-risk adventure business who'd know-ingly put themselves in danger. That was their choice, not ours. That had Avi not heard about De Bonnard's work, here at Saint-Rogatien, he'd never have rescued the Sand Druids? Possibly, but think of what would have happened had he not done this. The Sand Druids and perhaps all the other hominid species might have perished without our even knowing of their existence, which would have been a greater evil.

That he and Jadis should not have followed their hunches? That would have been a disservice to science, and a worse evil still. Jack thought of Ruxton Carr and regretted that Jadis hadn't met him.

That they should not have followed their hearts?

Inconceivable.

However, it remained the case that their discoveries had changed the world more profoundly than anything since the discovery of relativity, or evolution, or gravity, in which case Jadis was partly right—that we cannot simply discover things and unleash them on the world without taking some measure of responsibility. That was something that would just have to be borne.

There came to his mind a favorite line from *Middlemarch*, a book he'd read in the past few years and found—to his surprise—greatly to his liking, partly because he saw in Jadis an echo of Dorothea. It was something about the greater good of the world being forged by unhistoric acts. In the end, Jack said nothing. Jadis, calming, sat up and parted her hair. Her lips tasted of tears.

The next day, Tom barged into his parents' room to find them curled up like two spoons and fast asleep, even though the sun was climbing fast into a blue sky. Oh well, he thought, I can feed Fairbanks myself. On going downstairs he was puzzled to see the flexi-screen, rolled up and shoved into a black plastic bag outside the kitchen door.

Chapter 3: Abbot

Central North Africa, Earth, *c.* 6,355,000 years ago

But this momentous question, like a fire bell in the night, awakened and filled me with terror.
Thomas Jefferson—*Letter to John Holmes, 22 April, 1820*

The Abbot put his aching head in his hands. He was tempted to cover his ears, too—to shut out the bickering from either side—but he knew that such a gesture would have been unseemly. More to the point, unhelpful. Just like this unseasonable weather: so close, the black skies congealing into ugly thunderheads that piled ever higher over the savannah but never burst. His throat was dry; the hairs on the back of his neck itched; his head throbbed. And still the squabble went on and on.

"The records of our predecessors are quite clear..."

"Clear, did you say, Brother Cynewulf? *Clear*? Oh no, not nearly as clear as the mud at the bottom of the Great Lake."

"I was going to say, Brother Caedmon, before I was so rudely interrupted, that is, that the records are clear enough, to those with enough wit to decipher the glyphs, which are—I admit—very faded, and in an archaic mode that very few, these days..."

"Meaning what, pray?" Brother Caedmon sat back, his yellow-green eyes pitiless glints from beneath his hood. Brother Cynewulf adjusted his considerable and (in this heat) malodorous bulk in his seat, coiling himself up for a truly stinging rejoinder. Time, the Abbot thought, for a seasoned Man of the Goddess to show his quality.

"Shall we ring for some tea?" he said, tinkling a little bronze bell on his ironwood desk, the sparkling sounds peppering the glutinous atmosphere while doing nothing to dispel it. A small pithek shuffled into the room. It was clothed in the dirty white robes of the novitiate, several sizes too big. Every step it made exposed it to the risk of tripping on the ragged hem, its cowl falling over its face, pitching it forward, blindly. But the creature had learned to accommodate the over-generosity of its livery with a shambling grace, loping along in a state of imminent catastrophe, perpetually averted. Criticality in motion. "Mint tea, please, Mandergast? For three?" the Abbot asked, in as kindly a tone as he could muster. He had a soft spot for the pitheks, an affection that was the butt of many jokes made outside his hearing, or so the tellers imagined. In truth, he had a hard time explaining it even to himself — which was, of course, the only reason why he let the jokes circulate. "If you would be so kind?" The creature briefly bowed its heavily browed head, snuffled something indecipherable and loped off through the fug.

"I understand your concerns, my friends," the Abbot continued. "Really, I do, and with good reason. The timing of the Festival of the Apparition is far too important for us to get wrong. We all agree that it would be a tragedy for us to wake up one sunny morning and find we'd missed it. Too much rides on it." Not least our reasons for our continued existence, he mused: not least our very lives. If we miss it, the Annakhnu — or whatever they call themselves — would lynch us. Quite right, too. The sentiment, anyway, if not the execution. And there were other things, too. If only he could remember what they were, but this awful weather stifled all thought like a smothering shroud. "How many years, is it, precisely, Brother Cynewulf?"

"The records are quite clear, Father — *quite* clear," the corpulent monk returned, not without a venomous glance at his colleague, who pretended not to notice. "They say that apparitions of the Goddess occur once every two million, fifty-eight thousand, four hundred and sixteen years, two hundred and one days, forty-eight minutes and twelve seconds.

"*Seconds*?" snorted Brother Caedmon.

"Or thereabouts. And if they—the records—are correct..."

"*Seconds?*" Brother Caedmon repeated, the few remaining shreds of decorum sloughing from his now open contempt. The Abbot raised his hand to stay him. The strain of just this one, simple act, of thrusting his arm upwards through this heat, caused more sweat to spurt from his armpits and made him catch his breath. Brother Cynewulf, unaware of his superior's discomposure, continued.

"... the Blessed One will so honor us..." All three monks bowed their heads in unison. A knock at the door was heard. The Abbot looked up. He was conscious of the moisture dripping down his face and into his eyes as he did so. The fur on his neck and down his back was slick with it. He wiped his eyes and brow on his sleeve—the roughness of the burlap was a tonic as it scraped away the layers of sweat, grime and the sharp dust of the dry grassland.

O, that it would rain!

"Come, Mandergast." The pithek waddled in with the tea-tray. Ironwood, like most things here. But the tea-set itself was made from real glass and the samovar itself was chased with silver. The monks could practically hear the cogs in the little hominin's brain creak with the strain of coordinating its muscles and joints—all enfolded in its billowing robes—so as not to drop the precious load. The creature slid the tray onto the Abbot's desk with a flourish, and stood up, its face a picture of relief and triumph. "Thank you, Mandergast," the Abbot said. "You may go." The pithek shuffled off, closing the door behind it. "Bless," said the Abbot, looking after it, sighing with a species of contentment he couldn't quite identify or understand. He could almost feel

Cynewulf and Caedmon swallowing their laughter. He looked up and turned to the monks. Their expressions were as composed, as serious, as ever. Perhaps it was just his imagination, playing tricks.

O, this alien heat!

"Shall we be mother?" Silence reigned—silence, if that is silence which is broken by the tinkling splash of tea and the sucking noises of three monks slurping it through lumps of sugar.

O, the joy in tepid, sugary liquid!

The Abbot continued, now confident that a properly sacerdotal calm had been restored. "Brother Cynewulf?"

"Father? Oh yes. The Blessed One should turn up this coming Friday, immediately after Vespers. Or perhaps during it. There is, you will appreciate, a *small* margin for error."

The Abbot sensed the restlessness of Brother Caedmon once again reigniting, but waved him down again, for the moment. This time he managed to wave his arm in such a way—just *so*—that a small draft of air washed up his sleeve and irrigated his armpit. Lovely!

"Brother Cynewulf," he continued, "does your calculation take account of such things as... oh, I don't know, you're the expert... orbital eccentricity, precession, isostatic rebound, tectonic shifts, secular gravitational anomalies caused by planetary conjunctions and whatnot, not to mention dear old human error? A lot can happen in two million and whatever-it-is years. Not to mention the fact that our distinguished predecessors were not quite as we are now, and might simply have counted things differently?"

"I can assure you Father, that all such confounding variables have been accommodated. Our predecessors might have been different in their culture and their degree of learning, Father—far superior, in many respects—but they were as blind as we are when we are infants, and had the same number of fingers and toes." Cynewulf chuckled at his own joke, and the Abbot felt it politic to join in.

Caedmon, meanwhile, came to the boil. "Father, *if* I may..."

"You may." The Abbot puffed wearily and took another grateful sip of his tea.

"Thank you." The younger monk shot a smug look at his elder colleague. "My team and I have been looking at the evidence directly, as you know—*empirically*—and from our investigations of the laminations in the bottom sediments of the Great Lake..."

"Brother Caedmon," interrupted the Abbot, "We have already had the benefit of your most illuminating lecture. You have my permission, therefore, to cut to the chase."

"Yes Father. Of course. Anyway, direct and repeated counting of annual cycles in the layered sediments of the lake bed pulls up an interval of two million and fifty-odd thousand years, plus or minus a couple of *millennia*—never mind hours, minutes and... well, *seconds*. It's just not possible to be as accurate as all that."

"That's the benefit of having historical records, Brother Caedmon," interposed Brother Cynewulf. "Clarity. The answer at the back of the book."

"Clarity, my arse..."

"Brother Caedmon, *please*..."

"My apologies, Father. The problem is not only that Brother Cynewulf has this unfeasibly accurate interval since the last Apparition, but I'll bet that no matter how clear the records are, they'll say something enigmatic and open to no end of theological and, no doubt, scholastic interpretation. They won't say 'Oh yes, the Blessed One appeared today, about tea-time'. Will they? And what's more..."

"But that's precisely what they *do* say. Not the tea-time part, exactly, but the records are otherwise quite plain."

"Yes, but about *what*? What form did the last Apparition take, such that it might leave some mark—some physical, corroborative evidence—such that we'd be able to pick it up, unequivocally, more than two million years later? A calling card? A *fossil*? Your records say that *something* happened, dear Brother Cynewulf, but they don't say what. To be sure, the lake laminations do show some signs of disturbance just over two million years ago—but that's just the problem! The lakebed was disturbed, don't you see? Interrupting the usual process of sedimentation, screwing up the process of annual variations of deposition—which is what we rely on to create our chronology—and this not only makes for a big margin of error, but also obscures whatever it was that made the disturbance in the first place. We just don't *know*." Caedmon's voice rose as he spoke, in tone and volume, so that his final sentence came out as a pleading wail of anguish.

"Ah, knowledge," said the Abbot. "It's such a problem, isn't it? The closer one seems to get to it, the more elusive it seems. I have a feeling that at a time like this, we must take the best evidence on offer. Brother Cynewulf's records..."

"But Father, they can't... surely?"

"Take heart, Brother Caedmon. Look at it this way. Your limnological evidence—which is, I might say, greatly valued—does not actually contradict the historical interpretation offered by Brother Cynewulf. Does it?"

"No, Father, it..."

"Well then. In which case we have nothing to lose by watching out for an Apparition on Friday evening, will we? We'll all be in the chapel, anyway, won't we? And if the Blessed One doesn't arrive—well, we'll put away our pride, put away our shame—vainglorious emotions, both—roll up our sleeves, and look at the problem again. Won't we? *Won't we*?"

"Yes Father," chorused the two monks, as chastened as novices.

"In any case, I have a feeling that when the Blessed One chooses to grace us with her divine presence, we'll just know."

"We will... just *know*?" asked Cynewulf incredulously.

"It is as I said, Brothers. Knowledge is a funny thing. More tea, anyone?"

A rumble in the sky overhead sliced through the contemplative mood of the office. The Abbot looked up. The sound was instantly followed by a sharp tap at the door.

"Saved by the bell," he said. The Brethren Cynewulf and Caedmon looked at each other, their faces mirrored pictures of puzzlement.

-=0=-

Time was when the Venerable Alfred could have been sure of his solitude. That out here, in the whitewashed, wattle-and-daub hut he called his hermitage, he'd not see a living soul for months on end. Perhaps years.

Bliss.

With his small garden in which he scratched out yams and a few herbs; a well which, while niggardly, met his needs; and the thin shade of a ragged thorn hedge to keep out the worst of the Sun (and beneath which he could sleep, on hot nights, meditating on the stars through jags of branches)—he made himself a life which made up in contemplation what it lacked in luxury.

Well, almost.

And on those days when he visited the shore of the Great Lake to wash, to trap fish, or manage to snare a few stork or ducks or even a young keryx—well, then, he felt, his cup overflowed, and he made sure he offered the Goddess his most profound thanks.

If only he could be sure that she was listening.

How ironic, he often thought, while reciting his offices, that when he had been at the monastery—a long day's walk distant, across one now-withered arm of the Great Lake—the voice of the Goddess had been so hard to hear. Novices had yet to learn to adopt the necessary ruminative calmness, but—O! Frustration!—as soon as they had almost captured it, that elusive spirit, that frail voice, they would be burdened with the manifold distractions of mature responsibility. And if by some mischance they found themselves holding the office of Abbot, well—the voice would invariably disappear completely. It had happened to him, in just that way.

For more than forty years he had tended his cantankerous and dwindling flock in that windswept outpost, watching the Great Lake shrink, and the galleried pithek-shrieking forests melt into the ever-encroaching grass, just as his once luxuriant mane had faded to the smoothness of bald skin, naked under a bald sky. Eventually he'd had enough. That he 'wished to rediscover the voice of His Goddess' was how he'd explained it to the Synod, and they, with great sympathy (because many of them knew exactly what it felt like) allowed him to retire to this life of complete, undisturbed seclusion. And so he, Abbot Alfred, had given way to Abbot Aethelwald, and then Abbot Aelfric, and so to the present Abbot, whom Alfred could dimly remember as a callow novice, even though he could not quite bring his name to mind.

Forty more years passed. But still the voice of his Goddess remained too faint for him to hear. He had long since lost count of the times he'd abased himself before her image, grazing his knees, chanting until he went hoarse or fell asleep—his voice lost on the torrid air, unheard. He'd lost count of the other ways he sought for a sign of her, in the branching patterns of thorn trees against the Moon; the scatters of turtle or catfish bones, desiccating on the salty lake shore; the flutter of spoonbills set fly from the heat-hazy water; the swirls of wind-blown grass; the ripples of stones cast far out in the lake; the clots of clouds in the sky; even the patterns of stripes and spots in the pelts of the beasts he'd caught.

Nothing.

He'd begun to despair, but he put that most treacherous of emotions aside as he had so often counseled his flock. Perhaps his moment had passed. Or maybe he'd lost the knack. No matter—he would continue his offices as he'd done for so many years.

Until, one day, when he'd been hoeing his vegetable patch, and thinking of something utterly prosaic, such as how much his knees ached these days, he heard a voice behind him. It was the voice of a young woman, as clear as if she'd spoken directly into his ear.

"Oh, Alfred," she'd said, "you really are a very silly man."

And that was it. He'd practically had a heart attack on the spot. Recovering, though, with marvelous speed, he turned, just in time to see the ghost of a teasing smile and the fluttering hem of a bright red robe disappear behind his hut. Shockingly red, against the duns and blues and greens and whites of his world. Throwing down his hoe, he turned to follow, but when he got to the corner, there was nothing. Nothing at all, in the view of the wide burning savannah spread out before him. He walked all round the hut (this took all of twenty seconds, even with his knees in their current condition) and didn't see her. He'd half expected that when he'd given up, and had gone indoors, he'd find her there, crouched, in the hut's darkness.

It was not to be.

Had he been a much younger man he'd have stormed at the injustice of it all. Now, at the age of almost a hundred, he limped back to his garden and continued hoeing from where he'd left off. In the shade of his straw hat's brim, though, a single tear from one yellow-green eye ran down a deep fissure of his cheek and vanished into his straggly beard, evaporating. But he always kept an ear cocked. Just in case.

Only...

Hardly two months had gone by since the mysterious apparition, and some of his crops were coming up for harvest, when Alfred's solitude was shattered, and he feared he'd never hear her voice again.

Except that a small voice deep within reminded him that 'never' was a very big word, and its use by the clergy was at best disrespectful, at worst, heretical. Then something in him stirred, an old memory from long before his retirement, long before, even, his election to Abbot. From his youth, long ago, when there were trees with monkeys in them, and the Great Lake was wide, and not so salty. That there had been talk in some scholarly circles, then, that the next apparition of the Goddess was imminent, perhaps in their lifetimes, if only just. It could be that in that tiny, fleeting encounter he'd been blessed with something real, something premonitory, something that had made his long wait worthwhile—even though it did not seem so, at the time—and from that he took some measure of comfort and gave thanks.

What disturbed his peace, though, was an apparition of a more concrete kind. It turned up outside his gate one brazenly hot day just after noon, when he'd retreated into his hut to wait out the day's heat. The apparition was so remarkable that Alfred just had to come out to take a closer look. He grabbed his straw hat—and his machete, rosy with rust though it was, just in case.

It was a tall man, a warrior perhaps, except that his height was not matched with girth in proportion, and his face was white—*white*—and thin, with pink-rimmed milky-yellow eyes, and long, thick hair the color of bleached grass-stalks. He wore white robes, reminiscent of the novitiate, except that his were girt round with broad leather belts, and he wore a long bow and a quiver across his back, as well as a brace of short, stone-tipped spears, and wore stout leather boots. His height seemed greatly increased, though, to the old hermit, because the stranger was mounted on an enormous rhinoceros, braid-maned, perhaps six feet tall at the shoulder, its immense legs terminating in great hooves, its snorting snout tipped with a single, horn that tapered more than a meter skywards, terminating in a point that looked wickedly vicious, for all that it was strung with tassels and beaded cords.

The warrior dismounted, jumping to the ground. Small puffs of dust rose from his feet as they scuffed the hard pan. Indeed, Alfred could still see the clouds of dust raised by the passage of his lumbering steed, and there seemed to be other such puffs of dust on the eastern horizon. This strange, pale rider was not alone.

As Alfred watched, the rhino pitched its great head forward and snuffled on the bare ground for such forage as it could find. A huge, fleshy tongue lapped out, greedily scouring the cracked earth for salt. As it did so the rhino dropped a series of enormous turds, which sat on the parched soil, steaming. These would prove excellent for his crops, thought Alfred. He decided that polite engagement might be more profitable than mute retirement.

"Good day, Sir," began Alfred. The words seemed alien and uncouth, until he realized that he'd probably spoken nothing out loud for more than a year. "Might I be of assistance?"

The warrior spoke. Like his body, his voice seemed fleshless, all edges and sibilant hardness.

"*Bokh'rt'v*—greetings—most reverend *attaar'kha'av*" the warrior seemed to say. Alfred was sure he failed to understand at least half of it. But then, he reflected, he heard speech no more frequently than he spoke himself. The two men bowed to each other. Alfred was relieved that the nonverbal courtesies, at least, were mutually intelligible.

"From the East we come, my people, *ann'h'kh'nu*. What is the name of this land?"

This question threw Alfred, temporarily, for he had not thought of it for a long while. The problem was that nobody had lived in this country—nobody in it but for the monks—for a very long time. The nomads, always scarce, had disappeared with the trees and the freshness of the Great Lake. And the pitheks had no language of their own. Alfred began to think aloud. Now he had rediscovered speech, it was hard to stop.

"Name? That is a most profound question, is it not? Few have lived in this desolate region, and so it has not been blessed with a name. The Brethren in the House across the Great Lake named their community after its founder, the Brother who came here... oh, well, years ago, beyond count. Thousands. Perhaps even millions. And his name was 'Shinaar'.

"*Shinaar*," repeated the warrior, staring straight at Alfred with his unnerving eyes, their irises the color of soured milk. "*Shinaar*."

"Yes. Well, I suppose so."

"*Shinaar...*"

"Yes." There was an awkward pause, which Alfred felt obliged to fill with noise. "Might I offer you some water? Some food?"

"*Shinaar*. This is the place for which my people, *ann'h'k-h'nu*, have been seeking, *b'r'kh'ú*. Where the City of Heaven we will build."

"Here?" All Alfred could think was that his long solitude would be broken. That he would never hear his Goddess again. "Here?"

"Yes," said the warrior, who carefully folded himself downwards so he could kiss the ground at Alfred's feet. "Here." He rose, sand on his parched lips, tears in his egg-poached eyes. "*Here.*"

Chapter 4: Student

Gascony, France, Earth, April, 2054

What men or gods are these? What maidens loth?
What mad pursuit? What struggle to escape?
What pipes and timbrels? What wild ecstasy?
John Keats — *Ode on a Grecian Urn*

Shoshana Levinson shouldered her backpack and clambered wearily up the jetway. The six-hour journey crammed into a budget seat on the Stansted-Blagnac airship had been grueling. She should have saved up and got the train, as everyone had advised. Even the bus would have been better.

In the arrivals hall at Blagnac, she looked round at the small cluster of people, each one with face drawn, eyes expectant, waiting to see a friend or loved one emerge. A few — bored taxi drivers, mostly — held up signs. Although some were in uniform, it was easy to make out the skeletally tall Pamir Kaptars, their cream-and-dirt-orange manes either shorn or pinned back in laughably vain attempts to make themselves look human. Not that one should ever laugh at a Kaptar. Especially if you didn't want your head bitten off.

She stopped, scanning the reception committee, and now that her mental search image had become attuned to fur and hair, her own welcoming committee became apparent. It was a tall woman in a baggy sweatshirt, denim shorts and extremely aged sneakers, but distinguished mainly by an unkempt mass of hair that reached almost down to her waist. It was dark brown — almost black — but here and there streaked with gray. At first Shoshana couldn't make out her face, until the woman pushed the hair out of the way and stared at her with a gaze so dark and piercing that — just for a moment—Shoshana imagined herself in one of those anxiety nightmares in which you are looking for something, and everyone else unaccountably fails to notice that you are naked.

It was Jadis Markham. Of course it was. Shoshana recognized her from innumerable news pictures, none of which had captured the instant and overwhelming intensity that hung about her like a cloud. But then Dr Markham smiled, and everything changed. The eyes lit up like firebrands, and, but for the crows-feet, her face seemed to be that of a girl in her mid-twenties. Not at all like the serious, distinguished academic of fifty that Shoshana knew Dr Markham to be.

"Shoshana Levinson? Lovely to meet you. Quick—let's get out of here. The car's parked illegally." Shoshana hurried to keep up with Dr Markham's tall, easy strides. Nice legs, too, she thought, for a wrinkly.

"Hop in," said Dr Markham, gunning the motor as Shoshana flung her pack in the back seat of the open-topped jeep and climbed aboard. It was great to have shed the load, and to feel the warm springtime breeze of France on her face and arms, the loose sleeves of her t-shirt flapping, blowing away the shrouds of miserable London with each passing mile.

For a long time, Shoshana was too awed by her company to say anything. Jadis Markham was her heroine. She'd been reading about the fantastic discoveries at Souris Saint-Michel since she had been a little girl, and Jadis had been an inspiration for her even during her darkest hours—hours that had increased in both frequency and darkness until she'd made that final break from home. The fluke that had scraped her through the Cambridge entrance exam to read Archaeology, with a good if unspectacular high-school diploma, had a lot to do with that. She whispered a grateful prayer for the old-girl network, in which her college tutor had been a student of Professor Reynard at Cambridge. Shoshana knew that Professor Reynard had been one of the very first people to have seen the underground city at Souris Saint-Michel.

Shoshana was not to know that Professor Mathilde Reynard's life since SSM had been clouded by tragedy. Six years into their stint in Nairobi, her beloved Eric had died in agony, having succumbed to the new and lethal Naivasha-6 Hemorrhagic Fever virus, probably contracted from contaminated blood during an operation for a ruptured appendix that had itself gone badly wrong. Mathilde had counted herself lucky that she'd not caught this highly contagious disease herself—either that or any number of even more horrible diseases which, local gossip had it, were stalking the townships and the bush. Such talk was easily dismissed as folk superstition, especially in these days of crisis, but after what had happened to poor Eric, she did wonder.

Nairobi itself, beset by shortages, disease and a flood of migrants from the increasingly lawless countryside, was no comfort. Mathilde had fled, at first to Jack and Jadis' farmhouse where by happy chance Domingo was visiting, and being a good Catholic herself, she was able to discuss her concerns with him in depth and detail. The sensation of spiritual healing, of absolution, of uplift, had been palpable. She thanked God for confessors as sensitive and as articulate as Domingo (because, honestly, you hardly know it, to look at him). In time, a Chair at Cambridge came up, and her application was successful. But for the rest of her life she would regard the farmhouse at Saint-Rogatien as a haven untouched by care or worry, and would recommend it most warmly to any promising student, even one as inexperienced as this Levinson girl. Nothing like a good start in life, Mathilde thought, and if Shoshana was anywhere near as good as Jadis had reputedly been at the same age—eighteen, was it?—then she'd be fine.

Mathilde had seen Shoshana at interview, much as Jadis saw her now. Although Mathilde had told Jadis everything about Shoshana that could be found on paper, Jadis wasn't really prepared for the girl in the flesh.

Sizing Shoshana up with a glance in the afternoon sunshine at Blagnac, Jadis' first thought was that she'd have to be careful in case she drove some of the male crew to distraction. Shoshana was hardly more than five feet tall even in trek-booted feet, but packed every inch with what Jack would have called 'personality,' before he started referring (as corroborative evidence) to Magdalenian mother goddesses and the more fleshly works of Titian.

Jadis strongly suspected that Shoshana was well aware of her own appearance and its effects.

She thought of Tom.

No—no need for her to worry on Tom's account: he could handle himself quite well. He was in the middle of his second year at Cambridge with Mathilde, and had (according to her) broken a few hearts already. With his stocky, rugged good looks, matinée-idol French accent and permanent designer iShades, he looked more like a rock star than a trainee archaeologist. No, Tom was more than capable of looking after himself.

In fact, Jadis thought, as Tom was at Saint-Rogatien for the Easter recess, she might ask him to show Shoshana around. There had also been talk of Shoshana going to Israel in the summer as a volunteer on Avi's project, as Tom was also due to do. The fact that Shoshana had a smattering of Hebrew and had been to Israel already this year (according to her letter of recommendation) was a big factor in her favor. She could show Tom the ropes there as he would do for her at SSM. It could all work out rather well, but for one thing: Jadis wondered if Tom would be able to keep himself from showing Shoshana the latest and hitherto very secret discovery at SSM. She rather wanted Domingo to see it before anyone else outside the immediate team, because it was—well, puzzling. But Domingo had promised a visit soon, so perhaps it wouldn't hurt for Shoshana to get a sneak preview.

Jadis' first instincts about Shoshana, her appearance and how she might exploit it, had been entirely correct. Shoshana had been raised an only child in a conventional Jewish household in North London. Although her parents belonged to an Orthodox synagogue, she went to a secular secondary school where she had been very happy. But then came the day when, aged twelve, she'd returned home one Friday evening to find the mirrors turned to the wall, a blanket over the TV, and her mother in the kitchen in such distress that she was initially quite unable to talk.

"Where's Dad?" Shoshana kept asking her mother, receiving no reply but shakes of the head and more tears. Only when Aunt Jess, her mother's sister, called a little later did she learn the full horror—that earlier that day, Barry Levinson, aged fifty-three, moderately successful chartered accountant, loving husband of Myra and father of Shoshana, had been robbed, by assailants unknown, pushed under a tube train and killed.

Then the nightmare really started.

Over the days and weeks, the full history of Barry Levinson's past came back to haunt Shoshana and her mother. They knew that he'd come from a rigidly Ultra-Orthodox background but had somehow escaped. He had gone to University as Baruch but re-emerged as Barry, joined a middle-of-the-road Orthodox congregation and did his best to avoid his more intolerant and intolerable relations. His Achilles heel was his brother Howie, with whom he'd started his business and who was now a sleeping partner. Shoshana loathed Uncle Howie with a passion. He'd backslid into religious fundamentalism as his active interest in his brother's business waned—while still raking off a share of the profits.

But now Barry was dead, and the *mishpoche* scuttled like gaberdine-clad cockroaches out from under their stones with indecent haste. It was made clear to Myra that unless she married Howie, and Shoshana went to a decently Torah Jewish school and stopped hanging around with *goyim*—both demands made in accordance with what he felt was his religious obligation—Howie'd have to pull the plug from the business. Which, he didn't need to add, would require them to sell their home. What with death duties, and what Howie thought was reasonable recompense for the accountancy firm (which he'd have to wind up), this would leave Shoshana and Myra destitute. So Shoshana acquired a stepfather whom she hated, and Myra feared. Shoshana suspected that Howie beat her mother—and worse—for all manner of infractions to do with modesty, decorum, *kashrut*, the list was endless. If her new school wasn't bad enough—run by a load of creepy rabbis who didn't so much as teach the students as yell at them—attendance at synagogue was compulsory every Friday night and Saturday morning. She remembered when her mother was forced to shave her hair and wear a *sheitel*, and how she'd looked so beaten, so defeated.

Like most of her friends, Shoshana had had no reason to complain about the more tolerable strictures of her religion—it was part of her life. She had always been fascinated by the historical and cultural roots of Judaism, especially its antiquity. She'd enjoyed *cheder* each Sunday morning and was reasonably proficient at Hebrew, and it always amazed her that words like *shemesh*, meaning the sun, had been used continually and without change for more than three thousand years, the word having been used for the name of the Assyrian sun god: and yet the English she spoke in her everyday life had been recognizable as such for much less than a third that time.

But the new régime at home and at her new school convinced her that whatever the glories of its history, the purpose of Judaism now was to say 'no' to everything and generally to make life as miserable as possible. It was hardly her fault that this growing and understandable antipathy met the full force of her surging teenage hormones and her own fascination with her newly voluptuous figure — and the possibilities it offered.

And so she became a rebel. Hardly a week would go by without a stern conference in the sitting room in which Howie, in Homburg and *tzitzis*, would berate Shoshana about the damage that her behavior was doing to his reputation, and Shoshana shouting even more loudly that she couldn't give a flying fuck for his reputation, as he wasn't her Dad, and what the hell was he going to do about it anyway? Lay his *tefillin* even more tightly? Perhaps one day he'd do them all a favor and strangle himself with them. At which she'd claw her way out of the house and not be seen until dawn. Shoshana's only worry — but who worried about such things when they're a teenager? — was what this was doing to her mother. But her mother had let herself be a doormat for this creep to trample on, so maybe she deserved what she got.

Matters came to head when Shoshana was expelled. She'd been on a school trip somewhere or another, and Shoshana (whose position in the school bus had moved ever backwards to match her plummeting academic, attendance and behavior records) had apparently (and this was not in quite the roundabout form that her parents had been notified of the event) climbed into the back window of the bus and flashed her abundantly fabulous tits at the motorists following.

The sitting-room conference was much as expected. Howie raging, Myra standing behind him, pale and anxious, and Shoshana swearing and storming out. But the result of her motorway escapade had caught up with her. Wherever she went that evening she was followed by boys from school — and other, less savory characters — demanding that she 'get her kit off for the lads'. Outside a pub at about ten thirty she was surrounded by a gang of men she didn't recognize, one of whom she'd only just managed to fight off, but others had started to remove belts, get out knives... when the lights and blaring horn of a taxi scared off her would-be persecutors.

The driver was her cousin Frank, a burly ex-boxer who kept himself fit at the gym when he wasn't out cadging fares. He shared his one-cab business with an eight-foot Kaptar who went by the name of Big George. When not actually driving, the Kaptar rode in Frank's cab for security, to protect Frank. Big George never said anything, but he didn't have to. One snarl and a sight of those fangs was sufficient to scare off any potentially troublesome customers.

"Hey, Suze," said Frank, piling her into the back with Big George, "you're getting into bad company." Big George grunted, and made as much room for Shoshana as he could.

"Piss off, Frank," she said.

"Seriously, girlie-girl. You should wise up."

"So what do you think I should do, Frank? You seem to know everything."

"Do me a favor. Ditch the Dad. I shouldn't be saying this, but that *shlemiel*, he's a loser. I'll never convince Myra, but you, you're a clever girl. Think about it."

"Yeah, right."

Shoshana felt that the domestic situation, while bad, wasn't something she could do much about. And whatever she thought about Mum and her reaction to Howie — akin to that of a rabbit about to be mown down by a truck — she could hardly leave her. And in any case, where would she go? She was only just fifteen, had no qualifications, and with the way things were going, the chances of her acquiring any were slim and receding daily. Frank and George dropped her, still shaking, clothes torn, lip bloodied, at her front door.

"Now listen," said Frank, hanging out of the window, motor humming: "I'll let you off the fare if you sharpen up. When you've got your exams, then you can wave those big bazookas at whoever you want. Okay?"

Her chance of freedom came that very evening. It was Friday night and the house was totally dark, for *Shabbat*. The only sound came from the sitting room — smacks and small, choked yelps — where through the half-open door she saw her mother's form, cowering on the floor, Howie standing over her, whipping her with his belt. Shoshana's blood went cold: her head cleared and she sprang into action. She got out her cellphone, burst into the room, snapped on the light and took several pictures.

After that things turned out better. Shoshana clicked the pictures to her own private webspace, and threatened Howie, then and there, that she'd make them public if he didn't let her mother alone; if he didn't allow her to continue her education at a sixth-form diploma college; if he didn't stop her studying what he considered blasphemously Torah-threatening *goy* science — and if he didn't allow her to leave home as soon as convenient. Howie had no choice but to agree. The very next day, *Shabbat* be damned, she was living with her aunt Jess ("so relieved that you got out of that house, love, even though poor Myra...") and had taken cousin Frank's advice.

Two years of hard work later she had got her diploma and had scraped her entrance exam to Cambridge. She had been a borderline case, subject to an interview. Her meeting with Mathilde, however, was the clincher. The day after the result came through, she told her mother to flee to a women's refuge, or else. Then she posted the pictures anyway to her FaceSpace account. They went viral.

Howie got fifteen years, and the media had had a mild field day with the fiery, feisty (and notably busty) young woman whose testimony had done most to put him behind bars. Then, to kick off her gap year, she'd gone to visit Israel with some old friends from her *cheder*. Her life was now set.

Tom, for his part, had never been happier. He'd come home for Easter and was looking forward to his seasonal task—digging a bean trench for his mother, on her *potager*. Beans needed a lot of water and nutrients, and before they were planted, he had to dig a trench twenty feet long, three feet wide and two deep, fill it with compost and shredded paper ("Tom—I have boxes and *boxes* of old field reports you can use"), and backfill with the removed topsoil. The work was backbreaking, but after a term of study it was just what he needed to loosen himself up.

But what he enjoyed most about this ritual task was the sensory symphony that accompanied it. The soil was heavy clay, but his mother had worked it diligently for almost thirty years, so it was now rich and loamy. He loved the pungent smell of wet earth each time he pushed his spade into it, turning it—a smell, he thought, of the promise of growth coiled up tight and just waiting to burst forth. He loved the feel of the well-rotted compost as he crumbled it through his fingers. He loved the angular plosh and plash of the water as it hit the shredded paper, the gurgle as it soaked in. And all this against a background of breeze and birdsong. The only thing he missed—still missed—was the shuffling swish and pad of a golden retriever following him up the garden, the contented 'harumph' as the dog subsided onto the grass next to him—but his childhood companion had died when he was ten. Fairbanks' grave was somewhere over there, beyond the spinney, the retriever himself having long since made his contribution to the *terroir*.

So that's what Tom was doing as evening fell, when his mother brought home a gap-year student who wanted a little field experience. He knew that his parents were deluged with such requests, so he reasoned that this one must have been a bit special to get through the screening. Perhaps the fact that she was going up to his own department had something to do with it. His mother and Professor Reynard had always been close.

Not that Cambridge was anything like it had been when his parents had been there, as far as he could judge. They seemed reluctant to tell him much. Jack had just looked distant, as if lost in a dream. His mother either changed the subject or, if he'd pressed the point, said that he'd soon find out for himself.

Tom's Cambridge was not half the place it had been at the turn of the millennium. The smaller and less well-endowed colleges were closing, and because the town depended on its colleges, Cambridge itself was shrinking. There were two reasons for this, the first being a net decline in revenue from the admission of foreign students. Prosperous countries in East Asia and the Americas now tended to educate their children within their own borders. The African market had all but dried up, the death-knell being the collapse of Nigeria in 2039, before the two-pronged advance of the Khalifa and the Sahara desert.

The second was climate change, which was starting to have marked effects on the global economy. A combination of international carbon treaties (too little, too late) and shortages of oil meant that long-haul jet travel had ceased to become routine, except for the super-rich and business people with generous expense allowances. Everyone else had to put up with interminable train rides; worse bus journeys; and, worst of all, budget airships, most of them little better than flying sick-buckets. No wonder that when faced with the idea of travel, most people chose to stay home.

The droves of Japanese tourists that once crowded King's Parade and Trinity Street, weighed down by their Pentaxes, became small flocks and then stopped altogether.

Even had students and visitors continued to arrive in Cambridge as they had a few decades earlier, climate change would still have left its mark. Although Cambridge had always been a chilly place, the winters of the past decade had been harsh even by East Anglian standards. A dramatic season of storms each November presaged Arctic blizzards, a frozen Cam and snow on the ground continuously until April. After a brief Spring, late May onwards would be lived in a furnace, making the exam season all but intolerable.

And if his lecturers and fellow natural-sciences students were to be believed, the Autumn storm-surge season built on rising surface temperatures in the North Sea. With the consequent expansion of seawater, the grain prairies around the Wash were inundated each November, ruining all winter wheat and making the land too wet and salty to cultivate. Even cold-tolerant Nunavut and salt-tolerant 'Sahelized' wheat cultivars failed to thrive as dikes and drains were regularly overtopped. Some ambitious farmers switched to salt-hardened rice varieties, but after a couple of years the land became too salty even for these.

In the end, enormous acreages of East Anglia had been abandoned to fen and salt marsh, undoing more than a thousand years of careful reclamation in less than twenty. The coastline from Skegness to Blakeney in North Norfolk had become a vague and shifting thing, an uncertain and marshy merger of land, sea, and big, big sky. Whole towns, like King's Lynn and Wisbech, had been evacuated and abandoned; Boston was once again a sea port, as it had been before the American Revolution, when the Founding Fathers embarked at its quays; and the interior almost as far as Peterborough was dotted with half-submerged villages and the long-forgotten calls of bitterns.

The students had changed, too. The regular crowd was punctuated with traditional garb of all sorts, not just from the young sultans and princelings of the Khalifa. You could occasionally spot a Kaptar, one of the Almai or the various Sulawesians, even a Sasquatch, and there were rumoured to be a couple of Menehune at Christ's: the hominids had come to town. Tom was fascinated by all this diversity: he intended to study them in greater depth, someday. For tens of thousands of years, *Homo sapiens* had thought himself the only species on Earth capable of holding a conversation. But now there were so many different sorts of human, some of whom had been distinct species for far longer than dear old *Hom. sap*. What opportunities might this variety not present for a comparative anthropologist? That, thought Tom, was where his career path should be headed, though he'd not said as much as yet to his parents. He'd never yet seen a Sand Druid, though—they were pretty much all in Israel. But he was going to Israel this summer to work with Professor Malkeinu. He thought he'd heard his parents say that this new gap-year student had planned to do that too, so maybe he'd see one then. Thus happily occupied, Tom went on with his work.

He heard the scrunch of the jeep as it hit the gravel drive. He stretched, feeling his back muscles snap back into place, and, walking in through the *arrière-cuisine* and out through the kitchen door onto the drive, he went to greet his mother and the newcomer. He sensed the quick, decided steps of his mother as she alighted, the swish of her hair and her sharp smell. But there was a new and intriguing odor, too—yeasty, buttery, almost like—what was it?—cinnamon?—and in any case quite definitely female.

Tom had been around women all his life. The majority of his parents' colleagues were women; mostly young, all of them intelligent, many highly sexed and some very interested in Tom. But he'd remained aloof. Without consciously being aware of it, he was wary of forming any attachments on his parents' home turf. Cambridge was another matter. Once free from the apron-strings of home, he found himself endlessly fascinated by women: their compelling odors, intriguing shapes, and most of all, by their quite unbelievable textures. That women seemed equally fascinated by him offered plenty of scope for experience and experimentation.

But this one seemed somehow different, even in a world where every woman was, to Tom, so fascinatingly different from every other. To be presented with such an example on his parents' own doorstep seemed to break a taboo.

"Hi, Tom," she said. "Great to meet you."

Even her voice was a mess of contrast and contradiction. It was full of laughter and yet seemed rough at the edges, distorted by an ugly accent he couldn't place, its corners bracketing an otherwise appealing smoothness which, in its context, seemed incongruous.

He felt a strong and entirely uncharacteristic urge, then, to remove his iShades. Vision was a distraction he generally used only to corroborate things he'd already judged finely by other means. Eyes, he felt, were never trustworthy as primary sources of evidence. So he tended to keep his iShades on and ratcheted down, even at night. Women found this more alluring, somehow. Some women, anyway. This time, though, he had to make an exception. The odors and sounds seemed so varied, so jarring, and—well, so interesting—that he just had to see for himself how they would all merge together. And so he took off his iShades, squinted for a few moments in the still-bright evening light, and accommodated his eyes to the prospect.

It wasn't until about halfway through the journey that Shoshana plucked up the courage to talk to Jadis Markham. Every time she tried to speak her throat would dry and her tongue felt several sizes too large for her mouth. It was plain that Dr Markham—Jadis—wasn't going to go out of her way to make things easy. Shoshana had resigned herself to this. After all, Dr Markham did have a reputation as sharp and frosty as her first name implied. But as they progressed, Jadis would turn to her passenger, bestowing on her a series of increasingly warm smiles, which Shoshana interpreted as encouragement. Perhaps, Shoshana reasoned, here was someone who didn't say much unless it was worth saying. If so, this was a refreshing contrast to her own Jewish upbringing, counterpointed as it had been by incessant talk. She'd never met anyone who'd had the restraint to say nothing, as a default option. But her upbringing got the better of her, and she gave way to the urge to fill the void with a confessional stream.

So Jadis learned about Shoshana's recent experiences, and how she had been transformed by her trip to Jerusalem that winter, in which she'd shaken off her old *cheder* companions and went exploring on her own. How she had seen so many different kinds of Judaism, and other religions and peoples and species, all muddling along in a city so ancient that history just dripped from every crevice. She'd seen the western wall, but had also visited the *Al-Aqsa* mosque and the Dome of the Rock, preserving the last footprint of Mohammed before he ascended to heaven. She'd marveled at the crazy warren that was the Church of the Holy Sepulcher, in which each Christian denomination had its own jealously guarded corner ("and the poor Copts are banished to the roof, with the washing!") She had followed a troupe of Sumatran Pendeks as they walked the Stations of the Cross. It was all, she said, quite wonderful.

In the course of this, her own pilgrimage, she'd said, the anger she'd felt at her upbringing was distilled into a kind of sadness at how narrow it had been, and how the people imposing the narrowness seemed to have lost all perception of the joys of their heritage. Their relentlessly precise codification of Judaism had squeezed out all possibility of challenge or inquiry, so that Judaism was preserved simply for the sake of preservation, as if it had no other contribution to make. Rather than rage, she now felt regret for her stepfather and his ilk, about how they had walled themselves into a ghetto without hope of rescue.

"Welcome to the team, Shoshana," said Jadis, interrupting the flow, as she turned the jeep off the road and bounced up a much-potholed drive between two rows of tall poplars. "I hope you'll like it here. Ah! Here's Tom!"

As the jeep pulled to a halt in the courtyard, Shoshana saw a young man clad in scruffy khaki Bermuda shorts and a faded but still lurid Hawai'ian shirt that seemed several dozen sizes too big for him. His large hands were stained with dirt; his skin was as brown as mahogany, his black hair very thick and stuck up in peaks like a meringue silhouette, and on his face he wore mirrored iShades and a smile as big as his mother's. Confronted by this apparition she couldn't help but laugh.

"Hi, Tom!" she said. "Great to meet you."

She leaped from the passenger seat and found, now that she was facing him, that he wasn't very much taller than she was. Then Tom took off his shades — an act that Jadis seemed to find hugely amusing.

"Tom," she said, her voice full of suppressed mirth: "meet Shoshana Levinson. Can you show her around? Make sure she finds her room?"

"Sure, *Maman, d'accord*," Tom replied distractedly as Jadis hurried inside, his eyes fixed on Shoshana. "So, you're Shoshana."

Shoshana had the weirdest feeling that an insect might have had if pinned to a cork board by an entomologist, and finding, much to its surprise, that it enjoyed the experience. She gazed back at Tom's curious, unblinking cat-like gaze, and his sunny, easy-going smile. As she did so, she couldn't help but smile back: her own eyes widened.

Eyes.

The first thing (and the last) that Tom Corstorphine remembered about Shoshana Levinson was her eyes, whose gaze met his as soon as he'd removed his iShades. Tom saw that they were big, round and the deepest blue, a color so dark that they were almost purple, fathomless, full of intelligence. These were eyes that could swallow you whole. Dangerous eyes.

It took all of a quarter of a second for Tom to examine the rest of her. She had a long nose, a rather wide mouth, full lips and quite a lot of teeth, some at curious angles. Her skin—her skin?—this was the source of the smell he'd sensed as the jeep arrived. How would you describe it? That it looked just as buttery as it smelled was all he could think of. Her hair was curly and the very darkest shade of blonde. It was this that smelled of bread, with a hint of salt, and there seemed to be a lot of it. Tom put his iShades back on, held both hands out to Shoshana and said—"*Viens!*" Her hands were dry and slim and gripped his firmly, full of resolution.

Tom led Shoshana round the farmhouse, delighting in showing her every last nook and cranny, and making sure she knew where her room was in relation to the bathroom, the stairs and so on. "Just come and go whenever you want," he'd said. "It's your home."

Her room was a small but comfortable nook with a view over the front yard, containing a single bed, a stripped pine chest with a mirror on top of it, a bookcase next to the bed, stuffed to bursting with books, magazines and loose papers; and a bentwood chair. The wallpaper had a cheerful floral pattern but was spotted and peeling in places: lived-in and relaxed without being luxurious.

Most of the rest of the rooms seemed to have been variously used as stores, offices and bedrooms, or a shifting, ambiguous mixture of all three. There were books everywhere—unceremoniously crammed into bookcases, littering tables, piled in tottering stacks on the floor, wedged into doors, even in the bathroom.

At one end of a long, broad corridor hung with torn Hessian, flapping like rent tapestries (*"Aïe! Ils sont Les Horribles!*—I hope you don't mind cats! In this house they are everywhere!") was a large, open space with two windows overlooking the back garden. In the centre stood two huge and well-worn oak desks, facing each other, with an assortment of very old-fashioned flatscreen computer monitors on smaller tables to either side, in between what looked like the very latest Merlintech airtabs. Yet more shelves lined the walls, filled not just with books, but papers, filing boxes, stone tools, chunks of ancient masonry and all kinds of equipment, spilling on to the floor in untidy drifts. More papers were piled high on the desks themselves. Battered steel filing cabinets, drawers half open, disgorged further paperwork. "This is the office," said Tom, "where my parents do some of their thinking. Let me show you where they do the rest of it. Come!"

So Tom showed her the kitchen—a crazy mixture of a room that seemed to be part study, part greenhouse, part garden shed, with only the range, a sink and one small corner of a worktop to betray any culinary activity. So this was where the renowned Jadis Markham seemed to do most of her actual work—rather than in the study, which was where she just dumped it. Across the broad entrance hall was the sitting room, in which an enormous and utterly hideous sofa, its upholstery ripped and stained, stood before a massive stone fireplace, its grate heaped with logs. More logs were stacked haphazardly in the inglenooks. A faded though slightly unnerving framed print of two fighting cats hung above a mantelpiece crowded with pictures of Tom, a much younger Professor Reynard, and several other people Shoshana didn't recognize. One showed a very large and breathtakingly ugly man who seemed to share Tom's fondness for loud shirts. Another showed a small, dark-skinned boy, his arms round a big, goofy-grinned golden retriever.

Shoshana was awed. This crazy, untidy house was where it had all happened, where Jack Corstorphine and Jadis Markham had changed the face of human history. It was as if she was being given a tour of Einstein's office, or Faraday's laboratory—or, perhaps most of all, Down House, the big, rambling country home where Charles Darwin had thought about evolution and raised a family in one big, joyful mess. She was confused, elated, but most of all, tired.

Tom picked up on this immediately. "I'm so sorry," he said. "You're worn out. I haven't even asked if you're thirsty. Would you like some tea? *Tiens*—why don't you go upstairs, wash up, have a lie down, I'll bring you some tea." Shoshana didn't know whether to laugh, cry, to say yes or no—but Tom looked at her and smiled again—"*vas t'en*, go! I'll bring your things up with me."

Shoshana made her way up the creaking wooden stairs, tottered to her room, kicked off her boots and collapsed on to her bed. The candlewick bedspread and duvet beneath swelled up around her in a cool embrace. She felt as if all her batteries had expired at once, and closed her eyes. She hadn't slept at all on the flight—her memories of this morning were a dawn rush as Aunt Jess had pushed her on the Stansted Shuttle from Liverpool Street; the constant taking-off and putting-on-again of her rucksack during the innumerable security checks; the endless flight in which, unable to sleep, she'd seen three films but couldn't remember anything about any of them; and now, here, at this farmhouse, an overwhelming hive of clutter.

And her guide? Funny, but even though she'd seen him less than two minutes ago she couldn't quite picture him. Not because she didn't want to—but because he seemed so different from anyone she'd ever met. To be sure, her experience was largely limited to the young men she'd known since she was a girl, most of whom were pallid, predictable, serious and most of all weighed down with the tribal baggage of millennia, a load that they'd only seek to pass on to her, had she got too close. Tom, in contrast, seemed like a free spirit who could soar into the sky on a whim and go wherever he wanted, do whatever he liked, and if she wanted to come with, well, great. And if she didn't? Well, that was great, too.

She'd always known what to do with men, how to use them, how to manipulate them. It was easy, she'd thought, because all that men had ever done on first meeting her was stare at her tits, their gaze rarely straying thenceforth. Tom had instantly confounded this well-used and almost instinctive strategy. He'd looked at her face. Well, by 'looked'—she wondered if he'd really *seen* anything. His eyes were strange, huge, green like the sea, slightly cat-like, inscrutable. In contrast, he'd seemed more focused when he'd had those cool iShades on, and his eyes were obscured. Yet she'd felt that, even then, he'd looked right through her. No, not like he'd undressed her with his eyes like all those boys from

home, but something more genuinely appreciative, respectful even. Was that right? No, she couldn't put it into words.

Tom fumbled up the stairs with a tea-tray. What a jerk he
was being, dragging this girl round the house like he was a
six-year-old wanting to show it all off. How could he have
lost it so badly? He'd known lots of girls—lots—he had, in
truth, got well into double figures within his first year at
Cambridge—but Shoshana was as different as he'd thought
she might be. To be sure, all the Cambridge girls were tough
and self-assured, but Shoshana seemed, somehow, just as
tough as they were, and she hadn't even got to Cambridge
yet. It was enough trying to carry her rucksack (slung in the
crook of an elbow) and manhandle a mug of tea up the stairs
without being assailed by these confusing cross-currents.
Damn. He hadn't asked if she wanted milk—he'd made it
black with lemon and sugar. Oh well, perhaps too late now.

He knocked at the door with his booted foot. A tiny voice
from within bid him enter. As the door opened she rose
from the bed in a single fluid, curved movement that raised
all kinds of smells—the dust from an unused room; newly
washed sheets; one of The Horribles that had been hiding
(unbeknownst to Shoshana) under the bed; fly paper; and
her own odor, accented by exhaustion. She took the tea from
him, putting it on the chest of drawers, allowing him to drop
the rucksack.

"Thanks for the tea, Tom," she said. "I'm bushed. I think
I really will have that lie down, now." Her eyes lost their
focus, and she lowered herself onto the bed.

"Of course, Shoshana—of course!" he replied. "Sleep
well!"

The following day started early, and soon they were
bowling along towards Aurignac, Jack driving, Jadis shotgun, hair flying. Tom and Shoshana sat together in the back,
talking quietly. They seemed to be getting on well, Jadis

thought, and smiled to herself. Very well indeed. And was instantly catapulted into her own thoughts.

Eighteen months before, on the day that she and Jack had seen Tom off for his first term in Cambridge, they'd returned from Blagnac looking forward to having the place to themselves. But on the way home from the airport she had felt progressively more nauseous, so that by the time they got home she was clammy, hot and headachy, and unable to do anything other than lie motionless on the settee, and, unusually for her, actively complain of being ill.

Her health fluttered up and down for several months until she'd finally admitted defeat and went to the doctor, who looked her up and down critically before asking her age. This puzzled Jadis—Doctor Makembe had been her physician for almost twenty years, and knew perfectly well how old she was.

"Jadis," said the doctor, "we're none of us as young as we like to think we are." What was the doctor getting at? In her mind she was always eighteen and had just met Jack.

"Jadis—*Jadis*? Are you listening?" Dr Makembe continued. "You have to face facts. You're fifty years old. There is nothing wrong with you but the menopause. It hits us all, God help us." Dr Makembe raised her eyes to heaven. "I've just gone through it myself, so I know what it's like. I'll prescribe you an implant that'll help you get over the worst of it, and you'll be right as rain."

The truth dawned on Jadis only very slowly. Menopause? Fifty?

Where had it all gone?

The implant had indeed taken the edge off the horrible cocktail of nausea, sweats and anxiety, opening her mind to reminiscence. Funny though, she still felt like a young girl, deep down. Although she had heard from Mathilde that Tom was quite the heartbreaker (the pair of them giggled on

the phone like two teenagers) it had taken the physical reality of her son, encountering a young woman on her own
doorstep, in her own house, to make her feel old. Older,
when she recalled having watched Mathilde with Eric, more
than twenty years before. And Primrose. And Faye.

Lately, Jadis had been too busy to live life any more than
one day at a time. The menopause, and now Shoshana's arrival, had made her see her whole life all at once, as if spread
before her like a map. Jack had always been there, of course,
a constant like the sky or the sea, but the landscape itself was
marked with the milestones of discovery. And it struck her
with some force that Jack had first taken her to Souris Saint-
Michel twenty-three years ago. She had spent almost half
her life exploring it. And now they were going to look at
perhaps the greatest discovery of all—and the most worrying.

So worrying, in fact, that Jadis was beginning to think she
should keep it a secret forever. Only—should she? Should
she—might she—let Shoshana see it, what she and Jack had
kept a secret from almost everyone?

Yes. For lost youth. No, not that: for the best reason a scientist can have—for the sake of a fresh and unbiased pair of
eyes.

Shoshana's first view of Souris Saint-Michel was of a
parking lot with a scatter of cars, trucks and tourist coaches.
Between the parking lot and the lake stood a modest, low-
rise building that contained the visitor centre: the wonder of
the age had become a tourist attraction.

From the parking lot, visitors would board a robo-train
that would take them, a dozen at a time, into the city, round
a preset course and back again. They would see the Great
Pyramid; parade down the Champs Elysées, past the Hexagon where a series of still-inexplicable rites had been prac-
ticed (Avi Malkeinu had seen signs of similar ones under

Mount Carmel, and was equally mystified)—and into the Place de la Concorde, with its immense granite obelisk marking a thousand graves, each body clad from head to foot in exquisitely wrought flint-plate armor.

The two-hour circuit would, it had to be said, leave the visitor more mystified coming out than going in. There were ancient cities that matched Souris Saint-Michel in grandeur, even in scale—Teotihuacan, Xi'an, Knossos—but even if one could not grasp the purposes of their monuments, one was always reassured to know that such things might one day be fathomable by virtue of the fact that their builders were human. With Souris Saint-Michel this reassurance dropped away like the trapdoor beneath the hanged man, leaving a residue of vertiginous unease.

Compounding the mystery was the fact that despite almost a quarter of a century of mapping, logging every square centimeter of the city over its thirty-seven square kilometers, the team had found not a single recognizable work of art, and no sign of writing or record-keeping of any kind. No inscriptions, no engravings—nothing.

Now that the city had been charted to its full areal extent, Jadis had started on a new tack—digging downwards, excavating test pits beneath selected buildings and in certain streets. It wasn't long before she realized that SSM was much older than anyone had guessed.

Jadis had always assumed that the city had been built around 40,000 years ago, when modern humans invaded Europe, forcing the almost unimaginably ancient Neanderthal and pre-Neanderthal civilization underground.

Within a few months of the new project, Jadis had to confront the scale of her error. The city she had mapped was the latest of no fewer than fifteen cities, built one on top of the other, and even then, there were signs of earlier, pre-urban occupation. The deepest level beneath the pit known gnomically as TP255-9-2A, dug in the graveyard at the base of the Great Pyramid, was capped by a stalagmite layer laid down three and a half million years ago—meaning that the level itself was even older.

The *Nature* paper reporting this finding ('Extreme antiquity of the earliest occupation layers at Souris Saint-Michel' by Jadis L. Markham, Mathilde Reynard, A. Y. Malkeinu, John A. Corstorphine and thirty-eight others) was initially greeted with skepticism. Jadis found it hard to accommodate the fact that some people simply refused to believe her findings. She raged and fumed until the age was confirmed by three separate, independent teams of experts. But the conclusion was clear. Someone, or something, had lived in this cavern more or less continually from just before 25,000 years ago back to a time when no humans or indeed any known species of hominin had ventured out of Africa. And for those hominins in Africa itself, cities would be a dream beyond imagining, because for these creatures the first chipped pebble still lay a million years in the future.

The debate over TP255-9-2A had been so bruising that the latest discovery was still a secret, and why Jadis really wanted Domingo to see it before she made any announcement. For the first time in her life, she felt she needed some kind of religious counselor.

Jack drove the jeep across the car park and through the gate towards the cave itself, greeting the security guard with a wave. The road into Souris Saint-Michel was broad, smooth and brightly lit. Shoshana could hardly imagine what it must have been like when Jack, Jadis, Mathilde and the others had first walked through the pitch-black tunnels into the unknown.

The road narrowed—Jack had to stop at a signal to led a robo-train pass—until, widening again, it swept them up to a broad viewpoint, where the full extent of the illuminated city could be seen. To Shoshana, the lights seemed to stretch forever, to the left and right, as well as ahead, as if she were in a small plane coming in to land over a big city at night. She had seen this view many times, of course—it was the poster that had adorned every student bedroom for the past twenty years—but the real thing was eerie, ominous.

"Don't worry, Shoshana," said Jack, sensing her unease. "It's something to do with the lack of echo. When we first got here, it gave us the willies, didn't it?" He turned to Jadis as he said this: she sat quite still in her seat, and said nothing.

Jack swung the jeep down to the left, and they descended a long, broad ramp that took them into the city itself, past two more robo-trains and several groups of scientists, some of whom waved cheerfully as they drove along the Avenue Gaston de Bonnard to the foot of the Great Pyramid itself. Looking up from its base at its entire illuminated immensity, Shoshana was initially unable to grasp its scale until she glimpsed, on the very edge of sight, a few motes at its apex—and realized that they were archaeologists working at the summit platform.

"Everyone out!" said Jack, and they followed him towards the large plastic tent that covered much of the graveyard area. The tent, illuminated from within, looked like a giant Chinese lantern. Inside it was a hive of activity, both human and mechanical: a guard handed them all hard hats with emergency headlamps, and Jack and Jadis stopped several times to chat to the various surveying and digging teams. They all knew Tom of course, and some of them—particularly the younger women—gave Shoshana what she thought were rather resentful looks.

This was only a flying visit, though. Jack and Jadis led the party through a small flap in the far side of the tent to a metal platform at the very base of the pyramid, surrounded by a rail of thick steel scaffold-poles.

"Welcome aboard the Pyramid Express," said Jack, lifting a red-and-white painted chain-link partition so they could all squeeze on. Shoshana looked up the side of the pyramid and realized that they were on some kind of funicular railway that led to a point, far away, at the summit.

"I hope you're not scared of heights," Jadis warned Shoshana, her hand just glancing against Shoshana's wrist as she lifted her hard hat, and put it on. Shoshana murmured something inaudible. In truth she was terrified. She held on to Tom with one arm — and grasped one of the tubular steel rails with the other. Jack looked round to see if everyone was in, and pressed a small red stud on a control box. The Pyramid Express moved, smoothly but very slowly, up the slanting side of the monument.

They climbed for several minutes, and as they did so, more and more of the buried city came into view. A grid-line pattern of streets, all illuminated; scatters of polyhedral structures — most house-sized or less, others as big as small skyscrapers — attended by clusters of ant-like researchers, and larger, better-behaved groups of tourists, mainly on the bright skein of the robo-train. Shoshana felt that the climb was slowly pulling her free from the usual constraints of time and space. She thought she'd known enough about this site to be prepared for the vastness of it. The reality was a shock: even though she was wearing a fleece borrowed from Jadis, she started to shiver. Tom put a reassuring arm around her, and she pulled closer into him. It was then that she noticed that he'd put his iShades back on.

As they approached the top of the pyramid, the platform whined and shuddered to cope with a sudden increase in the grade. Shoshana could feel her palms sweat. With a final lurch, the Pyramid Express crested the summit and they all alighted on another small metal platform, jutting slightly out from the side of the flat summit platform itself. Shoshana did her best not to look down, but she needn't have worried — Tom, completely unafraid, steered her to safety. She felt herself breathing hard.

The summit platform was smaller than she'd thought, no more than about five or six meters square. Some of it was roped off, under excavation, and three or four archaeologists bustled about on this high eyrie, quite unconcerned by their vertiginous surroundings. They exchanged greetings with Jack and Jadis. In the very center of the platform stood a gray box, taller than a man. When she realized that it was the head of an elevator shaft, she laughed.

"Yes," said Tom. "Archaeology has its ups, and it also has its downs." Jack smiled, but Jadis, ignoring everyone else, looked anxious, agitated: her lips were compressed into a thin line.

The open meshwork cage rattled to a halt just ten meters below the summit. The Pyramid's summit platform was a hole of darkness against the greater dark, above them. Just to one side was an illuminated niche, dug into the rock of the pyramid. The kind of niche that you'd see in a museum, moodily lit to heighten the drama of a Sumerian clay tablet, an Egyptian death mask, or the Face of Agamemnon. Shoshana saw the faces of her companions in the light from the niche. Jadis's face was hard, nervous. Jack's — all bland composure. Tom's expression, behind his iShades — unfathomable.

At first sight, the mysterious object was a disappointment. It was a gray, rectangular tablet, about twelve centimeters from side to side and three tall, and perhaps a centimeter deep.

"Is this…?" Shoshana asked.

"No," said Jadis. "It's nothing you'll ever have heard of. I hope." Just for an instant, Shoshana got the full, actinic flash of Jadis' eyes—which turned, almost immediately to Tom, whose shaded face remained quite impassive.

"When we first surveyed the pyramid—and the city," Jack broke in, "we took a lot of readings of different things. X-rays, ground-penetrating radar, you can imagine. But we also brought in gravitometers, to detect any buried voids, mainly. Tombs, hidden chambers, that kind of thing." Shoshana noticed that he had, unobtrusively, slipped Jadis' hand into his own, and, equally unobtrusively, that Jadis seemed to relax.

"What we *didn't* expect was what we in fact found: a huge, localized gravitational anomaly buried beneath the summit of the pyramid. We found it almost immediately—the anomaly, that is—back in… when was it, Jadis?"

"As soon as we broke ground—2032," Jadis said. Shoshana could see the hard set of her jaw. "But… well, what with one thing and another, it's taken more than twenty years to investigate it. So now, at last, we have."

"And this is…?" asked Shoshana. Tom squeezed her hand. His grasp was hot, urgent—scared. She realized that he probably knew scarcely more about this finding than she did.

"Yes," said Jack. "About two months ago. We haven't moved it—we thought it best… *in situ*, you know."

"The problem," said Jadis, "is that we don't know what it's made of. It's no heavier than it looks, but the gravimetric readings are… well, they're unexpected."

"Do you know…?"

"How old?" said Jadis, "No—we haven't a clue. We've tried all the usual techniques, but nothing registers. It's maddening, it really is. It's obviously intrusive, so the rocks of the pyramid itself aren't of any help…" Jadis waved her arms in a gesture of exasperation.

"And every technique we try," said Jack, "even really arcane radioactive series designed to measure the age of the very oldest rocks—meteorites, asteroids, say—pull out nothing. It goes off all scales. It's *infinitely* old. It's *beyond* old." Jack's voice, so calm and friendly to begin with, was starting to show signs of strain.

"Maybe it *is* a meteorite?" Shoshana asked. She had the distinct feeling that she was flailing, losing it, but plunged on, nonetheless, "something that got buried here? Perhaps even before the city was built? Roofed over…?"

"That's what we first thought. Or tried to think," said Jadis. "But if it is a meteorite, it's made of nothing that any known meteorite is made of. Ion microprobe results make no sense. The closest thing we've been able to establish is that it might be metallic…"

"… even though there are no metals in it," Jack continued, "and even if it's made of anything we can understand."

"And, anyway," said Jadis, grasping Jack's hand. "Look at it, Shoshana. Really *look* at it."

She turned, then, to look directly at the mysterious object. The more she looked, she found that the object's size was hard to grasp: it seemed to shift, to shimmer, to grow and shrink as she watched. She found it hard to tear her eyes away from it, and as she gazed at it, it appeared to glow with what seemed to her a menacing luster. As if it were waiting for something. As if it were alive. After a while, and, looking more closely, she could make out an inscription— not letters, but circles, lines, crescents—engraved in lines almost too faint to make out, and as she looked, the circles and lines seemed to *jump out at her* and… and…

Tom caught her as she stumbled. She felt heavy, disoriented, nauseous. Jadis and Jack looked over her, evidently alarmed — and at each other, knowing. What Shoshana had seen was the first and only inscription ever found at Souris Saint-Michel. For want of anything else to call it, Jadis and Jack had named it 'The Sigil'.

Chapter 5. Merchant

Indian Ocean, Earth, c. 125,000 years ago

My loves leap through the future's fence
To dance with dream-enfranchised feet.
Siegfried Sassoon — *In Me, Past, Present, Future meet*

"All together now... *cheese*!" The three stevedores, brawny, burnished and bared to the waist, linked themselves together and hammed it up for the camera.

Click.

"Thank you all, so much!" said the photographer, smiling and bowing. The stevedores laughed and resumed their tasks, the overdressed tourist and his zuzim (now pocketed) forgotten.

What a grand sight it all made, thought Mr Haraddzjin Khorare, stowing his box-brownie in a cunning cache-poche of his own devising, in a pleat of his crushed-velvet knee breeches, where it rubbed along next to the talisman in its leather drawstring bag. How picturesque — the multitude of packages on the quayside; the people, of all kinds, bustling, shouting, picking things up, and putting things down again, and swarming aboard the magnificent ship that was the backdrop to the busy scene.

Mr Khorare, trader in textiles from the Very Great and Ancient City of Axandragór, looked up at the broad-beamed merchantman straining at the quay, gulls turning about its masts, a smear of smoke fuming from its funnel as the boilers were warmed; seawater spilling from the blades of its paddles, here on this Malabar shore, so far to the north and west of his home city.

Now, this coaling-station in Malabar had not the refinements of the Very Great City of Axandragór — where else had? — but it had a charm that made him tote the box-brownie at every opportunity. How his wife would clap her hands; how his kits would jump for joy, when their cambric-smocked father emerged from his darkroom clutching these images of far countries. Pity his umbrotypes could never capture the colors. These flowers; those parrots. But the moods. Those stevedores, now. Such matey, boyish jollity. And such muscles. Really, most picturesque.

The ship was called *The Tiger Sniffs the Rose*, and it would sail for Dilmun in less than two hours, carrying Mr Khorare's regular shipment of fine Axandragór stuffs to that benighted port. The burghers of that far shore were starved of stimulation — starved of taste, poor things, if truth be told (Mr Khorare took out an embroidered kerchief and dabbed a bead of sweat from his brow) — and he felt that it was his duty to enlighten them. But what they lacked in taste, they more than made up in price. Upon my soul! The Dilmunese were mad for Mr Khorare's textiles! So, as Mr Khorare watched a profit-and-loss account tip inexorably in his favor, who was he, he thought, to deny them? The best deal is when all parties were happy.

So that was that.

Except that it wasn't. Some of the profits were coming up a few zuzim short. Not many, it must be said, but ever a little more, month on month, and as Mrs Khorare often told him — look after the zuzim, and the shekels will look after themselves. Mr Khorare (with his loyal wife's encouragement) felt that the time had come for him to investigate the Dilmun operation in person.

There was a rush of steam and the bark of a klaxon, signaling all those who wished to board the *Tiger* that they should now do so. Mr Khorare clutched the talisman and the box brownie in his cache-poche and climbed the gangway.

Mr Haraddzjin Khorare spent much of the subsequent voyage hanging on the stern rail, feeling queasy. Decorum be damned: he'd doffed his velvet tailcoat, riding the tropic air with his lace-cuffed chemise undone. Just a button or two. So he was on many a heavy afternoon, the sea a bright featureless disc all around the tiny dot of the *Tiger* at its center.

One part of him put his malaise down to the turtle-and-loxodont soup he'd enjoyed at the Captain's Table several nights' running. The turtle was likely to have been all right. The gigantic leatherbacks were all harpooned by the *Tiger*'s own crew and hauled aboard, twenty men straining at the hawsers. The problem was the loxodont, which could never have been really fresh. Brains, scooped from the skulls of the giant straight-tuskers culled on the plains of Eurasia; shipped across mountains on the steaming backs of rhinos and down river on barges and across tropical seas, sloshing around in barrels for weeks and all of this before they ever saw the inside of a pickle-jar. Perhaps such dainties should never be taken lightly, least of all aboard a merchant steamer puffing its way across the open ocean. The intervals Mr Khorare did not spend above decks found him throwing up in the heads, or lying in his cramped cabin simply wanting to die.

A plainer diet restored his health, though not his spirits. Perhaps he was homesick for Axandragór with its crumbling canal-side palazzi subsiding slowly yet elegantly into the breathless equatorial shore, the ancient city looking ever outwards, pointedly ignoring the pitheks of the wild hinterland, in whom one could find no ready market for any garment that hadn't been ripped off the back of some hapless beast. Nothing tailored, certainly. And as for haute-couture, well… They'd probably eat it.

No, not homesickness. Not quite.

Mr Khorare heaved himself upright on his bunk, reached into the cache-poche and, sidling the box brownie to one side with his knuckles, grasped the bag that contained the talisman.

It was a curious thing, this talisman. It had been bequeathed him by his late father, along with the textile business. But while the transfer of several hundreds bolts of silk and calico and so on and so forth were all matters of public record, that of the talisman was not. Mr Khorare the Elder had urged Haraddzjin, almost with his last breath, to keep its existence a secret, and—and this is something that Mr Khorare the Younger found most curious—to 'follow the talisman wherever it might lead'. The first of these two instructions was easy to undertake. The talisman was simply locked in a safety deposit box at his bank.

The second whipped around like a hot cobra. No matter that it was sealed away from sight, the talisman haunted Mr Khorare's dreams. On many nights he'd wake on the divan in the grand townhouse that was the fruit of his (and his father's) labors; he'd sit stark upright in bed, the figured symbols on the talisman dancing before his eyes with their deep violet glow: the three circles, interposed with horned crescents, backed by lines radiating from the center circle—lines of an infinitesimal narrowness and yet a searing brightness that penetrated his mind even when his eyes were closed. Occasionally he could tear his eyes away to look down at the peaceful, many-breasted swell of the sleeping Mrs Khorare beside him, so casually in that state of oblivion he craved.

The talisman was calling to him to follow. In his innermost heart, the business trip to Dilmun was a pretext. The talisman had woken, and he was constrained to follow it. A furtive trip by tuk-tuk and gondola across the City found him at his bank, whence he retrieved the talisman. Had this proscription not been voiced by his beloved father on his deathbed, Mr Khorare should have felt with certainty that he'd been cursed. Mr Khorare recalled two most curious aspects of that final meeting with his father. The first was that he appeared to see the entire interview through his father's eyes, not his own. Second, at the same time, he had no sensation of ever having had a boyhood. He was sure he had had one — who hadn't? — just that he could not at that moment bring any of its specifics to mind.

Mr Khorare slid the talisman from its sheath. Now he had it in his hands, in broad daylight, it seemed such a small thing. A narrow cartouche, barely a handsbreadth across. The circles and crescents and lines were mute now, waiting. But Mr Khorare was sure that just below the level of hearing, they whispered 'follow'.

The merchantman *The Tiger Sniffs the Rose* out of the Great and Ancient City of Axandragór continued on its way across the wide ocean.

Until, one day, two things happened.

The first was that, one worrying morning of thick fog when all hands could hear the splash of surf breaking on sharp rocks alarmingly close, the magnificent dodecagonal Pharos of Hormuz, wonder of the world, loomed into view. Salvation was at hand; the navigator could check his charts, and could assure everyone that Dilmun's haven was no more than two days' distant.

The second was not such good news. As the fog dissipated to leave a day of unmatched clarity, a warm south wind speeding the *Tiger* through the Straits of Hormuz, two ships were seen far astern. At present they were no more than black smudges, like the hint of a harbinger of a storm many days hence. But with every watch they appeared bigger in the sterncastle 'scope. The ships looked huge — each twice the tonnage of the *Tiger*, if not more — and black, and black smoke belched from their funnels. No flags could be seen to adorn their masts or rigging — a clear contravention of the Laws of the Ocean — but they were each surrounded by flocks of birds like flies around a midden.

The mood on the *Tiger* was all nerves and edges. Officers, crewmen and passengers alike made febrile and over-loud noises to the effect that the two ships were doubtless, like the *Tiger*, merchantmen headed for Dilmun. Maybe they had run into trouble; forgot their flags, anything. And why should they not see other ships at sea in this region? Dilmun was after all a busy port, and the Straits of Hormuz very narrow. But the word unsaid, and yet posted in letters of blood and fire above every head, was — pirates.

The *Tiger* devoted all her draft to trade: she carried no cannon, nor weaponry of any sort. There was no option but to try and outrun their pursuers, if that was what they were. The Captain commanded every stick of wood be fired in the furnaces alongside the remaining coal; that the speed of the paddles be doubled and redoubled; and that every sail be pressed into use. A long and anxious night followed, in which nobody on board gained sleep save for crewmen constrained to regulation watch- and sleep-hours. Slowly, ever so slowly, the *Tiger* seemed to be gaining, so that by dawn the black ships seemed to be no more than tiny dots on the sternward horizon once more — and Dilmun was a whole day closer. For the first time in sixteen hours, the Captain and crew (and by extension, Mr Khorare) dared to think of exhalation.

Too soon.

For no sooner than all eyes had been turned away from the sternwards threat and looked forward once more, they saw that they had sailed, with marvelous speed, into a trap.

Athwart their forward passage, blocking their route towards
Dilmun, was a huge and ugly black galleon, in full sail and
broadside on, waving the blazon of skull and crossed bones
for all to see. It was close enough for the startled crewmen to
see the glints on the pirates' teeth, and for them to hear the
Pirate Captain's command to open fire.

Mr Haraddzjin Khorare watched the ensuing one-sided
confrontation with undisguised horror. Grapeshot whistled
through the air, ripping away arms, ripping away faces,
raining blood in great swaths across the pitching deck. After
the grapeshot came the pirates themselves, swinging over
from the black galleon on long ropes. They seemed to be a
motley bunch, people from all quarters of a world whose
diversity never failed to surprise him, from the sample of it
that was to be found regularly in the taverns and go-downs
of the Very Great and Ancient City of Axandragór. But
many of these creatures were of a kind that Mr Khorare had
never seen. They were big, heavy-browed, and clad in armor
of overlapping scales of flint.

Stoners!

Of course, like anyone with pretensions to a global out-
look, Mr Khorare had heard of Stoners, and what he heard
always filled with him horror. Typically, Stoners were rumoured to live in gigantic and wholly dark underground
cities, whence they issued to prey on pithekines and other
similarly unfortunate species. The government of Stoner cities was totalitarian, bloody and brutal, and they were perpetually at war with one another. Or so he had heard. He
had never (of course) visited a Stoner city, these being found
in northern and western countries far out of the usual mer-
cantile orbit. Being a reasonable man, he felt, perhaps, that it
might be harsh to judge an entire people on such few rumors
that percolated as far southeast as the Very Great and Ancient City of Axandragór. But Mr Khorare was cautious as

well as reasonable, and found it prudent to hide, for the meantime, inside a sail locker until all was over. He was, after all, a trader in stuffs and fancies, not a rugged buccaneer on some man-o'-war.

He might have been better, though, to have burst forth from his cramped cell with a battle-cry, and, grabbing some spar or stanchion, set about one of these burly, stone-clad warriors, making a brief splash of glory before one of their scimitars slashed him from groin to jugular and made an end of it. Such might have been better than this long, long wait, in which his chemise became drenched in sweat and the stench of his own terror, lace cuffs drooping. A foul odor issuing from crushed-velvet knee-breeches, accompanied by a viscid trickling sensation in his inner thigh, told him he'd soiled himself.

Without thinking, he reached into his cache-poche and withdrew his box-brownie and the silken bag containing the talisman. The brownie he placed carefully on the floor of the sail-locker. He didn't think he'd need it any more. He clasped the talisman, still in its bag, to his chest. It was warm, comforting. He closed his eyes. He remained in that position, curled up, serene, until the locker was wrenched open and a bright tropic light flooded in, followed by a pair of vast, grasping fists.

One of the rumors that always followed Stoners was that their pirate ships—indeed, their shipping of any sort—was always accompanied by a retinue of sharks and carrion-birds. Mr Khorare remembered the clouds of gulls that surrounded the two ships that had chased the *Tiger* into this trap—an observation that was among the first to have made all hearts sink. Why should this be? Well, the tales ran, it was rumored—again, only rumored—that Stoners took goods and booty, but never prisoners, not unless they were especially close to one of their own cities, where prisoners could be herded and, eventually, sacrificed. But out at sea, any prisoner was only good for one thing. For sport. To walk the plank. Mr Khorare now found in most brutal fashion that at least some of these rumors were, in fact, entirely true.

Mr Khorare, ropes coiling him in an almost unbearably heavy corset from mid-breast to waist, pinning his arms to his sides, was third in line. The talisman was in an inside pocket of his chemise. Like the craven he was, he had offered it in ransom to the Stoner pirates, but they didn't even laugh, or jeer. They just looked at him, their faces as unmoving as the flint scales of their armor, before hurrying him along to be bound. He had replaced it, in his inside breast pocket, where it glowed, flooding his body with what he'd swear was some kind of anesthetic. He felt numb, detached, happy to go whither they directed him, sure in the knowledge of — what? — a life everlasting. This utterly unwonted thought made him stumble, momentarily, before he was beaten over the head with a bone club and forced to walk upright.

The first in line was the Captain, who had been grievously wounded in the boarding. Blood caked over his pulped face, and he appeared to have lost a hand. As the Captain walked the plank, the wood thrumming over the sea, some of the Stoners fired arrows at his heels, making him hop and skip. He lost his footing, and, tumbling, slid off the plank before he had quite reached its end. Descending, he cracked his chin sharply on the plank, wrenching his head sharply backwards as he fell. Mr Khorare hoped that the Captain had broken his neck and had died before he reached the waves.

He heard the splash of the Captain's body as it hit the water, accompanied by a less-than-entirely-enthusiastic half-cheer from the Stoners. Piracy was all the same to them, it seemed; devoid of light, devoid of life.

The second in line was the cook, the only female on board, ropes tied to her ankles and wrists. What they did to her was terrible. Mr Khorare had to close his eyes tight, but her screams as they tore her to pieces made his mental picture as horribly vivid as if he'd had his eyelids torn off and been forced to watch the spectacle. Silence fell, and there was nothing left of her. Nothing, save severed hands and feet, dangling disconsolately from the ends of ropes.

Then it was his turn. Without his feeling a thing, he was prodded with spears to the end of the plank. Then he was blasted with grapeshot, from behind and at point blank range. He fell, in pieces, to the sea. The last thing he saw in his bloodied vision was the immense triangle-fringed jaw of a shark, yawning below him. That, and the talisman whispering—follow.

Chapter 6: Travellers

Israel, Earth, July, 2054

Day unto day uttereth speech, and night unto night sheweth knowledge.
There is no speech or language, where their voice is not heard.
Psalms **19**, 2-3

The journey to Israel had been even longer than Shoshana had imagined possible. After all, she and he small gang of old *cheder* friends had managed it perfectly well on a scheduled El-Al turboprop just the previous winter, and were at Ben Gurion just seven hours after leaving Gatwick. This time—only a few months later—it was as if they'd been thrown back to the earliest days of air travel. And, contrary to popular belief, she'd thought, it had been anything but romantic, even with Tom as her companion.

First had been the reconditioned Hydro-DC3 that had meant to go from Toulouse to Athens, but had been diverted to Brindisi. A freak Saharan sirocco had surged its way up the Adriatic, threatening to sandblast air traffic out of the sky, thus preventing the crossing to Greece. The plane took off again after twenty hours on the ground. This meant an enforced rest wherever they could find a spot in the crowded, overcooked airport, and a tiny allowance for food grudgingly doled out by the airline.

Things wouldn't get very much better next day, after they'd hopped from Brindisi to Athens. Their connections now all in disarray, they'd finally managed to squeeze on to a 19-seat prop to Ben Gurion, but this had to make an emergency stop in Nicosia where they were once again grounded overnight. As he told Shoshana later, Tom thought that one of the passengers had looked ill and had been behaving strangely, disappearing rather often into the toilet cubicle. When the stewardess finally broke down the door, her screams of terror would have been sufficient to have grounded the aircraft all on their own. None of the passengers knew what was going on, and were told no more. Suffice it to say that screens were raised, the plane landed and the passenger removed from the plane in a volley of sirens. After another hour of uncertainty, Tom and Shoshana and all the other passengers were escorted off the plane and put up in hotels.

"No, we don't know what was wrong with the passenger, either," said the airline agent at Nicosia, trying not to make eye contact, "but we were told not to use that plane again." She sighed, having explained this a dozen times already. "This means we'll have to charter another one from somewhere. It might have to be an airship. We'll take you to a hotel and call you in the morning. I'm sorry, that's really all I can say. Okay?"

The final hop to Ben Gurion in a rickety old R-300 floating barf-bucket passed, thankfully, without incident. Tom had fallen asleep next to her, so he didn't see that the airship had acquired a pair of IDF scramjets to escort it down. Shoshana was grateful for this attention—she remembered something similar on her last flight here. Air traffic into Israel had come under increasing threat from the Khalifa. So far it had just been routine saber-rattling, but one never knew when such posturing might acquire real teeth.

And so, two and a half days late, they touched down in the afternoon sunshine in the land of Shoshana's remote ancestors, and as they stepped out of the intermittently air-conditioned airship gondola and into the smoggy fug of Israel's coastal plain, Shoshana felt as if somebody had dropped a hot, wet blanket on her head.

When Tom saw Avi at the gate, he dropped his rucksack right there, rushed towards him, embracing him as enthusiastically as a small child might have, and as strongly as a cursed mariner whose albatross has finally been excised, beyond expectation or hope. Parting, they looked at each other, the broad smiles and shining eyes betraying a love and trust from which Shoshana had, temporarily, been excluded. Not that this was in any way intentional. Avi had been a frequent visitor to the farmhouse throughout Tom's childhood, and what with his open and playful demeanor, Avi had become, for Tom, a kind of elder brother, or long-lost favourite Uncle, and someone he loved to be around.

Joshing and punching each other for joy, they started jabbering excitedly to each other in French too fast for Shoshana to pick up any more than one word in ten, until, as one man, they turned to look at her: Avi, a broad grin in a handsome, brown face under tight, grey curls.

"Shoshana, I'm so sorry," said Tom, "that was very rude of me. It's just, well, it's Avi, it's been so long, and..."

Shoshana threw a mock-punch at him—Tom play-acted the stunned victim, staggering about—and she turned to Avi, shook his hand, and addressed him in passable Hebrew. Avi's expression became serious, appreciative, and he answered in the same language.

"You are most welcome, Shoshana," he said. "But what's a nice girl like you doing with a schmuck like him?"

She'd heard from Jadis that Avi had once been a ladies' man, but that he was now sternly, fiercely and firmly married to someone who Avi only ever referred to as "The Ballbreaker." Shoshana had been slightly shocked by this—Avi was almost as great a hero to her as Jadis had been her heroine. But when he met the man in person, she realized that Professor Avram Yitzchak Malkeinu, Israel's premier archaeologist, was just a big kid. She could see why he and

Tom got on so well together: they made a good pair of Lost Boys who'd sail off on an adventure together without a second thought, and Wendy would just have to trail along as best she could.

Not that she had any intention of giving up. Now she and Avi were chatting in Hebrew—for all that it was far less fluent and easy than Tom and Avi's rapid-fire French—it was Tom's turn to affect confusion, looking to Shoshana and then to Avi and back again as if they were Martians. Eventually the three of them ended up in a three-cornered embrace.

"Come," Avi said, "we have a long way to go before nightfall. And I regret it won't be comfortable."

Just outside the terminal building they had to wait for only a few minutes before a green army pickup squealed to the kerb, driven by a woman in fatigues as green as the jeep, who leaned out of the cab and blasted Avi with jagged and guttural shards of what sounded like abuse, in fluent Arabic. Avi turned to Tom and Shoshana.

"Sorry," he said, "what with all the flight delays, this was all I could get at short notice—you'll have to pile in back, I'm afraid. I have business to sort out... er... upfront." He looked slightly embarrassed. "I'll explain later, yes? But you have to hurry! We don't want a taxi marshal to book us for stopping too long kerbside."

Too tired and puzzled to remonstrate, Shoshana helped Tom haul their bags to the back of the truck, up on to the footplate and beneath the canvas. The windowless interior was baking hot. The bench seats on either side were entirely occupied with wooden boxes containing a strange assortment of goods. One contained burlap sacks, neatly folded; another was full to overflowing with lettuces; a third contained a jumble of greased and grimy car-mechanics' tools. Two uzis lay on the floor just behind the drivers cab. About a dozen green-striped watermelons the size of overinflated beach balls were wedged under the bench seats. The only concession to comfort was a filthy, stained mattress spread out on the floor. Being the only available space for them and their luggage, they stretched out on it together, wedged in between their rucksacks and the watermelons. And so they lay there, looking into each other's faces; sharing each other's hot breath; and laughing at the invisible but animated, frequently heated and occasionally violent conversation emanating from the driver's cab as the truck lurched crazily out of the airport and hooked into the highway towards Tel Aviv and thence Haifa.

There were also some long silences—one in particular when the truck pulled to the side of the highway for reasons that neither Tom nor Shoshana could immediately identify. Shoshana put her ear to the metal of the cab, beckoning to Tom to keep silent. Her eyes were sparkling with mischief when she resumed her spot beside him.

"I *think* I know what they're doing..." she said, conspiratorially.

"What?" asked Tom, puzzled.

"*This*," she replied, embracing him tightly and kissing him, initially with some force until she felt he'd really got the message. He drew her head beneath his chin so she could rest against him, cradling her head in his hands, hers clasped round his waist. Exhausted from the trip, Tom dropped off to sleep. Shoshana envied him his ability to catnap more or less anywhere, at no notice, leaving her to brood.

The long journey had given her plenty of time to analyze and review her feelings for Tom, and to marvel at how far they had come in so short a time. When she met Tom—when was it? Just three months ago?—she had been no stranger to men, or to sex. In fact, she thought, she'd probably had far too much of both, which was something she now regretted.

But what had first perplexed her most was that with Tom, uniquely, she was no longer in control, even though he made no demands on her whatsoever, and, more perplexing, was that this was something she welcomed.

She'd always had men exactly where she wanted them, and had begun to use them rather cynically, picking them up and dropping them when it suited her. To be sure, there had been downsides. The first few boyfriends she ditched usually followed her around anyway like lost dogs. Some of the later ones became petulant to the point of violence, and occasionally beyond it. She had come to regard sex in much the same utilitarian way, and with few exceptions, she hadn't enjoyed it very much more than any other pleasurable experience, such as—say—shopping with a girlfriend. On reflection, she thought this rather sad, and this thought alone pulled her up short: that before she'd come to the farmhouse, she thought that her life, while miserable in many ways, was the kind of life that most people learned to expect and took for granted.

It was only when she'd met Jadis and seen how content she seemed to be, married to the solid, dependable Jack, who plainly adored her, even though they'd been together practically since dinosaurs walked the earth, that Shoshana had any way to calibrate her own experience. Her teenage years had been lived in an atmosphere of brutal repression, and although she had known this to be true at the time, these same years had been the backdrop to her adolescence and puberty, and had done much to shape her character. She told herself that by using men as objects, she wouldn't end up an abused house-mouse like her mother. But in seeking the other extreme, she now feared she ran the risk of ending up in substantially the same place—beaten, and alone.

The kind of romance she saw in Jack and Jadis, lived in an easy, matter-of-fact and relaxed style, bound by respect, trust and love freely given and accepted — and certainly without the constant worry about rules, demarcation and the strictures of religious duty — was, she had thought, only ever found in slushy movies. But now she knew that it could really happen, and that she could be a part of it, if she wanted.

And with Jack and Jadis there came an added bonus prize — Tom — who had forced her to rethink everything she'd ever thought she knew about men and sex. She had the impression that he'd slept with at least as many women as she had with men, but with one crucial difference. Whereas she used men as a means to an end, Tom loved women simply for what they were. Because of this, his attention, while earthy, was always courtly, respectful — perhaps a little old-fashioned. And this was vitally important for Shoshana, who, until she met Tom had not quite realized that her desire for conquest was fuelled by a need for sexual satisfaction which, the more she strove to achieve it, the more it remained out of reach.

But there was another thing, too. Tom, having been raised in an atmosphere free from strictures, gave his love without expectation of return. It was this, as well as his obvious consideration for her (which he would have thought of, if he'd thought of it at all, as simple good manners) that had evoked a response in her that was far more than reflexive or mechanical. She felt that she wanted to demonstrate her feelings for him likewise without thought of any recompense, but simply because he was there, and she felt like it.

She'd known this instinctively within a few minutes of first meeting him, when with a casual smile he'd removed all her defenses and rendered all her usual stratagems at naught. But it had taken her much longer to admit it to herself, to fight her way through to this conclusion, past a host of snares and demons.

The first two weeks at Saint-Rogatien, before Tom had to return to Cambridge for what was still called the Trinity Term, had been exciting as well as deeply frustrating. They rose early each day and had no time for confidences. Tom rode off with Jack to the Merlin Institute Campus the other side of Aurignac, where he was learning about laboratory techniques for handling ancient DNA.

The Neanderthal skeletons at SSM represented the single biggest source of high-quality ancient DNA from any species anywhere in the world, and now that Jadis had opened up significant time depth, the team was beginning to shed light on Neanderthal genomic evolution over the course of hundreds of thousands of years in detail unprecedented for any species, living or extinct.

Shoshana, however, accompanied Jadis to SSM itself. Jadis advised her that, as a school-leaver, she should get more of a general flavor of an archaeological site rather than learn anything particular in any depth. Shoshana, though, was on her guard. After that first visit to SSM, nothing more was said about the mysterious inscription for several days. Shoshana sensed that Jadis, in particular, was uneasy about it, and that Jack and Tom dared not venture close to that subject.

Hence Shoshana's surprise when, four days after her arrival, when they were driving to the site, Jadis put Shoshana on the spot—what should she do with the Sigil? The Inscription at the bottom of the pit? Should she publish it? Shoshana was initially flustered and a little embarrassed to be asked, but Jadis didn't seem to be playing games. It was as if Jadis really did want to know, much as her Aunt Jess and (more particularly) her mother seemed to be relying more and more on Shoshana to make important decisions about their finances, their living arrangements—their lives.

So Shoshana reviewed the evidence as she saw it.

"Well, first, it's an artifact," she began, "the inscription can't be natural." Her mouth had gone dry. She licked her lips.

"Go on," said Jadis.

"The age—that's interesting. If it's older than can be measured by any technique…?"

"That's right, Shoshana."

"Then… well… what can be said, except that it doesn't belong there? It's…" she struggled for the right word.

"Intrusive." Jadis added.

"So what would I do about it? If you're asking me, I'd do nothing: keep it a secret."

"Why should I do that?" asked Jadis, who seemed genuinely intrigued. It dawned on Shoshana, then, why her views were being sought: it was because, as a scientific ingénue, her views were likely to be more honest than those of Jadis' immediate academic peers. Like the little boy in the story of the Emperor's New Clothes. This realization—that even to her heroine, one of the greatest archaeologists in history, her view might actually matter, filled her with a new confidence.

"Because… well, because the whole thing just sounds completely crazy," she said. Shoshana thought she might have misjudged this remark, but Jadis only smiled at her, willing her on. She gathered her thoughts.

"If the inscription isn't natural," Shoshana continued, "then somebody must have made it." She swallowed, forcing her nerves back down her gullet. "But who?" The first hominids in Europe that made tools lived a lot later, maybe two million years ago, max?" Shoshana was beginning to think she'd been trapped into some kind of oral exam.

"Keep going," encouraged Jadis, "so what does it all mean?"

"It means that you have…" she hesitated… "you *can* have no idea who made this artifact, not even a single suggestion. Apart from aliens. That's why, if it were down to me, I'd keep schtum until we knew more about hominid history. Maybe you could get some clues from the bones and other stuff in the lower layers you've been digging out? But—oh—that won't work, because the artifact is intrusive, so the other material won't shed any light on... Oh, I don't know, and you're, well, you're..."

"Shoshana, don't worry," said Jadis: "I won't bite. This isn't a trick question, and I really am interested in your opinion. And for what it's worth, I agree with you. I'll keep quiet. At least for now."

The conversation petered out, then. The jeep bowled along the lanes, Jadis' profile strobed in light and shadow, laddered by the poplars and planes on the dusty roadside.

What Shoshana really wanted to talk about was Tom, although she knew that this was the very last subject she'd broach. She'd known Tom hardly a week, but her heart was racing ahead, careering out of her control, and this was disturbing. She wanted to ask why he'd remained nothing more than polite. Warm and smiling, to be sure, but also just a shade uneasy in her company—even though his eyes, when uncovered, were on her constantly. It was agonizing, and she was dying to ask Tom what his feelings were, but if there really were a spell, she didn't want to break it; and in any case she felt she didn't know Tom at all well enough to put such things into words in case they might be misinterpreted.

Now, were Tom any other man, she'd simply have shrugged off all these worries and got on with her life. But the simple fact was that he had already won her and the question was whether she should just declare unconditional surrender (in other words, just show him) or let himself work it out on his own. But why was he so hesitant? Could it be because he didn't want to come on to her in his parents' house? Maybe, but he hadn't had the chance to take her anywhere else. Or perhaps he already had a girlfriend, and was trying to spare her feelings by toughing it out until he got back to Cambridge? This was entirely possible, and the realization made her recoil in anguish. How could she not have thought of this before? And so the first week continued, her eyes exposed to the wonders of the ancient world at first hand; her heart in a flutter of hypothesis.

She couldn't go on like this, she felt, as the second week drew on, and Tom was due to return to Cambridge at the end of the third, and then she'd be stuck here for eight more weeks, marooned, still in search of resolution. It would be intolerable. Some answers came when Tom came to her room with a cup of tea early one Sunday morning. He put the tea down on the chest of drawers and sat on the edge of the bed.

"I've an idea," he said. "I'm really sorry I haven't showed you around at all—we've just been so busy. So let's go for a picnic. Just you and me? A date?"

Although this was just what she'd been hoping for, her own feelings surprised her. Men asked her on dates all the time. Sometimes she agreed, sometimes she didn't, and quite often she agreed but later on found something more interesting to do instead. This time she felt she was a little girl again and her Dad (her *real* Dad) had given her a present she'd always wanted, or had taken her to some fabulous place, like the park, or the zoo, just the two of them. So the tears that now started in her eyes as she sat up and embraced Tom were partly of joy, and partly of regret, for she knew in that moment how much physical affection she'd been missing, for years on end: and that she'd finally traversed a parched desert into which she'd effectively been banished the moment she'd heard that her Dad had died.

So they raided the kitchen for bread, cheese, fruit and wine, and Tom drove them to a byway just outside Marciac, between fields of tall, ripening maize, that led to a small lake of clear blue with a small, secluded, sandy beach. Where Tom had been hesitant, he was now demonstrative: Shoshana decided not to inquire about Tom's seeming change of heart, and to enjoy what could well turn out to be a memorable day for them both. After they'd eaten, Tom stripped down to his shorts and ran full tilt into the lake. She felt that she had no option but to follow him: she dropped her shorts and chased after him, laughing, catching up with him in the water, and finding not a man, but a maelstrom of splashing and noise. He drenched her, ducked her, pulled her under, laughing all the while—and she did the same to him—until, just as suddenly, they stopped and were close together, quiet in each other's embrace, up to their necks in water. They emerged from the lake as if they were the first man and woman in the world, the first amphibians to crest the waves to discover a new land.

Jadis came into the yard to greet them. Shoshana was grateful that she didn't ask them about their picnic, as she was clearly bursting with news of her own.

"Domingo just called," she told Tom. "He's in the area, and he's coming for supper. Isn't that wonderful?"

Domingo arrived on cue along with Jack, just as Jadis was dishing up a farmhouse supper of new loaves, cheese, pâté and pickles. Jadis hugged the huge man even before he'd had a chance to cross the threshold.

"It's been such a long time," she said. "We really could use your advice…"

Shoshana recognized him as the very ugly man in the aloha shirt from the mantelpiece photo, although he was now bearded and grizzled, a vast mane of silver hair running down between his great shoulders. He was wearing a

Hawai'ian shirt now, rather faded and a little tight around the girth, and Shoshana realized where Tom got his from. For his part, Tom embraced the big man as if he were Father Christmas. Domingo produced a grin so full of teeth you'd have thought he was going to bite someone's head off, unless you also looked at his eyes, deep reservoirs of intelligence, each almost buried beneath an eyebrow the size of a small thunderhead.

Strange as it seemed, Shoshana thought, Domingo looked more at home here than anyone else, and she realized that one of the most important things in life was just that, a secure feeling of home. It was something she'd lost at a crucial time in her life, because the people who should have made her home for her had betrayed that obligation. But she could, if she'd let it, find it here, in this same farmhouse, as Domingo seemed to have done.

Her eyes must have lit up and they caught his: he shambled over to where she was sitting at the table and took her hands in his, enclosing them.

"You must be the delightful Ms. Levinson," he said. "I hope you'll like it here, just as much as I always have."

And so, she thought—he knew. Somehow, and as unlikely as it seemed, the middle-aged, deeply learned Catholic priest forged an instant connection with this young Jewess, a connection which, for these two people alone in the farmhouse, that spoke of early lives filled with wretchedness and hurt that was, for him at least, finally exorcised here, as it might be for her, too, were she to allow it. Her thoughts split up into a host of confused, separate but intertwining strands, one of which told her that her experience as a Jew would have been so much richer had the clerics at her school been a fraction as understanding as this priest.

She later discovered, to her astonishment, that this was the very same priest who'd drafted the Papal decree that encouraged Catholics to welcome any hominid species to God, transforming the Church. She'd learned about that, of course, wholly in the negative, damned by rabbis who were still arguing over the narrow definitions of who constituted a Jew, let alone a human being—the status of Sand Druids being an issue that was still to be resolved in many corners of Jewry.

Shoshana had known Jewish kids at her secular secondary school who went to synagogue regularly—far more than she ever did—and yet were barred from Jewish youth clubs and Jewish schools, not because they didn't believe in God, not because they weren't academically qualified, but simply because their *mothers* weren't born as Jews, or hadn't undergone the strictures of Orthodox conversions that were designed not to welcome new converts, but to do everything they could to throw obstacles beneath their feet. She remembered slanging matches with Howie about this, stinging him with the accusation that his kind of Judaism was a kind of Nazism in reverse.

"Some of my best friends are *untermenschen*!" she'd screamed: "And how about '*Ihre papiere, Bitte*?'" miming a Gestapo agent who, like Orthodox rabbis, were forever in search of hard, documentary evidence to prove one's Jewishness, as if faith and commitment were not themselves sufficient. "What do you think of that, Howie?"

Howie had either averted his gaze, or muttered words to the effect that teenage girls who lacked respect for their elders couldn't possibly be expected to understand. But in Domingo she saw an elder who commanded respect without demanding or expecting it. Now she'd finally met him, she wouldn't have been at all surprised if she found herself wanting to escape from her Judaism altogether as her father had once tried to do—but she realized that this was impossible. If you are born a Jew, that's that. And, as Howie often added—no matter how much you paint yourself white, you're still a *schwarzer* underneath. It wasn't meant to be racist, he'd said—that was just the way *Ha'Shem* made the world, and we had to accept it.

Supper was as full of merriment as any meal at the farmhouse always was when Domingo was around. He was now a Cardinal and one of the Pope's closest advisors, but had been granted a few days' leave before accompanying the Pope on a state visit to Israel. Domingo said he'd hoped to meet Avi, but expected that his schedule would keep him firmly at the side of His Holiness. Shoshana learned that this was Professor Avram Malkeinu, an archaeologist almost as famous as Jadis and Jack, and when Jadis told her that Domingo and Avi had been the Bad Boys of *Le Dig* at Saint-Rogatien more than two decades before, Shoshana was torn between laughter and astonishment.

"To be sure, Shoshana," said Domingo. "And, believe it or not, our beloved Rolling Stones will be playing a concert in Tel Aviv during my visit. Even at the same stadium at which His Holiness is due to celebrate mass. Though not, I regret, siimultaneously. However, I expect that the exigencies of politics and antiquity shall conspire to prevent our attendance. Ah, well." He sighed, somewhat theatrically, Shoshana, though, given the sly twinkle in his eyes. She stifled a giggle: Domingo picked up on her amusement, and seemed tickled in his turn to learn that she would be making her second trip to Israel at about the same time, with Tom, and that they'd be spending a couple of weeks exploring Avi's dig sites on Mount Carmel.

"Please give that young rogue my best regards, won't you?" said Domingo. "And—here's a thought—if you you… ah… young people get the chance to see Messrs Jagger and Richards, don't pass it up. I shall expect a full report, of course." His eyes clouded—"we had such wonderful times here, Avi and me, and everyone, such wonderful times, in the good old days..." He looked at Jadis, who was smiling back: "Ah me! For a beaker of the warm south! Now, what was it you wanted me to see?"

And so Jadis told Domingo about the inscription, the strange Sigil, ancient beyond measure, that had been the source of the long-puzzling gravitational anomaly at the summit of the Great Pyramid at Souris Saint-Michel. Domingo betrayed no emotion, but asked if he could see an image of it. Jack went upstairs to the office to fetch a drawing, and, clearing the table, they unrolled the sheet of white paper, weighting it down at the corners with pickle jars and coffee mugs. The inscription was several times actual size, Jack explained, blown up so that every detail could be clearly seen.

"The real thing's only about twelve centimeters by three," he said, "stamped or traced on the artifact itself, which is hardly larger — and the lines are so thin that they're actually very hard to make out without some degree of... um... strain."

Shoshana was almost sure that Jack glanced, just for an moment, in her direction. She remembered how giddy she felt when she'd stared at the inscription. It was only now that it occurred to her that everyone who'd looked at it felt much the same. But rather than feeling that she'd been the victim of some peculiar initiation ritual, she was glad that Jadis and Jack and Tom had allowed her to see it at all. Her presence here, at this conspiratorial kitchen table, was evidence that she'd been welcomed into a very exclusive club indeed.

She looked at the tracing, and the company fell silent. The inscription lay within its own rectangular frame or cartouche. Inscribed within the rectangle were three circles: one at the left-hand end of the frame, one at the right, and one in the middle. Between each circle stood a crescent, like the crescent moon, their horns pointing outwards, away from the central circle. Fine lines radiated from the central circle to all corners and edges of the rectangular frame.

There was a long pause. It was Domingo who broke the silence.

"First, there can be no doubt that this is intentional," he said. "Nothing natural makes patterns as geometrical as this. And I'd hazard that what we're seeing is a picture, albeit stylized, of a total eclipse of the Sun."

Jadis nodded, as if she had suspected the same thing, but desired some kind of confirmation. Shoshana was amazed. She had no idea what the pattern of lines and shapes might have meant.

"Imagine that this circle on the left"—Domingo pointed at it—"is the solar disk. Then, reading from left to right, it is occluded from the left by the Moon, and we can see the eclipse as it progresses in the crescent. In the central circle, we see totality. The disk is completely covered except for the solar corona…"

"That must be the radiating lines…" said Jack.

"Exactly so. And as we go towards the right, we see the Moon moving on, leaving the rightmost disc as the Sun, once again… ah… uncovered." Domingo paused, still thoughtful, as if he hadn't finished.

"But, my friends, I am puzzled. Usually, records of eclipses in ancient astronomy refer to particular eclipses…"

"That's what I thought," said Jadis, "and had I the confidence, I'd ask an astronomer to look at this, if I knew any, but I don't think it would be possible to tie this to any one eclipse, particularly as we can't establish the age of the artifact."

"And even if we could," broke in Jack, "the inscription could have been made at any time after the material that constitutes the artifact itself was formed…"

"And," concluded Jadis, "we haven't any idea when that might have been. Not a clue."

"You do have one clue, my dear Jadis," said Domingo. "Or, perhaps, two."

"I do?" Jadis looked shocked.

"Yes, of course. First, if age of the artifact cannot be measured, that means that it must be very old indeed. Perhaps older than the Earth. And, second, if the… ah…. nature of the artifact's material resists investigation, it could be that it is made of something ordinary that's been… ah… transformed by some unimaginable physical process. But you'll have thought of all these things, of course."

"Yes, Domingo," said Jadis. "And that's why we're at a dead end. I'm reluctant even to share this finding with anyone, let alone people outside our field."

"I quite understand," said Domingo. "But one should not depair. I believe that the Merlin Technologies Astrometry Institute—your sister body—might be well placed to offer some advice. My colleagues at the Vatican Observatory have forged some useful links with them lately," continued Domingo, "very useful. I've become quite a fan of their work of late. However, I can understand why you might want to sit on this one, for a while. Too much like *Chariots of the Gods*, eh?"

Jadis smiled, weakly: the work at SSM had trawled up its share of cranks and conspiracy theorists, and reprints of Von Däniken's hoary old aliens-and-humans bestsellers from the 1970s were enjoying a new vogue. This was just the kind of thing she wanted to avoid, and she was grateful that Domingo understood.

"In any case," Domingo went on, "I am not sure whether any astronomer might have been able to help, in this instance. This picture, you see, works however you look at it — up, down, or from right to left. I suspect that this isn't a record but a pictogram, a statement of eclipses in general, rather than any one that might be identified."

"But why?" asked Jack. "Could it be some kind of sympathetic magic?"

"Like cave paintings of mammoths and bison, you mean?" asked Domingo. "Summoning up success in the hunt? It's an interesting thought, my dear Jack. But who'd want to conjure eclipses? In all societies they are seen as omens of terror. The ancient Chinese, you know, had an engaging myth about eclipses. They thought the Sun was being swallowed by a dragon, which was very large but also very shy. The legend was that if enough people came outdoors to shout at it, the dragon would be frightened away. Isn't that lovely?"

Jack joined in Domingo's mirth. " — and what do you know," he said, "they must have been right, because it always worked."

Domingo became serious, with a suddenness that startled them. "Yes, dear Jack, it *has* always worked — *so far.*"

"But that's just it," said Tom, "the sign-makers didn't want to encourage eclipses, to bring them on…"

"No, it was the other way round," said Shoshana: "They wanted to ward them off, at all costs… to find a way of chasing the dragons away…"

"*D'accord,*" said Tom. "It could even be a warning."

And at this, Tom and Shoshana turned as one to look at Domingo, who looked stunned, pleased, and then, as if recalling something he really ought to have remembered earlier, profoundly worried.

"My dear Jadis," he said, "I fear that your young *protégés* are quite correct, though I cannot say why. And so my advice, if you want it, is to keep this discovery quiet, at least for the moment."

He would not elaborate further, but asked if Jadis had any more of that good coffee, and some more of her 'world-famous' Gascon chocolate cake? Jadis always fell for people complimenting her on her cooking—something at which, in contrast to her expert gardening, she felt rather deficient, and therefore responded eagerly to all encouragement.

Later, lying in bed, Shoshana was abuzz from the visit of this strange and strangely compelling new visitor, but before long she thought back to the picnic with Tom. How he'd broken his reserve. How they'd made love, right there, on the beach, and afterwards, how she felt that she'd come home at last.

When, a week later, Tom left for Cambridge, she felt as she'd expected—empty, wretched and lost. She returned to work trying to act as normal and cheerful as she could. But in her heart she knew that this wasn't the real Shoshana, but just a phony. Inside she felt about as useful as a squashed football. Without Tom around, she was even more exposed and alone, as a guest in the house of his parents, whom she hardly knew, so of course she couldn't tell them of her feelings for their own and only son. Had she known him better, she could have certainly talked to Jack: but Jadis was, for her, on a pedestal, and nobody confides in a statue.

A couple of days after Tom left, Domingo had passed through on an another flying visit, returning to Rome from one Papal errand or another, and she had wanted to talk to him then—what was the word, *confess*?—but she thought it would be just too weird. Her religious world was very much constrained by her past, which she realized was not just a straitjacket, but a star to steer by. She could not abandon it for something so alien, for all that her instincts screamed at her that this man was likely to be a good listener, and that her worries would go no further. In any case, by the time she'd plucked up the courage to approach him, he'd gone.

So she was left in the house of strangers, trying to be on her *Shabbat* best behavior. Until, one evening about two weeks later when she found that she could manage this charade no longer. She and Jadis were sitting at the kitchen table, Jadis lost in a spread-sheeted morass of figures, Shoshana pecking her way through a file of site reports and papers on SSM that she felt duty bound to study, making notes on her Airtab. But the time came when she found herself reading the same lines over and over again, and no effort she could make could get her to the next one. It was as if she'd hit a wall. A tear of frustration slid down her cheek. Jadis looked up then, peering over her reading glasses.

"Shoshana," she said, "what's the matter?"

"I'm sorry, so sorry" she replied, and then, without meaning to, "I miss him so. I'm so sorry, but I miss him so much…." She started to get up, her intention being to pack her rucksack and ask to be taken to the airport, for now her secret was out, she was fit to stay in the farmhouse no longer. She could hardly be banished from Eden if she chose to leave of her own accord.

At first Jadis said nothing, but rose, came round to Shoshana's side of the table and put her arms around her. "Oh, you poor, poor girl," she said. "If only I'd known. If only you'd told me…"

A little later, Jadis had steered Shoshana up to bed, and sat by her on the bentwood chair, and talked to her—really, for the first time. Shoshana was relieved that Jadis did not inquire about Shoshana's past life or present needs (she felt that she'd have withered up with embarrassment), but sought to reassure her that the farmhouse was her home, and always would be, whenever she wanted it. Shoshana realized how much and how hard she'd been fighting against this gift, this offer to relieve her of her past life, as something too good to be true. But here was Jadis, making it entirely plain that if she wanted Eden, all she had to do was accept it, with no thought of recompense.

"Come and live here—move in!" said Jadis. "It's a big house. There's always room for one more." So Jadis told Shoshana of the story of how she met Jack, and told her just how much she'd missed him when he'd first left for France, and that she understood what Shoshana now felt for Tom: that you wanted someone so intensely that you felt actual, physical pain. Jadis recalled how the absence of Jack was like a twisting knife in her abdomen; and Shoshana, without words, but in the way she sat up and hugged Jadis, admitted that the way she felt for Tom was just the same.

"I know, I know, it all seemed so silly from this distance," said Jadis, "and you should excuse the ravings of a silly old woman. But I remember that pain, Shoshana. Even the memory of that pain is painful, for all that it happened before you were born." Much to Shoshana's surprise, Jadis started to cry, too, as if letting out some private anguish coiled up for years that could no longer be contained.

"Shoshana," she said, quite deliberately, so she wouldn't seem patronizing, "No matter what happens—and especially no matter what happens with Tom—I'll always be here for you, if you need me. Always."

Chapter 7. Settlers

Central North Africa, Earth, c. 6,355,000 years ago

And hear at times a sentinel
    Who moves about from place to place,
    And whispers to the world of space,
In the deep night, that all is well.
Alfred, Lord Tennyson — *In Memoriam*

That warrior was the first of many people of the same kind. At first they rode straight past Alfred's hermitage, heading for the faint ridge on the western horizon that he knew was a high and extensive range of mountains, though Alfred had never been there himself. Some of the tall, milky-eyed people stopped at his gate, offering gifts of food and drink, which he accepted with good grace.

After the warriors came the herdsmen, steering droves of anthracotheres and other beasts less familiar to Alfred, all towards the west. They did not stay long, but when they did, the herds, snouting and squealing, seemed to stretch from one horizon to the other, and Alfred began to fear for his thorn bushes, which began to look even more threadbare than ever. The tide of animal droppings in the herds' wake, though, more than made up for it, both as fertilizer and as fuel. Wood for firing was ever harder to find, and nights on the savannah were cold.

The years passed, and the savannah became ever more populous. The wilderness around Alfred's hermitage became tamed with fields, stockades and homesteads. The people — the Annakhnu, as they called themselves — were polite enough, and kept out of his way, for the most part. But he found (to his surprise) that he'd become 'adopted' by the clans who lived in the homesteads close by, who treated him with great reverence, and often came to him to discuss knotty ethical, spiritual—even familial and marital problems. He heard, through his regular Annakhnu visitors (he hesitated to think of them as 'parishioners') that the Brethren in the community of Shinaar were accorded similar respect, for which he was also grateful, though he did not really understand why these quiet, polite conquerors were so accommodating. Perhaps they did not see the Brethren as sufficiently numerous to constitute a threat.

He did, though, become tolerably proficient in the newcomers' language, and when that happened, some species of comprehension began to coalesce from the alien fog. At first the effort of speaking the language was very great, rather like being forced to make an extended series of regurgitations, just to say the simplest things—and this in a dry country in which saliva was at a premium.

But it was through this language that he learned of the deepest beliefs and wishes of the Annakhnu, which was this—that they would not 'come into their own,' as they put it, until their new city, now slowly accumulating on the heights to the west—had been blessed by some celestial portent. The Annakhnu spoke of this in terms of the most dramatic and florid phenomena: of lightning from darkened skies, and visitations of fiery chariots from heaven. Such events, the Annakhnu said, were imminent. Their shamans looked for them every day, casting runes now to plot the precise hour, the exact minute. And that was when something dark, something exciting, stirred in Alfred's brain. Unfortunately for Alfred, this revelation, when it awoke, found that something even darker and potentially more deadly was already in residence.

The school of babbling children had gone, their lessons over for the day. Alfred saw them career in gay, gangling masses, like a flock of pinwheels, towards the heron-gray horizon, yelling their excited good-byes. Alfred loved the children. He loved teaching them basic arithmetic, astronomy, geometry. It was tiring — it was *always* tiring — but now Alfred felt more than usually drained, worn into catatonia, and he felt a headache starting to unfurl just behind his eyes. At first he thought it might have been the weather: oppressive, unnaturally hot, spectacular thunderclouds building in stacked formations high into the sky. But never a drop of rain, no measure of the easeful relief that rain would bring.

He stood, propped up at his gate as the bright motes of the children shrank and vanished against the threatening vastness of cloud, his hand raised in valediction. He looked up at it and wondered why it was still there, pointing up like that, into the sky. There was another arm, now, an arm at his shoulder, not his. It was Leila, a tall and stringy Annakhnu woman of middle years who, with her sister, had lately taken it upon herself to look after the ageing hermit.

"*Aba*? Father? Are you all right?" Her questioning became shriller, more urgent, but somehow he couldn't find the strength to answer, no matter how hard she clucked, how insistently her claw-like fingers clutched at his robe. The words he wanted to utter formed in his mind like the burgeoning waters in a mountain spring, but by the time they reached his mouth they had dribbled away into nothingness. Evaporated. He stood there, the Sun setting, the Moon rising, his arm still raised, and the thin cream-eyed face of Leila, framed by a cowl, peering round at him, concerned.

"Father?"

He felt a thin string of drool trickle down his chin, but for some reason he couldn't work out, he did not feel inclined to move a hand or an arm to wipe it clean, as if the hands and arms he felt he had once had at his disposal did not really belong to him and he had to ask permission for their use, but couldn't now remember whom to ask. The arm pointed skywards was, now, gently lowered, and he could see that the person lowering it was Leila. By now Leila's sister had arrived. Lilit, as bustlingly plump as Leila was thin, cleaned his face with the busy concentration of a dung beetle. The feeling of her sleeve on his chin tickled and he wanted to laugh. A thin cackle emerged from what he imagined was his throat. Leila and Lilit laughed too, the laughter of the relief of the rain that did not come. With great gentleness the two women turned him around and steered him, step by step, into the hut.

He lay there for several sticky, stinking days—he counted two phases of the Moon—and at first he could hardly move. The sisters bathed the sheen of sweat from his skin, his fur, cleaned his nether regions. He wished he had the voice to thank them for performing this unpleasant yet necessary office. Instead he made a kind of odd snuffling noise. They seemed to understand and for that he uttered a prayer (necessarily silent) to the Goddess, in her avatar—as it always appeared to him now, in his memory—of a hem of red, disappearing behind the white wall of his hut.

In his motionless state he began to assemble further thoughts, at first with the inelegance of a child's first towers of toy blocks, forever teetering and falling, but after each fall, a greater confidence, a surer resurrection. And his thoughts ran as follows: that all this heathenish Annakhnu chatter of signs and portents and fire from the sky coincided, *suspiciously* coincided, with the imminent Apparition of the Goddess. In the great scheme of things, it probably mattered little whether the Goddess arrived this year, next year, or sometime in the next ten thousand—because such intervals are neither here nor there given that the Blessed One visits only once every two million years or so. Alfred remembered the academic debates of his youth, about equinoctial precession; and galactic longitude; and compensating for changes in the Earth's gravitational field; and the significance of the amount of oxygen in the tests of microscopic diatoms dredged from the bottom of the Great Lake, and further arcana of that sort. Alfred could never work out why that mattered, but it had nevertheless remained stuck in his mind, like that speck of food that always manages to lodge between one's incisors, especially when one is trying to have a serious conversation with a superior cleric. Alfred thought all such debates sterile at the time. After the passage of eight decades he did not feel inclined to change his mind.

But even so, when all these things had been considered, why had the Annakhnu arrived *now*?

The flashes of day and night, darkness and light, counterpointed with the comings and goings of the two women and, somewhere between now and then, a painted Annakhnu shaman, until, one day, he found he could sit up, get up, and move about, and that he could reclaim his arms and legs as his own. He danced the dance of a much younger man, whirling around the hut, first with one sister, then another, yelling his inchoate praise.

A day dawned of great joy when he found he had recovered the ability to speak. The capacity was yet limited to a vocabulary of one, but the word was well chosen, he thought, and he made it do the work of many.

"*Hashek'na!*" he screamed, when they tried to bathe him.

"*Hashek'na!*" he roared, between mouthfuls of the soup they were trying to feed him, undeterred by the explosions of flying vegetable and fishy gobbets that punctuated each such announcement.

"*Hashek'na!*" he sang, as he capered around the hut, driving the sisters to distraction, screaming this single word, over and over, the word that in the Annakhnu language meant "Goddess."

He slept well that night, despite the pummeling heat, and for most of the following morning. By the afternoon—like all afternoons, now, black with billowing cloud—a second word had found refuge in his damaged brain, where it snuggled up against the first and made friends with it. As evening fell he rushed naked out of the hut, the sisters clucking in pursuit, his robe uselessly brandished before them, as he reached his garden gate and pointed up at the sky.

"Calm yourself, Father," urged Leila, "please, at least put your clothes on."

"Goddess here!" He looked up into the vault, his voice subsiding into a childlike wonderment, as Leila busied herself trying to force the old man's robes over his head.

"Goddess here! Goddess here! Here! Here! *Here*!"

Lilit, however, glanced to westward, following the hermit's staring eyes. Her own now opened as wide as his: her mouth went slack with shock.

"Sister, look—"

All three of them stopped and looked, then, at the evening sky. A sky seared with flaming brands, raining from heaven. And from within the flames and shards of falling scoria, something else. Something that the three people standing at the thorn-branch gate could hardly comprehend. It fell, silver-bright, through the clouds, hovering over the savannah some distance to the west. What struck Alfred most of all was the eerie silence of it all, as if all sound had been stolen from the world.

It looked like the Moon had fallen out of the sky.

-=0=-

"Come in!" barked the Abbot. The door opened on Mandergast, followed by a pale-faced novice, clearly awed by the company. The first rain in months began to fall, the first drops clattering heavily on the windows.

"No, don't get up," the Abbot said as the Brethren Cynewulf and Caedmon stirred to rise from their seats, as if to go. Then, to the novice, "We won't bite, my son. We're quite friendly, really. We limit ourselves to one novice each, per day—even the ferocious Brother Caedmon, here—and we've already eaten." He smiled and patted his large belly. "Though, these days, I must confess, I never can eat a whole one."

Caedmon began to snigger; Cynewulf to roar; and even the novice, after an interval of what looked like utter terror, saw the joke and joined in, a treble cadence above the general monastic din. Mandergast remained mute and still. The Abbot knew that his servant had seen all of this before, many times, and it presumably puzzled him as much now as it ever did.

"Now, my son, what was it you wanted to say?"

"Yes Father. That some people have arrived from the western savannah, and should like to see you."

"'People,' my son?"

"Yes, Father. Two Annakhnu ladies, Father, and one of the Brethren, I think, though he's very old. I... I think he's ill, Father, he..."

A thought passed behind the Abbot's eyes and disappeared into his mind's gloom. A memory of one of his predecessors. Almost a memory of himself. Retiring. A hermitage. Years and years ago. And inexplicably, a flash of sudden scarlet against a white, sun-brightened wall.

"... threw up on the floor of the refectory. The Annakhnu ladies made quite a fuss. Novice Aelle and I cleared up the mess. The ladies wanted to help. Brother Cedd came then and calmed them all down."

"Do you know who they are? And why they have come?"

"No, Father. He wanted to see you, Father. The old Brother. He insisted, though it was hard to understand him, Father. He talked mostly in Annakhnu, I think, and even then his words were difficult to... like, slurred, and... well..."

"Thank you, my son. Please go back to the refectory and ask Brother Cedd to show our mysterious guests to suitable accommodation, to ensure they can wash, and have such food and drink as we have. I shall be along to see them shortly."

After I have prayed, he thought.

"At once, Father." The novice bowed, and left, followed by Mandergast. The Abbot indicated to the Brethren Cynewulf and Caedmon that their interview, too, was at an end — for the moment — and he was soon alone in his office once again. Alone, the rain-dark clouds beyond the windows, the savannah sky now filled with ruinous thunder.

Alone, in the dark. As if he could describe his life in any other way. He had appalled himself at the scale of his own complacency, that it was only in the past few weeks that he had sought to ask questions of his own life. No, not of his faith, for that was unshakeable. His motivations — his calling, his ministry — were likewise supported by his complete conviction of their utter rightness. No, none of these things was in question. His troubles were more personal.

He rose quietly from his chair and left his office. The cloistered corridor outside was quite dark. The shockingly bright jags of lightning that seared through the regularly spaced windows only deepened the darkness between. Had he not already known this way with his eyes shut, the Abbot would surely have felt as if he were voyaging rudderless through inky space, leaping blind from one star to the next.

At first he had great difficulty simply articulating the nature of his malaise, just finding the words to express the unease that had condensed in his mind. As a first approximation, he'd say that he was having problems reconstructing his life as a narrative.

He had come to the Brethren as a teenager, about thirteen or fourteen, and had never sought to look back, beyond that. He had always assumed that the stories they'd later told him were true — that he was a foundling, the sole infant survivor of a village razed in some long-forgotten skirmish far away, and had been passed, hand to hand like a parcel, across many countries, perhaps even continents, before arriving at the doors of this last resort, the lonely Mission by the Great Lake.

He was troubled, now, that until recently he had never sought to corroborate this history; worse, even to question it. Perhaps the details were too vague to allow any investigation any purchase without prodigious expense of effort, and anyway, what would have been the point? The Mission had made him everything he was, everything he would be, so to look back would have been fruitless, painful even, and why bring any more pain into a world already long overburdened with that commodity?

However, he was troubled to find that when he did try to look back, setting out to plumb his own mind, concentrating hard — in the way that he had long been taught, as a meditative exercise — he could retrieve no memory of any life before the Mission. None whatsoever.

Could it be that through technique, and slow time, he had simply learned to forget? To expunge his past, replacing such remote recall with antennae that might better detect the faint echoes of the voice of the Goddess? No, that could not be it: conversing with the Goddess was something he had always found ridiculously easy, at least compared with the problems experienced by every one of his colleagues with whom he'd shared such intimacies.

But of any life before the Mission there was no trace. Not so much as an impression; an atmosphere; a tableau whose location and the identities of the large cast of characters had been forgotten, for all that the whole might be brought vividly to life; the sense of the milky closeness of a maternal primary breast, or the sudden waking, as an infant, to the eternal sunshine of childhood's lost play. No subsequent impression, no odor, no sound, had had the effect—as he had heard it did with others—of the sharply realized recall of times now lost.

There was more to this malady, however, more disturbing yet than a mere poverty of memory. For it was only since he became Abbot that he'd begun to have the flesh-crawling sensation that he'd been along the same tracks before. Not the recall of memories of an earlier life, but of a life—of lives—lived, here and now, in very much the same way. A sense of *déjà-vu* which could be at times very strong. Yes, it was only when he became Abbot and started to read the private diaries of his predecessors that this sensation started to feed on itself, amplifying to a pitch that was disabling in its intensity. It was at times like that when he would go to the chapel and fling himself on the timeworn flags before the statue of the Goddess, shivering, penitent, confused—and frightened.

For when he read those words—of Abbots Aethelwald, and Aelfric, and Alfred; and of Abbots Aelfwine, and Guthlac, and Breca, and Unferth, and Sigelweara, and the Abbots before them, and so on beyond count, back, and back, and back into archival mists so ancient that the words, even the alphabets in which they had been written, were hard even for greater scholars than he to decipher—he found that he could read and understand them all, every word, with perfect clarity.

The conclusion was as outrageous and impossible as it was parsimonious and inevitable, but he had put it off for as long as he could. But events were overtaking him, now, or would if he let them, and he'd seen the same records that Brother Cynewulf had seen, and he would have supported his subordinate completely in his interpretation that the records indeed spoke very plainly, except in one thing. That Cynewulf had missed something of the idiom: the records were even plainer than his colleague had thought. They were now emblazoned on the Abbot's mind in letters of fire.

And it came to pass that the Goddess appeared in the Chapel as a young woman in robes of red.

And she blessed us and made miracles among us.

And she called us brave men, loved, and foolish, but she said all these things with a bright countenance.

And she said that she would reappear at the appointed time in exact same guise.

And she warned us to beware of false gods and false goddesses who would appear otherwise and yet lay claim on our allegiance.

And she spake, saying: 'For I am a Jealous Goddess, apparently, and even though I've probably fucked it up for everyone, as I usually do, I'm not going just to lie back and be two-timed by a load of silly old men like you, lovely though you are, each and every one. So you guys had better watch out. Grrr!'

Such were her Holy words.

The Abbot knew this very well, of course, because he'd been there, had welcomed the Goddess to the Earth in person, and had written these lines himself. While thinking these thoughts he'd walked round the great cloister and found himself, steered as if by automatic pilot, in front of the towering ironwood doors of the chapel itself. The doors were shut, and would remain so until vespers, still two hours away. He could sneak in and prostrate himself before Her image, cooling his forehead on the broad flags at her feet, seeking solace. Indeed, that had been his original plan, or so he thought. But no—he had promised to pay a call to the refectory where the new arrivals would be waiting. He was sure of the identity of one of them, at least, and he was keen to learn the reason for their sudden flight to the Abbey. "She warned us to beware of false gods," he muttered under his breath as he continued on his way.

The refectory was a large space, low-ceilinged and dimly lit, lined with long tables and benches of ironwood. Millions of meals and rough sackcloth sleeves had smoothened the tabletops to a soft gray sheen. The Abbot rarely went to the refectory, preferring to eat in his own quarters. Some might have said that this was appropriate enough for an Abbot who presumably had little time to spend in idle chat with his subordinates. The truth was that the Abbot would have loved to have indulged in gossip—the lifeblood of a place like this, and key to its successful government—but he just happened not to like the smell of the place, a mixture of rancid tallow and slightly-gone-off vegetables.

As the Abbot entered, the refectory was beginning its evening bustle. Pitheks were laying bowls and platters and knives for the evening meal. At one end of a long table, though, a group of larger forms was clustered, huddled round a candle, and he could see and hear that they were already at their meal. He recognized the stork-like figure of

Brother Cedd, wringing his hands in his characteristic posture of anxiety. Seated, though, was a monk of great age, flanked by two Annakhnu women, clucking like birds, who were trying to feed him soup and mashed-up pieces of bread, leaving their own meals largely ignored. The yellow light of the candle flame threw the old man's face into sickly ridges of papery yellow, exaggerating the folds and lines. The man's green-slitted eyes, heavily lidded, seemed enormous in his thin face, as if he'd been startled. A long, thin mouth — a mouth which looked as if it was once used to vigorous and intelligent discourse — now moved slackly, disgorging as many morsels of food as it swallowed, the remainder dribbling into his scruffy beard, chased down by the more rotund of the two women, wielding a cloth like a flail. The old man looked up as the Abbot entered and stopped as if caught in a sudden sunbeam. He swallowed, hard, and tottered to his feet, the two women on either side rushing to steady him. The man made a series of stertorious grunts and finally uttered, into the cavernous hush of the great hall —

"Well, bugger me, it's…"

The Abbot waved him to be seated, as he heaved himself over a bench and sat down next to the thinner Annakhnu woman (whom he later learned was called Leila), the old man seated further along the bench. The Abbot avoided looking directly into the old man's eyes, for fear of seeing more of what he'd learned in the briefest instant as he'd entered the refectory — that in this frail hermit, and former Abbot, was a man in search of himself; the man who he had once been, before the mantle moved on. The Abbot now realized, with sinking heart, that if he'd had any life before this, it had become subsumed into the persona of the head of the Order, eternal, unchanging — but should he ever abandon that role, and yet cling on to life, he could only ever be a lost fragment, disoriented, abandoned to the wilderness, forever seeking the Goddess but never finding her. Poor, poor Venerable Alfred. The Abbot's heart was filled with pity.

"Venerable Alfred," he said, "I am sorry."

"You… sorry?" The old man looked every bit as confused as the Abbot imagined he might be.

"Yes." The Abbot took the old man's hands in his, reaching across the table. They were cold, stringy, thin sinews gnarled with pale, fatty lumps, like the plucked necks of fowls. He looked down, still, not daring to meet Alfred's eyes. Anyone passing the tableau and not knowing the identities of the players would have placed the Abbot as a supplicant before the bright face of an ikon.

"Why sorry? Goddess here. *Here*,' said Alfred. "We saw. Leila and Lilit and me, we saw her. Like moon, falling from sky onto savannah. We saw… we saw…"

"Alfred," replied the Abbot, "you know that cannot be true. You know that the Goddess warned us, to take special care of false gods and goddesses…"

Alfred took up the line, now, and the change in his voice was startling, changing in mid-sentence from a querulous, infarctic dotard to a sage with full mastery of a considerable mind and store of words.

"Yes, Father Abbot, 'to beware of false gods and false goddesses who would appear otherwise and yet lay claim on our allegiance.' I know this well. In which case…" Alfred withdrew a hand from the Abbot's grasp and pulled it to his face. His eyes were like green, alien worlds. "Oh, Goddess, save us, you don't think…?"

"Venerable Alfred, tell me what you saw."

Alfred told the Abbot of the shining disk that landed, hovering a few feet above the plain. Of the holes that opened in the disk, and the lines of hundreds upon hundreds of men armored all in bright silver—for that's what they looked like—who emerged, and streamed away towards the west, towards the Annakhnu's City on the Heights: and the decision that he and Leila and Lilit should cross the cracked bed of the once outflung arm of the shrunken Great Lake and rouse the Brethren to action.

"Father Abbot—I see now," said Alfred. "These must have been the false gods of whom the Goddess herself specifically warned us… and they will be coming this way soon. I…. I…. am a fool, Father, a deluded fool. Forgive me. It is many years indeed since I heard Her True Voice."

"I absolve you, Alfred," the Abbot said. "And your errand is not yet vain. For I know that the Goddess is indeed here. Or will be, very soon."

"She will? Goddess here? Goddess really here?"

"That is what I believe. That the Apparition will fall in three days' time. And you will be able to hear her—see her—at long last. If only we shall all survive that long."

"Why, Father Abbot? Why should we not?"

"Because, I expect, all those false gods and goddesses will try to importune us first, just as the Goddess herself foretold. And they probably won't take 'no' for an answer."

Chapter 8. Transfiguration

Israel, Earth, August, 2054

I say to you that I am dead!
Edgar Allan Poe—*The Facts in the Case of M. Valdemar*

Their home for the next fortnight would be where Avi had spent the greater part of his childhood, and had now been his research base for the best part of two decades. What was, essentially, a field station of the Merlin Technologies Institute for Historical Geomorphology had taken over the accommodation blocks and kitchens of the collective farm where Avi had once played in the dirt, shot his first hoops, made out with his first girl.

The kibbutz itself was only glad to be rid of it all, for the Institute's generous rent had allowed the *kibbutzniks* to pave over groves of olives and oranges and build spacious, modern apartments. For where once the inhabitants had been farmers, making a living of sorts from limes, turkeys, a small herd of Friesians and (its pride and joy) an orange-juice processing plant, they had now largely shaken the dirt from their hands. They had exchanged their tractors and denim coveralls for high-tech, high-paid jobs in Haifa, as far from the Soviet-style kibbutz image of agrarian toil as might be imagined. Farmland was no longer needed—flats and houses most definitely were.

But Avi's parents still lived on the kibbutz, so for him it would always feel a little bit like home. He had, however, moved on: his own home was an army barracks the other side of Haifa, where he lived with his formidable wife Rivka, a military communications specialist, and he had to commute in through the morning sprawl.

Tom and Shoshana were quartered in what was affectionately known as the 'Old Town' — the original heart of the settlement, built back in the 1920s and hardly improved since. This was a double row of about two dozen dilapidated wooden shacks, each row facing the other across a broad dirt square, in the centre of which was a vast and ancient olive tree. Long ago, somebody had strung lines of colored bulbs between the shacks and the tree, and a haphazard collection of tables and chairs had accreted beneath it. This was the social center for the younger kibbutz volunteers, whose parties would often last until the early hours. Tom and Shoshana were assigned a shack at the far end, closest to the washrooms and the avocado plantation that bordered the settlement, beyond which lay the track leading up to the first and closest of Avi's many dig sites, spread all over the Mount Carmel massif.

The shack was certainly nothing fancy: just an iron-framed bed on a chipped linoleum floor, a table and a couple of chairs, bare wooden walls and roof, and an entertaining nightlife featuring cockroaches, columns of ants, geckoes, and on one occasion, a title bout between a scorpion and a praying mantis. Tom and Shoshana loved every minute of it. The evening they arrived they'd joined in the general merrymaking of the polyglot volunteer throng that lasted well after midnight.

Tom knew one or two of the other students attached to the Institute, and felt a great thrill to be able to introduce Shoshana, who was in her element. She loved parties, chat and bustle, and felt that she'd had far too little of that kind of thing lately. Sure, the farmhouse was now her home, a long-sought anchor for her life and a special place in her heart. But a girl has to get out, now and then, to laugh, to dance and to flirt. Having recharged her batteries, she spent the energy regained, much later, with Tom, who she led into the warm leafy darkness of the avocado field, whence she flew him to the moon and back.

Thankfully, Avi allowed them the next morning to acclimatize. When they finally ventured out of doors, they found a world refreshed by a light rain that had fallen in the early hours. Their first sight was a pair of hoopoes displaying to each other in the morning sunshine among the litter of candles, bottles and overturned chairs in the square, whose hard-packed ground exhaled the tangy richness of new-washed earth. Avi had to teach that morning at the Technion in Haifa, he'd explained, and wouldn't be able to show them round his latest dig site until later. He wanted to show it to them himself, so they should take the opportunity of resting up after their long journey and wild night. He was surprised, though, to learn that they actually wanted to sit in on his early morning class, so all three of them rode in together (this time in the relative comfort of a pickup) to see Avi in action.

The class was almost as wild as the volunteers, but it was a wildness kept always one ever-shifting heartbeat from abandon: Avi held the first-year students in the packed hall teetering on a tightrope of chaos. For Tom, who couldn't understand any of it (it was all in Hebrew), it was almost like a comedy show, a clown act. Avi's eyes, his hands, his expressions—they'd made him laugh when he'd been a small child—all were now being put to good use. Tom wished his lectures in Cambridge were half this much fun. Professor Reynard had warned him what to expect from Avi's 'Bones 101' class, as she called it. "It's a bear-pit!" she'd laughed; "the noise! It's amazing he actually teaches anyone—but somehow, he always does. They love him."

Shoshana, who picked up maybe one word in five—the Hebrew was much faster and more colloquial than she could comfortably follow—lost herself to Avi's compelling kinesis.

The irrepressible, gray-locked teacher bounded across the podium, up the aisles, cajoling and returning, pitching and fielding questions and answers in a constant, rolling exchange with first this student and then that; gesticulating, eyes flashing, whirling constantly to point at the screen or write something in rapid-fire cursive Hebrew strokes on the whiteboard: this was teaching as free-form ballet. After the lecture it occurred to her that Avi had not stood still for the whole hour. He was all animation, all movement, like a particle whose motion defines its nature, and for which the concept of rest-mass is meaningless except as a convenient fiction for theorists. She could see why Avi's classes were so popular.

Thus reinvigorated, Avi took Tom and Shoshana on what he called a 'special VIP tour' — just them, nobody else — to his latest dig site. He had to do his routine inspection of several others first, like a butterfly flitting ceaselessly over flowers in a meadow, tasting each before moving on. Over the years Avi had opened up more than fifteen new sites on Mount Carmel, digging at each new one himself for a season before his curiosity drove him on, passing on each site to a student to run more or less independently. It was a hit-and-miss way of working, but the hits had outnumbered the misses, and in so doing he'd produced an entirely new picture of the prehistoric Middle-east. Tom and Shoshana got a concentrated burst of all this: twenty years of work compressed into two hours.

The eastern end of the Mediterranean is, as it always has been, a crossroads of clashing civilizations, at the centre of an ongoing human ferment that produced agriculture, the great early empires, and the three great monotheisms. But for those who care to read it through the eyes of landscape, its history can be read further back, long before the very earliest stirrings of agriculture on the shores of the Sea of Galilee more than twenty-six thousand years ago. It had long been known that the caves on Mount Carmel hosted among the earliest populations of modern humans to have emerged from Africa, around ninety thousand years ago. As the climate shifted over the millennia, the cave complex harboured waves of Neanderthals and modern humans, each replacing the other.

That had been the view, at least, until Avi arrived and started unpeeling the deeper secrets of the Mountain.

And so, as the Sun reached its searing height and started to descend seawards, they reached the end of a dirt track high on the north face of Mount Carmel snaking just above the most far-flung suburbs of Haifa, the Mediterranean gleaming in the distance. A small complex of buildings—just two prefabricated huts and a machine shop—framed a steel door in the side of the hill, as innocuous as if it were the entrance to any suburban double garage. Two or three field workers waved to Avi, exchanging a few words, as he pulled the pickup to a stop.

"But first—lunch!" Avi took a cool box from the back of the truck and carried it up a narrow, gritty path to the shade of a small cypress grove. It was an idyllic spot. The trees shaded a small, scrubby lawn that gave them complete cover and yet allowed them a magnificent view towards the sea. There was the usual kibbutz travelling brunch of cucumbers, tomatoes, bread, cheese and fruit. As they ate, Avi told them of an email he'd had from Jadis.

"You two are getting first look at a lot of big news," he said. "So? Spill the beans to your Uncle Avi. What's the latest about eclipses?" So they told him about the Sigil, the inscription that Jadis' team had found at SSM. Avi had heard something of it from Jadis, but he was especially keen to learn what Domingo had made of it. "Hey, Shoshana, what do you think of my good friend Domingo? Quite a guy, eh?"

At the mention of Domingo's name Shoshana blushed and looked down. She did, however, recover some of her composure to say that Domingo passed on his good wishes to Avi, and that he hoped they could meet in Israel.

"Sure—he's here next week," said Avi. "The Pope is doing an open-air mass thing in Ramat Gan Stadium, so I guess Domingo will be busy—how did he always say it? Yes—'matters on a higher plane.'" Tom laughed at Avi's impersonation of Domingo's voice, its intriguing mixture of cultured tones and bear-like gruffness. "Actually," said Avi, "I think Domingo's *really* here as a warm-up act for the Stones."

Tom and Shoshana both laughed. Shoshana imagined Domingo, red-capped like a cardinal but still in an aloha shirt, doing a stand-up routine before a stadium packed with screaming rock fans.

The prospect of the Rolling Stones' latest comeback had been the talk of the kibbutz volunteers, some of whom were trying to get tickets to the stadium show—scheduled for the day after the Pope's open-air mass—and the opening concert in a promised eighteen-month world tour. Tickets were hard to come by and those few that were still on the market circulated for small fortunes. Stones tours happened once every five or six years or so, with such inevitability that people had long since stopped wondering whether Keith Richards (a sprightly hundred and ten, thanks to some timely yet experimental rejuve treatments) and Mick Jagger (just turned one hundred and eleven, and as lithe and athletic as ever) had traded their souls for longer-than-usual life-spans, and had accepted that they were probably immortal anyway. The big wow was the much-trailed reappearance of 'Brian Jones,' who, the rumor had it, was either an imposter; a product of a secret Korean cloning laboratory; or both.

As for the Sigil, Avi agreed that Domingo was probably right that it should be kept secret. "I hope we never find any prehistoric art here," he said. Imagery of any kind was becoming very hard to square with the bubbling religious and political situation. The Orthodox rabbinate would never stand for it, he explained, "and with the Khalifa breathing down our necks, well…"

Everyone in the archaeological world—and indeed the world in general—was still reeling from the rumors that just two months earlier, the Khalifa had dynamited the beautiful ancient city of Petra, because a visiting Imam from Yorkshire had declared its statuary 'offensive'. But as no western journalist was ever likely to be able to verify anything that happened inside the Khalifa, the rumors remained just that.

"Just imagine if we found religious iconography from a non-human species here, in Israel?" said Avi: "It would blow the whole lid off everything. The Imams are on a hair-trigger—they want Jerusalem so badly they'd need no more excuse than that."

Avi did not mention, of course, Rivka's pillow-talk, about the immense armies parked in the desert beyond Jordan and along the parched banks of the Yarmuk; the airfields packed wingtip-to-wingtip with the products of a decade of round-the-clock production in remote desert factories from Tripoli to Tashkent; the gigantic rail-gun howitzers and mobile missile launch-pads lining up on the Euphrates. The European Union, mindful of vocal support from the Khalifa from within, and still trying to digest a skittish Turkey, was turning a blind eye. America was in one of its more isolationist moods: Israeli mutterings that given the unity and armed might of the Khalifa, she'd have no option but to 'go nuclear,' made the US ambassador nervous and run for cover. It was all behind the scenes, of course—if it hadn't been, His Holiness, and probably the Stones, would have taken their immortality elsewhere, and there'd have been panic in the streets.

Yet panic or no panic, Israel was quite alone and poised to fall—and Avi, by digging up some figured stone or other, would be damned if he'd be the one to push it over.

But Avi was thinking of a far more ancient war when, after lunch, he took them down to the machine shop, found miners' helmets from the team store, and ushered them through the metal door. "Forget eclipses," he said. "They're for little old ladies like my old friend Domingo. What I'm going to show you is strictly adults-only. It will blow your minds."

The door led into a short tunnel, down a slope and into a broad and brightly lit cave, dotted with geometrical monoliths, as impressive as SSM, but on a smaller scale.

"We've found lots of these all over *Ha-Carmel*," explained Avi. "We call them 'SSM-lites'. Each one was probably a clan base for an extended family, maybe for a few dozen generations. But *this* one, this is odd: usually there are cemeteries, like the ones at SSM. But there are no bones here at all, not one. It's as if they've all been dug up, or swept away."

They walked past the ranks of silent monoliths, perhaps for three or four hundred metres. Above their heads, the cave roof gradually sloped down to meet them. "So, after I and a small team discovered this cavern last year," Avi continued, "we kept pushing inwards, further and further, looking for the bones we knew must be here, until we found— this!"

Avi's timing was as perfect as it had been in his lecture early that same day, for just as he finished his sentence they saw that they'd reached the edge of a black ravine, and that the cave roof had arced over their heads to plunge before them, downwards into the abyss.

Avi steered them to a path a little way to the right that led them down the slope of the ravine, which was neither as steep nor as deep as they had first thought. Perhaps twenty meters below the level of the cavern floor, they found a lower, larger cavern opening before them, stretching as far in all directions as their lights would penetrate. Unlike the cavern above, this lower cave was yet to have a full lighting system installed. At present there was something like the emergency lighting system in an aircraft—a pattern of tiny LED lights on the ground marking out paths where it was safe to walk, their weak, local illumination making deep and eerie shadows of small objects close by, throwing them—hugely magnified—into the illimitable lightless voids beyond.

Avi led the way down to the cave floor, and it wasn't long before they started noticing bones. First in ones and twos, then a few together, until, by the time they were thirty or forty metres in, there were drifts of bones in great waves, in high dunes to the left and right, their extent made all the greater by the fact that only a few caught the localized ground-level beams from the pathway lights, the rest fading upwards and outwards into the musty dark, present only by virtue of horrible suggestion.

But what little they had seen was quite enough. Few of the bones seemed in any order at all. There were skeletons, and parts of skeletons, bones scored and charred, shattered, scattered and thrown awry in a massed idiot-dance of death. The litter of carnage seemed to go on forever—it was a sea, an ocean of bones. Shoshana and Tom drew close to Avi, who had stopped before a vast and teetering pile of skulls. They were utterly silent.

"Yes, my friends," he said, his voice subdued, his upper face in a shroud of weird, Hitchcockian shadow cast by the pathway light at his feet, "it's quite something."

"How far does this go on?" asked Shoshana, dry-mouthed, querulous.

"We—that's me and the team—we think it links up with another cave system on the east side of the mountain, but we're not sure. We haven't got there yet. We've penetrated three kilometers into the cavern so far, and it still goes on and on, just like this. Where we're standing is just the start. As of now, we can see no end to it."

"Just… bones?"

"Yes, just bones," said Avi. "Okay, there are a few simple hearths, too, no more than bonfires, really, but we haven't found any buildings. The bones are mainly… but—hey—let's get out of here before I explain any more. I don't mind telling you, this place freaks me out."

So they retraced their steps, and even Tom, who had lived his formative years in darkness, was never so pleased to have reached the surface as he was then, when they ascended the slope to the cypress grove to greet the Sun as it began its downward slope over the Mediterranean.

To Shoshana, the Sun, while welcome, seemed sickly and apologetic. She felt cold, preternaturally cold: she hugged herself to warm up, and then clung tightly to Tom. When they'd sat down and had assumed a measure of equanimity, Avi started to talk again, and this time it was with a seriousness that surprised them.

"Now, if I tell you a few things, you must promise—*promise*—not to breathe them to a living soul. I shall tell your mother, Tom, because—well, *davka*, just *because*. But what I am about to tell you must never get out. Not until I'm ready. I'm not sure that I ever will be."

They promised.

"But first, I must ask you both a question. Why is it, do you think, that humans came out of Africa maybe a hundred-fifty thousand years ago, but took another hundred thousand *at least* to get into Europe?"

Silence. And then Shoshana said, warily, like a shy student at her first tutorial—"because the Neanderthals were already there?"

"Good," replied Avi. "But that's only a part of the story. All the reasons we hear—and, I am ashamed to say, the reasons I still teach in my class—are horseshit. That the first modern humans were still too primitive to go north, or that they first went east into Asia before venturing into Europe, blah blah blah. All just glimpses of the truth, but not the whole of it. I think I can now supply the missing piece, from that pit of bones."

And so he told them a story.

How much was truly based on the evidence, how much informed conjecture, and how much he'd just made up, they would never know.

When the first modern humans had stumbled, innocent and blinking (said Avi), out of Africa more than a hundred thousand years ago, they had the misfortune to run straight into a Neanderthal civilization at its most powerfully rapacious, centered on Mount Carmel—which, like the landscape of southern France, was largely artificial. The massif had been a warren of subterranean cities, sometimes bursting into ramparts on the surface, always at war with each other. After many millennia the squabbling clans united one single chieftain—let's call him the King Under the Mountain—whose armies of stone-clad warriors commanded Mount Carmel and all the lands round about. The Kingdom had blocked access to Europe, and had found in the steady stream of newcomers a life-saving resource.

For the might and extent of the Kingdom was increasingly a sham. Although at its very peak of power and majesty, it had in fact started to decline long before, rotting from within. The troops had to go ever further to exact tribute to bring to Court of the King. The forests, long depleted by a civilization still dependent on hunting and foraging, were in retreat. The Kingdom might well have been unified, but it was starving to death from the inside. Until, that is, a ready supply of man-flesh wandered stupidly over the horizon, just in the nick of time.

The decline of the Kingdom was suddenly thrown into reverse, and for a while the Neanderthals grew to yet greater power by refashioning their whole economy around human beings. They enslaved them for tens of thousands of years, rounding up more wherever they could find them, farming them for sacrifice to whatever gods they worshipped: using them for food, and for sport. Even when dead, no part of a human being was wasted, for waste was a luxury that this decadent Kingdom could not afford. Apart from the meat and offal, marrow and brains, their body fats could be rendered down into oil, their skins used to make baskets and boats, their bones and teeth wrought into tools, furniture, musical instruments, even toys for children.

More and still more humans had come from the South to replenish this never-satiated Moloch. Whenever humans became scarce locally — or wise to the Neanderthal threat — raiding parties were sent to find them, penetrating the Nile Valley as far as modern Ethiopia. And so the bloody story continued, for age upon age.

Until, around forty or fifty thousand years ago, new tribes of humans appeared in the South. These were tall, wild and fierce, completely different from the flabby, cowed race that the Neanderthals had dominated for so long. And they were bent on conquest — and vengeance. They would tolerate the raids no longer. No more human tribute would be sent north. They had come north to see the Kingdom Under The Mountain for themselves, and to wipe it from the face of the Earth.

Sensing the threat, the King Under The Mountain had ordered that all his humans, his chattels and broodstock, be gathered together in this cave, and that they should all be slaughtered—rather that, than for them to be taken. This deed was done, and the bones of these humans could be seen in a vast drift in the centre of the cave. There were tens of thousands of them. Men decapitated, their brains bashed out. Babies broken in two. Women spatch-cocked like chickens when not otherwise impaled, beheaded, sacrificed in a last and desperate throw. The floor of the cave became slick with offal and broken bodies and tides of blood. The brutality of it was unimaginable. Some of the humans fought back before they died, but not many.

The only thing the King Under The Mountain feared, almost as much as the vengeance of the Gods, was the wrath of the Neanderthal Chieftain he'd usurped many years before and driven across the Jordan. The hated rival was now back, his legions marching on *Ha-Carmel*. It was a fine judgment as to who would arrive first, the Neanderthal raiders from the East, or the Men of the South. In the event, it was the Neanderthals. In this very cave, they started to do battle with the King's troops for control of the remaining humans. We can tell this (said Avi) from the presence of two kinds of flint armour; the presence of skeletons associated with Remillardian artifacts; and that some of the humans appear to have been pulled in two, as if victims of an internecine squabble for who would get to make the bloody ritual obeisances first. Evidence from hearths and scattered coprolites suggests that some of the Neanderthals paused from their warfare to engage in impromptu banquets of raw human flesh.

The battle was futile, for when all the humans were dead, and the Neanderthals had just about finished slaughtering one other, the Men of the South arrived to finish the job, if indeed there had been a job to finish. Within a few years, the great Neanderthal civilization of thousands of centuries was destroyed. And *Homo sapiens* found that the gates of Europe were open wide.

By the time Avi had finished his story, the Sun was sinking into the Mediterranean in a florid gash of barred clouds. Tom and Shoshana looked pale with shock, like rabbits in headlights.

"Look," said Avi, "I don't apologize for telling you this, or for bringing you here. If I hadn't, you see, you'd never have believed me."

"Avi, how much of this do you know to be true?" asked Tom, in French, and barbed with anger.

"What's the truth of it?" replied Avi, coolly. "Well, I know this much. That the bones accumulated in a single event, for accelerator-mass-spectrometry dates taken from all over the cave all cluster around a single date, about forty-odd thousand years ago. And the bones? Tom, you saw them."

"Look, Avi," Tom returned, his voice brittle, "you cannot frighten us with this… this lurid rubbish."

"Tom, you're a scientist," said Avi. "You are rational. You have every right to be sceptical until you have sifted through the evidence for yourself. But even if a tiny fraction of what I have told you is true—and just look at the evidence before your eyes! The bones!—you can bet that once people get hold of it, there will be all kinds of stories, elaborations, used and perverted to all kinds of ends. And let me tell you another story. When you were very small, the effects that the discoveries at Souris were having on the world almost drove your parents apart."

Tom and Shoshana sat up at that, and Avi returned to the fray, with increasing vigour. "You didn't know that, Tom?" he said. "Well, perhaps you should. And let me tell you more things you didn't know. It happened not so long after me and Rivka rescued the last of the Sand-Druids from certain slaughter in Chad. When Faye Callaghan and Primrose Tsien—dear friends of your parents, and also of me—were lost in Tibet.

"We didn't know what happened at the time, but it turned out that they were ambushed by Almai. When they finally got the truth out of the ringleader, he confessed that our friends—my friends, whom I loved—had been blinded, their tongues ripped out, their hands and feet chopped off, and then they were systematically *fucked* until they *died*, in the cause of Almai traditional religion! So how do you like that?

"And it gets better! They were then dismembered and eaten raw! And what's more, the schmuck who did all this confessed all on Prime-Time TV! He thought he was doing them a favor. And yes, guess who was watching? Yes, Tom, your *Maman* and *Papa*. It tore your mother to pieces, so much so that Jack could hardly cope—he was *this close* to walking out on her. You were about six years old."

Avi sat down behind them both, embracing them. "So now you understand. I'm sorry it had to be this way. Now you can see why I can never make this public. Just imagine what it would do, not only to us, but to the world? It was my old friend Domingo who created *Undique humanitas*, the document that welcomed the hominids into humanity. With impeccable timing he announced it the day before the Almai confessed to murdering our friends. Jadis hardly talked to Domingo for weeks afterwards. It took all his diplomacy— and that's more diplomacy than you'll ever see from any-one—to talk her down. And those two are *real* close. So if news of this battleground ever gets into the media, just imagine what will happen. *Undique humanitas* will be no more than a straw in the wind. They'll be hanging Sand Druids from lamp-posts. The Kaptars will have to run for their lives in case they get flayed alive and made into rugs. Those cute little Pendeks, you know the ones? They drive all the cabs here in Tel Aviv. They'll be locked in their cabs and torched alive. And when all the hominids are gone, where then will the lynch mob turn its fury? Who'll be next, eh? Humanity will destroy itself."

They drove back to the Kibbutz in silence through the deepening night. "Don't worry, and sleep well," said Avi, stiffly. "I'll come get you in the morning."

But sleep was hard to find. They tried to make love, but could not raise much enthusiasm, so they simply rested close together. Shoshana insisted on keeping the light on, so Tom put on his iShades, so that even though he'd had his arms around her, he seemed very far away. As usual, he was the first to fall asleep. Shoshana sank eventually, turning off the light and allowing Tom's arms to curl round her like angels' wings.

Shoshana's sleep was troubled. She had a dream in which she'd looked down at her body, which was made of glass, and found a black blob the size of a golf ball in her insides. The blob grew as she watched, turning from a rough sphere into a star shape and sending out threads and tendrils that ramified through her whole body until they burst out through every orifice at once, swelling at the ends into buds that disgorged enormous blood-red flowers and bloated fruits that rotted where they hung. She should have been horrified by this, she thought, but found it no more than mildly unpleasant. But then she looked up at the Sun and it was black. She screamed.

-=0=-

Domingo had had to be on his mettle a few days later when the cavalcade of Papa Linus Secundus, Episcopus Romanus, rolled into town. As the Pope's Personal Private Secretary, Domingo had the closest possible access to His Holiness: and although Linus II was affable enough, Domingo felt that they weren't really getting along at the moment, or, at least, not as well as they usually did. Even when they'd tried to compensate for this loss, by setting time aside deliberately to brainstorm about things—like when they'd forged *Undique humanitas* together, fifteen years before—Domingo had the sensation of intellects sliding past each other. It could simply have been their different backgrounds, now coming to the fore at a time of heightened tension.

Linus II had once been a street kid from North Dublin. To be sure, Domingo himself had come from a lowly background, and perhaps it was no more than a difference in climate: the parched heights of the Sierra Nevada versus the damp and vivid green of the Emerald Isle. Yes, perhaps that was it.

But it was more likely, Domingo reflected, to be the current circumstances themselves. Domingo was sure that His Holiness, who was usually in pink and rosy health, was looking pale and peaky. It could have been the journey, which had indeed been exhausting, with many delays enforced by technical problems and the weather. And maybe His Holiness had picked up a cold along the way. He'd have to attend to him carefully.

The night before the Open-Air Mass, His Holiness was attending a private reception at the official residence of the Prime Minister of Israel, so naturally Domingo came too, along with a small squadron of dark-suited, bulging-pocketed Swiss Guards. They were to stay the night.

If Domingo found his boss a little distant, he had hit it off immediately with the Prime Minister, a man of sparkling wit and intelligence. His name was Seamus O'Shaughnessy.

"If I might say so, Prime Minister...." Said Domingo.

"Yes, I know, I know," said O'Shaughnessy. "It's an odd name for a nice Jewish boy like me. But I am an Israeli, a sabra, born right here, if not very well bred. My folks, though—they're another matter, They're as Irish as the Blarney Stone, and in fact I spent most of my boyhood in the Old Country. That's where I met His Holiness, in fact. We go back a long way. A long way indeed. The tales I could tell. Now tell me, Your Eminence...?"

"I beg your pardon, Prime Minister," said Domingo, smiling. "It's Cardinal Domingo Sanchopanza. Or, for those with sufficient leisure, Domingo García Vasquez Santéria Sanchopanza de Orellanzana von Hohenzollern und Taxis. But my friends just call me 'Pongo'."

The Prime Minister laughed, but his face immediately darkened. "Tell me, Cardinal... er... 'Pongo'. His Holiness— our friend—doesn't look quite as chipper as I remember."

"*Anno Domini*, Prime Minister. It gets to us all in the end."

"Assuredly, Your Eminence, but the Davy O'Leese I remember from the Old Country would never have refused a second pint of Guinness as he did at the reception, freely given, nor a third, and would have been carousing until dawn, even on days when he'd be taking mass. He was just a Parish Priest, then, but you know, all the same—I'm worried."

The Prime Minister's observations struck a chord with Domingo. It wasn't, then, just his own imagination, fuelled by proximity, mistakenly reading the tiniest difference in his employer's countenance as the symptoms of something terminal. Even when considered objectively, His Holiness looked more than just tired. He was gray, like freshly burned ash, and he kept having to wipe away beads of sweat that persistently broke at his hairline (like blood from a crown) which, if not stopped, rolled glutinously down his face like something out of *Death In Venice*. Yet he'd waved aside any offer of help.

"I share your concerns, Prime Minister," Domingo confessed. "I thought it was just me, but, well…"

"So what can I do?" asked O'Shaughnessy.

"Nothing much," said Domingo. "All I can do is persuade His Holiness to take some ibuprofen after vespers and hope for the best."

Hope for the best. That was all he could reasonably do, Domingo thought to himself, anxiously.

The next day, however, Domingo assured his host that the Pope seemed to have taken a turn for the better; was excited about the open-air mass; and looked forward to downing a glass or two afterwards with his boyhood friend. The Prime Minister for his part regretted that he couldn't make the motorcade to Ramat Gan, and would indeed miss the service — urgent committee meeting at the Knesset — but waved off his friends, old and new, with all the good wishes he could muster.

It was not until his committee meeting was over that O'Shaughnessy heard the appalling news.

The committee meeting had gone on even longer than planned, even accounting for the usual delays, diversions, filibustering and procrastinations. Knesset sessions always overran in any case, but this must have been a record. The ongoing problem of the Khalifa loomed over everything like a pall of smoke from a burst oil well, dragging everything out, sapping all energy. Israelis were usually practical to beyond the point of rudeness, getting on with the job in hand, no matter how trying the circumstances. But tendrils of fatalism were beginning to creep in, even here, to the corridors of power. Nobody had said it out loud, but you could see it in peoples' eyes—that they were living in the Last Days.

So sighed O'Shaughnessy almost three hours later when his trim and pretty aide led the way from the council chamber and into the fresh air—when the Prime Minister noticed, in that contrast between acrid staleness and tart freshness, just how hormonally horrid the atmosphere had become in camera. There is nothing as evocative as the human sense of smell, and O'Shaughnessy was drawn straight back to the pallid, perspiring face of his old friend Davy O'Leese (he could never quite believe he was the Pope, even now). The pressing business of governing a fractious country had driven all thoughts of the open-air mass from his mind.

Caught in reverie, he hardly noticed the aide, concern on her face, trying to engage his attention. "Sir," she started nervously, as if half-afraid of pulling the Prime Minister from his daydream, "Sir, I have some news…"

But she was too late, for in that moment he caught a TV monitor in the Council Chamber Ante-Room, tuned to Kol Israel News One, the staff glued to the set. The picture showed the Pope being stretchered offstage to a waiting Magen David Adom ambulance. Cut to screaming sirens, police cordons, crowds of concerned worshippers bearing candles.

"What happened?"

"The Pope, Sir," explained the aide, momentarily casting her eyes floorwards, "He'd just got to the end of the *Aleynu*—I mean, sorry Sir, the *Agnus Dei*—and then…. he just…"

"Collapsed?"

"Yes, Sir." Well, God be thanked that Linus had pretty much finished the job before expiring. "Get me to wherever they took His Holiness please—at once!—And see if you can get his Personal Private Secretary on the line."

More police sirens. More crowds. Streets darkening towards evening, a light wash of rain. Helipad. Whirring, whining racket.

"Prime Minister, I'm so glad you called," said the deep, resonant voice of Cardinal Domingo Sanchopanza, incongruously squeezed into the Prime Minister's earbud. "We're in the emergency room at the… er… Hadassah Hospital."

"How does he look? His Holiness?"

A pause. "No more than… uh… fair to middling."

"I'm on my way, Your Eminence," the Prime Minister said. But the line was dead.

And, finally, the sliding doors of the Emergency Room, a section thrown hastily under guard, with Cardinal Sanchopanza standing outside, deep in conversation with several doctors. The white-coated throng parted to admit O'Shaughnessy and two bodyguards, adding to the crowds—two Swiss Guards stood outside the section in which the Pope was currently confined. Something was, clearly, up.

"I know that there are… er… protocols about isolation," Domingo was saying to one of the doctors, "but please might I be allowed to see His Holiness, as his aide, and in such moments, his confessor? Perish the thought, but I might have to administer the last rites."

"I understand, Sir," came the reply, "but really, I'd advise against it. The patient is in a bad way. Really bad. Unconscious. He's very ill indeed, I'm afraid, and getting worse. We'd need to stabilize him, or try to, before… I very much regret…"

At this point O'Shaughnessy felt he ought to at least try to tilt at a windmill to help his new friend. "Oh honestly, Doctor," he said: "how ill can he be? Flu? Coronary? Overwork?"

"None of the above, Sir," said the doctor, whose name badge read 'Dr Mohamed Al Hajj, Resident,' turning to the Prime Minister with such cool professional detachment that he appeared not to recognize him for who he was. "Or, at least, we don't think so, Sir. In truth, it's like nothing we've seen before. But I understand you were with him last night—you might have seen some symptoms?" *Death in Venice.* "Anything you can tell us, anything at all, could be immensely helpful."

A small crowd gathered. Ambulance drivers, paramedics, nurses, secret servicemen, Swiss Guardsmen. A gentle, steering, hand. Cardinal Sanchopanza. A quiet side office, a desk, some chairs, a wastebasket overflowing with paper and food wrappers, medical charts, vending-machine cups, a pennant for Maccabee Tel-Aviv, a CCTV screen labelled 'Isolation Room 1' in embossed red tape: and the smell of sweat and fear. And now a Muslim doctor from Gaza City, a Cardinal from the Vatican, and the Prime Minister of Israel. Three great religions in one tiny office. Not the usual ER crowd. But not the usual patient either. And not with any of the usual complaints.

O'Shaughnessy sat, his collar increasingly tight and sweaty. He loosened it as Dr Al Hajj ushered out the secret servicemen who unobtrusively took positions outside the closing door. "Please, Prime Minister, and… er… Your Eminence," the doctor said. "Please, look at the screen. Pay close attention. Then you will see."

The screen was flickering and monochrome, but even with such a low-quality image you could hardly describe what was happening as in any way normal. His Holiness was in a hospital gown, lying on a gurney—or, rather, manacled to it, so great were the convulsions sweeping through his body.

"Can't you do something, Doctor?" asked Domingo.

"I'm afraid we've done everything usual in a case of—say—coronary arrest, or even just fatigue. We've tried sedatives, but we're afraid to overdo it. We've had to restrain him as you see…"

"But what of his mouth?" snapped O'Shaughnessy, impatiently. "Couldn't he bite through his tongue?" They gazed in horror as the blurred image of the silent scream of the prostrate Pontiff bounced from the curved screen, caromed off their astonished corneas and bounced back again.

"That's just it—his mouth is locked wide open in tetany. We couldn't close it again if we wanted to." O'Shaughnessy was about to apologize for his earlier asperity, his heightened mood—the doctor was clearly doing his best—but the three watchers were overtaken by events.

The Pope, jaws agape, eyes bulging, suddenly sat up. He did so with such force that his hands were both neatly severed by the unyielding restraints. Blood squirted everywhere in looping, jetty gouts.

Al Hajj went white.

"Get someone in there—quick!" he screamed into a gooseneck mike beneath the monitor. Big, burly nurses in Class-4 outbreak suits appeared on screen, trying vainly to restrain the Pope while not being repeatedly hosed in blood from his scything stumps. Retreating, they too gazed mutely at the scene, for even though the Pope had now stopped moving—as suddenly as he'd begun—they made no attempt to move in on him. They, like the three observers in the office, could only stare at the patch of inky blackness that had appeared at the Papal throat, and which had begun to spread even as they watched.

None could now intervene. No action seemed advisable, even possible. As the wave of darkness lapped slowly up the patient's neck, over his ears and jaw line—and down over his collarbones and under his hospital gown—it took on the dull sheen of taut PVC, as if the now motionless and un-breathing form were being slowly melted into a body bag. The blackness seeped over both cheeks, his nose, and — encircling his mouth like an 'O' — bridged that, too, closing it off in a broad meniscus. After another twenty seconds, the head — the eyes — were completely encased. It was this wave of blackness that finally choked off the blood dripping from the wrists, and, after another twenty seconds, closed in over the tips of his toes.

Only the hands, once the hands of a healer, hands that had given the benediction times beyond count to grateful multitudes, remained beyond the dark tide — severed, life-less, bloodied, on the gray floor of the isolation room.

The three watchers exhaled in unison, as if a terrific tension had been released.

Too soon.

The nurses on camera moved out of shot as a further monstrous transformation took place. The black caul around the Pope tightened and thickened, drawing his knees up be-neath his chin, squashing his face between them so that the black membrane, once in contact with itself, fused together. The Pope was sealed in, redoubled, and yet the dark shroud contracted still further, squeezing his legs and head inwards and downwards so that they lost all recognizable shape and distinction. The stumps of the arms were drawn in until, af-ter a minute and a half (the watchers had in fact lost all track of time: this fact was only noted later from CCTV records and corroborated by comparison with dozens of similar cases that the hospital would see over the coming hours, be-fore a Khalifa fighter jet, its pilot in the grip of the same af-fliction, plunged into the hospital, blowing it to smithereens) the Pope now looked like nothing more than a shrinking, melting black candle.

And still the collapse continued, remorselessly, until what was once a man had entirely disappeared, replaced by a featureless black sphere of radius precisely 15.68 centimeters, and which would prove refractory to all forms of penetration or inspection immediately available to the hospital.

At last, Linus had become an oyster in negative, a black pearl against the white folds of the hospital gown, spattered with blood as nicely as in any Passion. As for transfiguration—well, that had to be another matter entirely. For the time being, as the transformed Pontiff toppled from the gurney, bounced once, and rolled beneath a rack of life-support equipment: *Noli Me Tangere.*

Chapter 9. Reed-cutter

Southern Mesopotamia, Earth, c. 125,000 years ago

Thynke howe short tyme thou hast abyden here.
Thy place is bygged above the sterres clere,
Noon erthly palys wrought in so statly wyse.

(Think of the short time that you have abided here.
Your place is outmatched by the clear stars above.
No earthly palace is made in such a stately fashion.)

John Lydgate—*Vox ultima Crucis*

Waves, soft-lapping, like the passage of purest cotton across the face. A breeze now, as soft and stinging as sheerest satin. Light, bright as any braided gold. The man who had once been Mr Haraddzjin Khorare of the Very Great and Ancient City of Axandragór opened his eyes. He looked up to see the Sun, clear, overhead, in a teal-blue sky. He found that he was floating, wavelets caressing his ears. The water was quite shallow, though: for once awake, he startled, thrusting his hands downwards at his sides for them to sink in soft ooze. He sat up, waist-deep in the dark water. Hard stalks of reeds pressed all around, imposing a monotonous yellow verticality on the scene, like cheap interior décor.

Mr Khorare, who had yet to appreciate the fantastic miracle of his survival, entire, when he had previously been shredded into fist-sized chunks for the hungry throats of sharks several hundred miles to the southeast, wondered instead why the afterlife smelled like a midden, and had such tasteless wallpaper. Either that wallpaper should go, he thought to himself, or so should I. He blinked, but the scene remained obdurately the same, in which case, he thought, his wager with himself was lost, and he should seek some more interesting vista, elsewhere.

He rose, unsteadily, his knees creaking beneath the tatterdemalion shreds of his crushed-velvet knee-breeches, the black water sliding away in viscous runnels along its fluted pleats. But the view on standing was hardly more edifying, given that he sank in the mud almost up to his knees, and the reeds still towered overhead. It was not in the character of Mr Khorare to feel despondent, and yet he did begin to wonder what he should now do. At that point he felt a warmth in the inside pocket of his chemise (whose quality, he was pleased to note, was such that it maintained its integrity, despite now looking more like a string vest). The talisman was still with him, and, if he stood still and concentrated, it would tell him which way he should go. He sloshed manfully in the prescribed direction, pushing the reeds apart as he went.

It was, though, very hard work, and he was soon parched, hungry and exhausted. He should have liked to have sat down, but the only place to sit was in the malodorous ooze itself, and as he was now dry from the knees upwards (if caked with mud from the waist downwards) Mr Khorare was most reluctant to get wet once more. And the mazy sea of reeds, while allowing no sense of any forward direction, was still open to the wearyingly pitiless sun, which started to burn his head and neck. After a while, though, he found that the water became shallower, until it became hardly deeper than his ankles, and in places gave way to a kind of blancmange of semi-solid ground, streaked with green slime and pocked with small herbs between the reeds. Frogs and small jeweled lizards darted away from his feet as he passed. The reeds became shorter, so that he could, in places, begin to see above them — though the view was, regrettably, only fractionally less monotonous than it had been before. And yet he took heart. The view, while still dull, was beginning to change, and that, thought Mr Khorare, must be for the better.

After a while the reeds began to thin and he tramped through a wide land of tussock, bog and little creeks so overgrown and hard to see that he had to look carefully as he walked in case he tripped and pitched right in. This was not a place, he thought, where one could just bowl along, wherever or however one liked, as were one on one's regular morning constitutional. The creeks became wider and deeper as he progressed, until he reached one that was probably too wide for him to jump, but was deep, with high, sheer, treacherous-looking sides beetling over the curl of black water in the ditch at its base. He was just maneuvering himself to sit down on the tussocky edge, so as to probe the consistency of the bank with his toes, when he heard a voice.

"You're late."

Startled by this irruption of sound, Mr Khorare turned to see where the voice had come from, overbalanced, and tipped into the creek. His fall was broken by the pungent ooze just above the water's edge, but, unable to stop, he continued to roll downwards until he came to rest in the water with a splash. He sat up. Wet again. All over. Harumph. A brown hand came down and grasped his, pulling him upright.

"Come on, then, now you're here."

Mr Khorare found himself following the source of the voice of the hand upstream. Walking along the creek beds—if you knew where to tread—was quicker than trying to leap across them, or squishing up and down their steep and slippery sides. He was, in particular, following a broad back, clad in a garment of rough-looking burlap, surmounted by a shaggy brown head, and supported by massive, beefy legs. There was no way that he could, as yet, see the figure from the front. He was barely able to keep up with it, given its speed, let alone try to overtake it. He did try, though, to engage the figure in conversation, but his ejaculations of "I say!" and "now, look here!" and so on and so forth in like fashion went unanswered, so he was perforce intimidated into silence.

After several twists and turns they reached a broad, shelving beach of muddy gravel that allowed them access, at last, to something akin to dry land. Just above the creek edge, on a grassy platform, stood a hut of sun-baked mud-bricks and thatched with reeds, on top of which the carcases of fish and other creatures were drying in the sun. Mr Khorare's unexpected companion stooped and disappeared into the hut's darkness. From the outside, where Mr Khorare still stood, the hut seemed entirely spare and without ornamentation, and seemed so to Mr Khorare's eyes until he saw an engraved mud-brick hanging above the lintel. The engraving was of three circles, and two crescents, with radiating lines. His hand snatched straight away to the inside pocket of his ragged chemise, and pulled out the talisman. A face appeared at the door. It was broad, leathery, and with a weak, receding jaw—a Stoner—but for all that, the face of a woman.

"Well?" she said, "Are you coming in, or are you just going to stay out here all day?"

"Excuse me, I meant no offence," Mr Khorare replied. His limited experience of Stoners did not, he had to admit, presage anything other than a most grisly fate—especially here, in the wilderness. But Mr Khorare felt that polite and mild compliance ought to be worth the effort, even here.

"None taken," said the woman, disappearing again. This time Mr Khorare followed her. Now, he had no clear idea what to expect from the inside of a hut of what looked like a lone reed-cutter, except that it would probably look no more sophisticated than the outside, only darker. Which is why the sight of the interior, as it greeted him, quite took his breath away.

"Think of me as the… oh, I don't know… as the Genie of the Talisman," the reedcutter said, a few minutes later.

"But that, Madam, is just a description, a title, a soubriquet, if you like," replied Mr Khorare. "I am—I was—a man of affairs, in a business where reputation measured a great deal. Reputation gathered to my name."

"Mr Khorare, do you not think that the contrast between the externals of this dwelling and the interior are not sufficient proof that I'm not the genie of *something*?"

Mr Khorare had to admit that she had a point. He leaned back on the rich oxblood leather of the chesterfield, looked out at the brilliant white landscape, and took another sip of the spirit from the tumbler in his hand. But he was still uneasy.

"Quite so, Madam. But the same might apply to the facts of your person. I am sure—quite sure—that you are not, nor have ever been, a Stoner."

"Congratulations. But if you look like anything else in these parts, you're likely to get eaten, or at least killed. As you've found out."

Mr Khorare chose to let her final comment pass. "But if you will not tell me your name," he continued, "can you not at least tell me your species?"

"Mr Khorare—would you really ask such personal questions of your host, were you a guest in their drawing-room in the Very Great and Ancient City of Axandragór?"

"Well, no, I… well, no I shouldn't, but that great city is far away. And I ask your forgiveness for my frank curiosity, Madam, and crave your indulgence nonetheless. Consider, if you will, my trade. I clothe people of fashion and taste in stuffs, in ginghams and velvets, taffetas, organzas, brocades, buttons, frills, ribbons, ruffs and bows. I have been engaged in such a business for a long time and have achieved tolerable standing and a degree of wealth. From which you should know that my contemplation of the superficial is based on an extremity of profundity. In short — it matters to me what people look like. Clothes make the man, Madam — or, if I might speak plainly, the woman. But as you remain quite immune to my requests, Madam, I hope you will excuse my being quite candid — that skirt doesn't suit your figure."

The woman laughed and melted, before his eyes, her brutish lineaments and figure changing into a form younger, taller, and much paler, with big, strangely round black eyes and long, black hair. "Is this better?" Her smile, while still not furred enough to mark her as human by his lights, illuminated the room.

"Much."

"But despite being a better fit to the clothes, Mr Khorare, how do you know that this is any more my real form than *this*..." (a black sphere chased with silver filigree, on balloon-wire wheels, pulled along by two silver-plated steam-powered automata) "or *this*..." (a loxodont from the Eurasian plains, caparisoned with rich embroidered brocades) "or *this*...?" (a vast spider form that seemed far too large for the room, with a dizzyingly imprecise number of limbs, its body towering above him at what seemed an impossible distance).

"Point taken, Madam." Said Mr Khorare. "I apologise for my impertinence."

"No need. And really, I am fascinated that you should ask. Nobody has before. They usually imagine that I am some avatar of somebody else, somebody they've known. But nobody has ever asked to see the *real* me. So, to be honest, Mr Khorare, I'm flattered. Would you like to see what I really look like?"

"Do you advise it?"

"No, not particularly. I don't think you'd make much of it. If I simply flashed it up before you… well, it would just seem like a meaningless jumble of angles with nothing to fill them. Or a sea of holes."

"You're a 'sea of holes'?"

"No, not quite that, either. If you're sure you want to see what I look like, I'm going to have to… to have to… to have to…"

Mr Khorare felt himself lulled into a seamless peace, and woke up—if that's what it was—on a tropical beach, at night. Really, it could have been his private vacation home in the Archipelago, a few dozen miles from the Very Great City. But above him wheeled a sea of stars like a Catherine Wheel, and as he looked up into it, he felt something of himself being sucked rapidly upwards into the sky.

-=0=-

Finding a comfortable spot for a bivouac was proving a hard task. These low hills, rising to the east of the great river that eventually debouched into the marshes now far behind him, in the south, were dreary enough by day, with no vegetation taller than knee-high knots of heather. By night they presented an endless series of slopes, each just too strongly canted and stony for comfort—Mr Khorare had discovered, to his cost, that any flat ground in this region had achieved this state by the slow accumulation of mud. The sun was setting, far across the river, on the fifth full day after his departure from the altogether remarkable hut of that Stoner reed-cutter—genie, mage, sorceress, whatever she was—and the light was fading, when, joy of joys, he found it: high on the slope, a small, dry, flat space in the west-facing lee of a large rocky outcrop. Shelter enough from the chill winds rolling off the range of mountains to the northeast, and space enough to pitch a bivvy and perhaps brew a kettle.

The bivvy practically pitched itself — a flick of the wrist and it was up, blowing and billowing until he'd found the strong, thin lines and metal pins to secure it to the soil. He'd already located a spring nearby, and was able to fill a kettle, made of a light, silvery metal, and use a portable stove to set a fire beneath it. All this equipment had been provided by the reed-cutter. A few things to speed him on his way, she'd said. And some of the dried, preserved food — especially the apricots — had been at least as good as anything he'd tasted on his travels. But what interested him the most — a professional interest, one might say — was the fabric of the bivouac itself. So sheer, so light — lighter than silk, as light as a feather — and yet, unlike silk, entirely proof against rain and wind. Night after night Mr Khorare lay beneath it, looking up at its perfect seams, wondering what sort of material it might have been that could repel moisture and retain warmth without any need of a nap, or grease, or, indeed, anything much at all. His wonderment at the fabric far exceeded that of the portable stove equipment — a fire, wherever he was, instantly — also thoughtfully furnished by the reed-cutter.

And what was his journey, then? The reed-cutter (he still preferred to think of her in such homely terms, not being able to comprehend what she claimed to have been her true nature) was quite adamant — as his late father had been — that he should follow the talisman wherever it might lead, for it was (she continued) vital that he deposited it at a certain place, at a certain time. She would not say when and where these loci were to be found — to do that would (in her words) 'throw the game'. All she'd say was that he'd know them when he found them. Curiously enough, this was sufficient to allay any remaining worries on Mr Khorare's part.

Mr Khorare did, however, establish that he would in all probability never get back to the Very Great and Ancient City of Axandragór that was his home. The reason, however, was curious—for, according to the reed-cutter, he would probably outlast it. The reed-cutter had only laughed at his expression of puzzlement.

"Oh, my dear Mr Khorare, you are such a silly man!" she had exclaimed: "do you not think that it might not be such an easy thing for fate to so casually expunge from its tapestries, as if swatting a mosquito, a man who has survived pirates, grapeshot, sharks and even decapitation?" Mr Khorare felt he had to concede, although he did wonder what decapitation had to do with anything. He was thinking these thoughts as he dowsed the fire (by the simple expedient of twisting a knurled metal knob!), inchwormed into the sleeping-sack—another marvel of stuff offered by the reed-cutter—and fell into a happy sleep. Let the fates fall where they would.

It was in the gray of early dawn on the next day that Mr Khorare thought he heard voices. In fact, if truth be told, he thought he'd heard voices during the night, but had dismissed them as phantoms of his own dreams, or as animal sounds from far away. But as light now stole into his bivouac sufficient for him to see by, he became more conscious of the voices all around, clearly to be heard—but very far from human. He sat up in his sleeping-sack, rubbed his eyes and listened intently, holding his breath. All around the tent there was a low rumble of sounds. At first Mr Khorare was hard put to it to tell them apart from wind roaring in the rocks, except that, with attention, they resolved into the deliberate, punctuated packets of spoken language, for all that Mr Khorare could not recognize any of the words spoken.

He imagined that were wolves and jackals to have had speech, it would sound like this.

Feeling now rather scared, Mr Khorare put on his corduroy trousers, cotton shirt, synthetic jacket, socks and boots (yet more marvelous stuffs supplied by the reed-cutter from her inexhaustible store of wonders) and peered out of the bivouac. The view was westward, downslope, and what he saw amazed him.

Huge, humanoid forms were streaming down the hill, on either side of his sheltered slope, and in front of him: a parade of backs, walking away towards the river, where—in the distance—he could see a black knot of activity and birds circling high in the sky. The humanoids were much taller and rangier than any of his own kind, or even—he guessed—any Stoner. All of them were clad from head to foot in close-fitting suits of shaggy gray or off-white fur—either that, or these humanoids were naturally very furry, and were otherwise naked, aside from the peppering of leather helmets and other articles of a military nature, including long clubs of bone and other weapons of horn or ivory.

These creatures, whatever they were, were marching, downhill, to war. None had yet looked back, and for that, Mr Khorare was very grateful. He hoped that he could remain secret until the entire army—if that's what it was—had passed by, so that he might be able to slip away unnoticed. But the great, shaggy, armored forms continued to file past, much as they had done, it seemed, for the past several hours. There must have been thousands of them. And the more there were, the more noise they seemed to make, the sparse barks of words joining up into a more uniform, unified bellow, a war-cry of defiance. But if these creatures—and Mr Khorare thought he knew what they might be, now; they looked very like the fierce Almai of the mountains of Tibet—

if these creatures were indeed marching to war, where was the enemy? He imagined that it was the target of this long march, the camp—if that's what it was—in the valley below, and to the west. All he had to do, then, was wait until the horde had finally passed by, and he'd be able to watch the battle in relative security from this high point.

Matters turned out very much as he'd expected, at least to begin with. The host eventually transmuted in nature from warriors to wagons, a straggle of bone-railed sleds, and the squeals of female and young Almai, their domestic animals and all manner of the incredible variety and quantity of impedimenta that nomads felt they had to convey on their long migrations. In this gigantic, mobile fleamarket, Mr Khorare in his modestly camouflaged bivouac felt even less conspicuous than he had before. But even these last of the Almai camp-followers had moved on downslope, and Mr Khorare was left quite alone, once again—all such Almai voices that could be heard now came from far away, and his proximate company was the lone wind, gusting through the rocks and heather, as it had been before.

The morning waxed in warmth, and all such change as Mr Khorare could discern concerned the sounds he heard, solely, which changed from the basso roar of defiance and the superimposed chatter of women and young, to the more variegated palette of sounds associated with battle engaged, though the nature of the Almai's enemy remained unknown to Mr Khorare.

At this point Mr Khorare felt that it was time for him to pack up his things and resume his course, roughly north by northwest, following the line of the river to his left and the mountains to his right. Packing took a remarkably short time and all Mr Khorare's belongings were soon stowed in a knapsack of a smallness and lightness that always amazed him. In addition to their other properties, the stuffs provided by the reed-cutter folded up so tightly that his entire bivouac could be held in the clenched fist of one hand, his rolled-up sleeping sack in the other. The entire cooking stove, when folded up, was no bigger than a modest firewood faggot, were any firewood needed. Well satisfied, Mr Khorare shouldered his pack, strode confidently out of the lee of the sheltering rock, and walked straight into a trap.

His first inkling that something was wrong was the impact of his nose against a standing stone which he was sure hadn't been there the night before. Recoiling, he looked up, and found he'd run into the flinty breastplate of a heavily armored Stoner. Looking around, the soldier had three companions, and was identical with two of them. These were clad from wrist to ankle in long coats of leather studded with overlapping flint scales, and wore flint-studded leather helmets on their heads. Each carried a dagger of honed antler points, and a long spear tipped with a blade wickedly carved from the antlers of giant deer.

The fourth rode behind the phalanx of three, mounted on an coelodont of great size, likewise armored in leather and flint. The rider wore much the same armor, and carried much the same armaments, as the foot-soldiers, except that his helmet was ornamented with auroch horns on either side, and its nose-guard was decorated with roughly cut crystals of amethyst, he thought, or garnet. And this Stoner, too, wore something else that his colleagues lacked: a facial expression. Where the faces of the troopers were as stony as their costume, that of their leader was horribly animated into knots of muscle, warped into an asymmetric leer. But most surprising of all to the stunned traveler was his voice—as patrician, as modulated, as articulate and as sarcastic as any of the grasping, defensive elder statesmen and merchant emperors that haunted the Chamber of Commerce in the Very Great City, resisting change, using their gifts of withering rhetoric to impede the young, hinder the new, thwart the ambitious: the forces for whom the fetid stasis of death was life, and all life-giving change was the wind of death.

"So, Mr Khorare," the Stoner chieftain said, dismounting. "We meet at last."

Chapter 10: Sand Druid

The Wilderness of Judaea, Earth, August, 2054

Ah! why, because the dazzling sun
Restored our Earth to joy,
Have you departed, every one,
And left a desert sky?
Emily Brontë — *Stars*

Tom tried to swim in it on his front, but found that his body was almost skating across the surface. With only his chest and knees submerged, his hands and feet couldn't gain enough purchase to move.

Shoshana tried the more customary seated method, like in all those photos of people taken while relaxing in the water; in hats, sometimes with tea-trays, but always reading a newspaper. But those pictures had been taken decades before, when the Dead Sea had less deadness in it than it had now, and she found it hard to keep herself from bobbing out of the water like a cork. In the end they just lay on their backs, side by side, propelling themselves by gentle sculls with their hands. They felt like two tiny pond-skating insects, whose world is forever confined by the unforgiving, rubbery tyranny of surface tension. The water itself had a curious texture, both oily and salty, and it made their hands sting where they'd suffered even the tiniest abrasions, the result of Avi's whirlwind field school — the incessant handling of bones and stones.

For the first few days they'd stayed pretty much in the kibbutz, learning to recognize and classify animal bones and stone tools. Tom knew much of this already, and could have gone, pretty much, to any of Avi's roster of currently active dig sites. But he welcomed the chance to be with Shoshana, the relative novice. Not that they spent much time chatting: the effects of the Battle Cave had left them both profoundly thoughtful, and—as they couldn't tell anyone else about it—they preferred to be thoughtful together, rather than separately.

At the weekend Shoshana felt that what they needed most was a change of mood, insisting that they both catch a bus to Jerusalem, for she wanted to show Tom around. "You'll never know how amazing it is until you get there," she'd scolded, when he showed even the tiniest reluctance.

The visit, however, had been a frustrating failure. The *suq*, usually overflowing with bustle and noise, was sullen and subdued. When Shoshana had visited it the previous December she'd found it as entrancing as Aladdin's cave, the stalls and open-fronted shops on the narrow alleys crowded with the same scenes that you might have witnessed five centuries earlier, or ten.

There were stalls selling nothing but orange juice, squeezed for you then and there, on the premises; itinerant coffee-sellers dispensing thimblefuls of their scalding, cardamom-scented brew from ornate silvered urns carried on their backs, the urns tinkling with tiny bells. There were dimly-lit alleys in which the all shops sold nothing but *halal* meat, the butchers hard at work in full view of the customers (although Shoshana hadn't wanted to look too far past the hanging racks of carcasses), and the exchange of greasy money and gossip was accompanied by the decisive sounds of slicing and dicing. Shops that had seemed unfeasibly small at the front gave on to room after amazing room, piled high with the most exquisite carpets, each with vivid patterns of confounding intricacy. And there were, as there always are, merchants selling basketloads of the tackiest souvenirs. She particularly remembered one especially enthusiastic stallholder chasing her down an alley with a plaited leather whip—"for your husband!" he'd yelled, as she scooted round a corner: "for your wife!"

And the smells! Coffee and cardamom, cloves and cinnamon, onions and garlic, leather and wool, and meat, and fruit, and textiles, and people, and animals, and (most of all) money, all in one great intoxicating sensory onslaught.

But now most of the shops were closed, their filthy, graffitoed shutters down, and Tom and Shoshana as among the very few visitors felt that they were unwelcome. That they were being watched. It smelled only of rotting fruit cooking in hot trash cans.

Another disappointment was that the Temple Mount was closed, so they couldn't visit the *Al-Aqsa* mosque, nor the shining blue-and-gold jewel of the mosque of Omar. Riot fencing barred the gates to the mosque precinct, to which a trilingual sign had been attached. In English it said 'Closed for Renovations,' but Shoshana swore that the Hebrew version was more eloquent and included words like *forbidden* and *security* and *danger*. What the (even longer) Arabic sentence read, they were unable to fathom. But the IDF troops guarding the gate looked grim, and neither Tom nor Shoshana felt like inquiring further. The Western Wall below the Temple Mount had also been barred (not that Shoshana had any desire to mingle with the 'black hats,' as she'd called them), and was uncharacteristically deserted; the Church of the Holy Sepulcher bore only its complement of the variously denominated clerics, outnumbering visitors and pilgrims at least six to one. And nobody, not even Shoshana, visited the Copts on the roof with their lines of washing. "Tom, I'm so sorry…" Shoshana began, "but I think Jerusalem is *closed.*"

Her disappointment was deepened by the feeling that she'd taken Tom on a wild goose-chase, and by her confusion, that this really shouldn't be happening. It wasn't a religious holiday, as far as she was aware, because she'd checked—this was, after all, Jerusalem, where any given day might be a religious holiday for someone—and those few tourists they'd seen had looked lost, as if they were really expecting to be in Milan or Cozumel or Blackpool but had taken a wrong turning. They decided not to stay the night as they'd planned, but to head straight back to Haifa, where things seemed more, well, 'normal'.

The second week started with an early-morning call. Avi was to take them to a site he was working on personally, where they'd have a chance to help excavate part of a Neanderthal cemetery for a few days. On the way, they'd told Avi about Jerusalem, how muted it was, how—*threatening*—as if they'd been partygoers who'd unwittingly stumbled into a private funeral. Avi looked troubled, and what little he said seemed couched in riddles. "Okay, make this your very last day," he'd said. "Tomorrow you're free to go. Your time is short. See as much of my wonderful country as you can, while you can."

And so the very next morning they'd taken their leave. They'd both hugged Avi, who seemed more tense, more serious than the overgrown puppy who'd greeted them just eight days earlier. He didn't say anything, because he didn't have to—but he looked like someone who knew he was entering the Last Days.

They would never see him again.

First they went to Tel Aviv. "If Jerusalem can't cheer us up, then Tel Aviv will," promised Shoshana, and this time she had been right. They cadged a spare sofa for a couple of days in a flat currently occupied by Alina Jacobs, the elder sister of one of Shoshana's old *cheder* friends, and whom she'd met the previous December.

Alina was an expat from North London who'd made *aliyah* and was now working as a real-estate agent, selling expensive seafront condos to other soon-to-be ex-residents of North London. Her boyfriend, David, was a fighter pilot and on duty increasingly often, as he was now, she knew not where: so she welcomed the company—and the chance to show off Tel Aviv's wild side. For two whole days without stopping they'd all got drunk and expired on the beach; they'd drunk some more and partied and bar-hopped and clubbed until dawn. It was just what they'd needed to beat the Battle Cave Blues.

Two days later, Shoshana woke late to find herself crammed on the sofa next to a man who seemed utterly dead to the world. Drink-sodden nights out had been the back-drop to her life since she was twelve or thirteen, but oh, poor Tom—until he'd gone to Cambridge, he'd had very little experience of drink at all, and was now flat out, comatose. She rose and wandered blearily to the kitchen, in search of anything like an aspirin—for she was convinced Tom would need one when he eventually surfaced.

But she herself needed one right now. Over the past few days she'd been seized by pains in her lower abdomen that felt like someone had filled her with kerosene and set it alight. She was convinced Tom hadn't given her a dose, be-cause, despite his promiscuity, he just didn't seem the type—and anyway, she'd been vaccinated against every-thing imaginable, including pregnancy. Her mother, in one of her rare outbursts of decision, had insisted on this. Part of the problem (not that it *was* a problem!) was that there was such a *lot* of him, and after several weeks of frequent sex, her more tender regions had been stretched, bruised and abraded. At least, there were times when she could regain some measure of control, like when she had been riding him, last night, settling gently down on top, shimmying down to find a comfortable level, swivelling around until she felt she fitted over him like a glove, and…

"It must be love," said Alina, joining her in the kitchen, catching her thoughts. Shoshana suddenly realized she'd been standing quite still, with a silly grin all over her face.

"You're so lucky to have found Tom," Alina cooed, filling the kettle and putting it on the stove—"he's *gorgeous.*"

"You don't know the half of it," replied Shoshana, gesturing like the angler whose fish has got away "… or the whole of it…" and the two girls collapsed on each other in fits of mirth.

"Is he… really?"

"Yes, he *is*—and he's *lovely*—and I'm so *sore.* Have you got any aspirins or something?"

Alina rifled around in a cupboard until she found a small bottle of pills, and gave them to Shoshana. But as she handed them over, her expression switched from morning-after playfulness to a soft yearning of regret, of loss. It was her turn, too, to look distractedly into the distance.

"What's up?" Shoshana asked.

"Oh… it's nothing." Alina turned off the gas beneath the kettle and upended the boiling water into two cups of spiced, unfiltered, heavily sugared black coffee. "Hey, drink this. It's *botz*, I know. Usually it's my Mum's PG Tips but, you know, needs must."

She turned away when Shoshana looked at her, wide eyes full of questions. But it was only for two or three seconds. When Alina turned back, her own eyes—pale, ice-blue—were blazing for all that they looked inward.

"David came home last night..." she said. Shoshana remembered a time lost amid the small hours when, being more than half asleep, she half-thought she'd half-heard the frantic gasps and sighs of sex from another room in the small flat. "… but he was gone well before any of us woke up." Silence. And then, Alina standing in her own kitchen, began to shake, wiping tears on the sleeve of her bathrobe.

"Oh, fuck it, Shoshana," said Alina, "everybody's selling, nobody's buying, I haven't had any decent commission for months, and if I could go back home, I would." She subsided onto a chair. "And there's more. Something David said. He told me to… to… well, he said I should be prepared for the worst. He said we should party and drink and fuck each other silly, because tomorrow… well, who knows?"

So that was it, what had been eating Avi and the whole of Jerusalem, and why deep in the desperate night Alina and David had screwed each other's brains out, like they'd never have another chance. Israel was the last man standing against the Khalifa. Alina, stood up, wiped her face and made herself busy with cups and plates. "But don't mind me," she said.

"We'll pick ourselves up. Nobody else will, after all. Now, do me a favor—take that gorgeous stud-muffin of yours and bugger off out of here as quickly as possible. In two days the city will be gridlocked for the Pope, and then the Stones, so escape now. Go and see the Dead Sea before it's gone. Masada too…"

The defiance of her eyes continued her sentence: Masada will be enough to show you that we've been fighting off bastards like these for practically ever, and we'll be here still, when the Khalifa is dust and forgotten.

Alina saw Shoshana and a groggy Tom on to the bus, and within half a day they were here, at the Dead Sea, trying to swim in it like any two fun-loving tourists, for all that the Khalifa loomed from mountains in plain sight. After a while the sunshine and salt were becoming oppressive, so they sploshed and clambered awkwardly from the clingy brine. The water evaporated immediately, leaving them crusted in a thin armour of salty plates.

After using the creaking, paint-peeling showers, they laid themselves side by side on the stony beach. Tom gazed at the yellow hills in the distance, lost in his thoughts. Sho-shana, the words of her Tel-Aviv friend still echoing around her mind, wondered how many Khalifa field-gunners were staring back. Shoshana decided to do something useful instead and went in search of food. Breakfast at Alina's now seemed like ancient history.

Shoshana found a snack stand not far from the edge of the main road out. She joined a small crowd milling around it—mostly soldiers taking a few hours' snatched leave, plus an assortment of back-packers and boho tourists. One had stood out from the rest, at first because he was extraordinarily tall, and second because of what he was wearing. No backpack, no uniform, but a long, brilliantly white, hooded robe that stood out sharply against the general sea of green and tan. Because he had been a little ahead of her in the snack-bar queue and had his back to her, she did not take much further notice of him—until she heard his voice, as he ordered *falafel* from the seller. It was less a voice than a completely dry and tuneless hiss, like someone suffering badly from laryngitis. She looked up then, and met an unreadable expression from the stallholder taking the order. The transaction completed, the hooded figure turned.

And then she saw his face.

Framed in a lion-mane of scruffy, yellowish hair on an unusually tall, narrow head was a thin parchment-white face in which two eyes glinted amid curiously folded eyelids. The eyes were palest grey, almost white, as if he were suffering from cataracts. The nose was long and beaked, with narrow, slit-like nostrils. The mouth was disconcertingly wide, but very thin and almost lipless.

The first thing it said to Shoshana was "excuse me," in English, but with a curious accent that she couldn't place, before standing aside to allow her to place her order at the snack-bar counter. The stranger seemed eager to talk to her — out of politeness, she supposed — and offered his name, which sounded like the noise that might be made by a cat with emphysema caught on the point of death while trying to cough up a rusty bicycle pedal. When she looked like she might embarrass herself trying to pronounce it, he came to the rescue.

"Of course," he said, "my friends just call me 'Bob'." He smiled, his lipless mouth broadening to a somewhat startling size, revealing a lot of yellow-brown teeth.

"My name's Shoshana," she replied, brightening. "I'm a student, from England. But today I'm just a tourist!"

Bob tried to repeat her name, but through his lips it emerged as the crackling of kindling in a frozen winter bonfire. Yes, he too was a tourist, but only from a *moshav* outside Dimona, he explained. Yes, he whispered, wasn't it a funny feeling swimming in the Dead Sea? The hacking gasps following this sentence Shoshana interpreted as laughter. And, yes, he was Jewish.

"For sure!" he said. "I'm a Hebrew Israelite!" Taking Shoshana's quizzical expression as a cue, he continued. "Of course you mightn't have heard of us. There aren't many of us, after all. A few in America, of course. Florida. And who are we? You are justifiably curious, young lady. No, I don't mind at all. We're the Lost Tribe of Judah. To be sure, you'll have heard lots of people say *they're* the Lost Tribe. But we're the real deal, straight up. We've been Jewish for hundreds of years, thousands, maybe forever! Would you like a cigarette?"

And so Shoshana put two and two together, and made a vast, intuitive and daring leap. She was standing before a real, live Sand Druid, and she wouldn't miss her chance.

"Yes, I've heard of the… er… *Annakhnu,*" she said.

Bob smiled at this brave and rare example of anyone else trying to pronounce their own great and holy name. He bowed to her in appreciation. Thus emboldened, Shoshana continued: "I've been on Mount Carmel," she said, "studying with Professor Malkeinu. Do you know him?"

The two turned away from the snack stand and sat on one of a number of heavily weathered wooden benches nearby. Bob looked at her, his reptilian stare from deep within his hood glowing with an inner fire.

"Avi Malkeinu is our returning prophet," he said. "He is our avenging angel, our savior. Without him we would be as ashes and dust. If you know him, you are to be blessed." Then he rose from his place, knelt before her, took her hands in his long, bony claws and kissed them, and said, at the back of his throat but with passion for all that it was close to silence:

"*Avinu Malkeinu, aseh imanu tzedakah v'chesed v'hoshiyainu.*"

With a startling jolt, Shoshana was transported back to North London, to every Yom-Kippur morning service she'd ever been reluctantly dragged into, amid all the other children and the women, and she found herself mouthing this most solemn Hebrew prayer along with this stranger: our Father, our King, treat us with charity and kindness—*help us.*

After two beats Shoshana joined in Bob's prayer, singing it to a haunting, minor-key tune full of imploring, keening loss, of sorrow and of hope; the melody she felt she'd known since her earliest childhood, before her Dad died, in the morning of the world when all was fresh and new and happy, and which she'd always found inexpressibly moving. How could her stepfather have been so narrow, so proscriptive, when here was this alien in this scruffy desert who had internalized their religion so completely?

Who, then, was the Jew?

If Jewishness could encompass Bob the Sand Druid and Howie the *schlmiel* in a single sweep, then *everyone* was Jew-

ish, all humanity—and beyond it. And more than Jewish.
She thought back to Noah, the tower of Babel, a record of an
age before there were Jews, when people had lived together
on the Earth, humans and the lost *nephilim* and who knows
who else, in an idyllic time before they had challenged God
and had been punished with the realization of their own
sundering diversity, to give—what? Sand Druids; Neanderthals in the Battle Cave; the Almai that had eaten Avi's
friends in reverence; the Pendeks that drove all the taxis in
Tel-Aviv; Souris Saint-Michel; the mysterious Sigil of un-
guessable age and mysterious purpose; Tom, Avi—and herself.

Domingo had been right—religion did not transcend
humanity, it *defined* it. Any creature that raised its head
above the murk and sought the face of God, however hope-
lessly, and however lowly, alien or strange it might be, was a
human being, by definition. This inner blast of revelation did
not stop, for now filling her head were words she'd learned
in her diploma-college biology class, that came now as if in
answer—from a source that would have had Howie Levinson squirming with horror: that there is a grandeur in this
view of life, having been originally breathed into a few
forms or into one; and that from so simple a beginning endless forms most beautiful have been, and are being, evolved.

Shoshana sat in stunned silence with the ghost of Darwin
and the memory of her Father and Mother and her *avoteinu
v'imoteinu* back to Abraham and Isaac and Jacob and *Homo
erectus* and apes and all the creatures that had crawled out of
the slime, all there on the bench with her, looking up at her
young face in expectation of an answer that did not come.

Before she could say anything else, the Jew whose name
was Bob but was really something utterly remote and inhuman stood up, collected his paper-wrapped falafel, and

walked with a loping, stork-like gait to a waiting *sherut,* which drove off in a clash of gears and dust.

"Tom, I'm sorry…" she started, having brought the cooling falafel and warming coke back to the stony, salty beach, inwardly cursing that she always seemed to be apologising to him all the time, "I… er… ran into a Sand Druid."

"A… what? A *Sand Druid? Tiens!* Where is he?" Tom sat up, scanning the grove of scrubby trees and bushes that screened the snack stand and the road from view.

"I'm sorry Tom," she said. "I wanted to bring him to you, I know how much you wanted to meet one, but when I looked up, he'd just disappeared. Like he was a dream, like he'd never… like I imagined the whole thing."

"It is nothing, Shoshana."

"It was weird, Tom, he was so, like, *other.* But he *knew,* Tom, he took me back to when I was a little girl in the synagogue: I could see it all, Mum, Dad, everything — it was all there before me, in my mind."

Tom paused for a long time. "You know," he said, "it's like something Domingo once said, when I was little."

Shoshana looked up. "What?"

"Well, you know Domingo and I have always been close. He's been more *mon père* than Jack, in some ways, like he's always looked out for me, even from far away. And one day — I think — yes, I was about nine or ten, and Fairbanks had died. Who was Fairbanks? He was my dog, and my best friend." Shoshana recalled the picture of the little boy with his arms around a big golden retriever on the mantelpiece at the farmhouse.

"I was very distressed," Tom continued, "at losing my good friend. But, you know, my *Maman* and *Papa* have never been very religious, and they didn't seem to have… to have the right things to say, when Fairbanks died…"

"Like you needed a ritual?" prompted Shoshana.

"Yes, that's exactly it, a ritual. To be sure, they tried: you know what people say, 'Fairbanks is looking down on us from doggy heaven'; 'Fairbanks is free from pain now,' and so on. But nothing they seemed to say worked for me. *Rien. Alors,* so I was as upset as ever—remember, I was only a little boy." Shoshana loosened up a little at this, wrinkling up her nose with laughter, leaning up against him.

"In the end they just shrugged and told me to wait for Domingo. So next time he was visiting, he did a ritual for the dog in the garden. Just for me. Nobody else was there. I don't know, maybe my parents kept out of the way on purpose. But I swear, Shoshana, he must have made it up as he went along." Tom laughed in remembrance, Shoshana now embracing him as they sat on the beach.

"But it was just something he said. That although his church said that Fairbanks had no soul, we two—you know, if it was just *entre nous*—we could always... er... 'stretch a point for special friends,' on one condition: that if, and only if, we'd loved Fairbanks as though he was a person—then God would love him too."

Shoshana said nothing, but looked across the still, flat lake, regretting once again that she'd never had the courage to take Domingo into her confidence. She marveled at the sensitivity—the informality—of a ritual that the priest had made up to ease the bereavement of a child. But the sentiments were not patronizing, and very far from childish. They were eternal. Domingo had understood that if a sense of religion defines any creature as human—that was the basis of *Undique humanitas,* which must then have been still quite new and raw—then something else is necessary, too. For religion implies awe, and devotion, even fear: and these things are impossible without love.

So Domingo had made the obvious connection. That if we love someone, or something, we are in effect transferring something of our souls to them, just like every scribbler of every cheesy love song ever written had always understood.

But there is a flipside. Only those that can love have souls to share. And her blood ran cold with revulsion at the religion of her upbringing, at least as interpreted by her stepfather—as hard and stony and lifeless as this salty desert shore. Domingo realized that religion must have rituals if it is to survive, but can only remain meaningful if there is space for these rituals to be stretched, and for love to find its expression within their confines. For without love there can be no soul, and no humanity, and therefore no religion.

But Judaism, the Howie Levinson Way, was all about ritual coming first, no matter what, and love was a long way down the list. His religion had survived for thousands of years despite the earnest attempts of many to destroy it—but at what cost? Without love it was meaningless, with the pointless, bureaucratic cruelty of any Kafka short story. The tragedy was that this inhuman austerity was quite unnecessary. For what she'd seen in Bob's burning, alien eyes when she'd mentioned Avi Malkeinu was nothing but awe and devotion, and love. She would have prayed for her stepfather's soul, if she thought he'd had one.

The Sun was beginning its descent down behind their backs. It was time to move on, to Masada. They'd learned from Alina that you could usually hitch a ride there from the Dead Sea, straight up the highway. A small crowd of people was already milling around the bus stop beyond the snack bar, and some them said they were Masada-bound. Staying the night at the summit of the ancient hill fortress was officially discouraged, but unofficially tolerated as an item on the student-boho-backpacker List of Things To Do.

So Tom and Shoshana joined up with a small group who'd fallen in with a muscular young man with an American accent who'd just become an Israeli citizen and had completed basic training in the army. His name was Danny Forbert. There was also a sandy-haired and studious-looking Englishman who Tom thought he recognized, but couldn't place. He seemed to be miles away, listening to an earbud. At first Tom assumed he must have been following the cricket.

The rest of the party was made up by a pair of back-packers, both Mexican. One was a slim and well-groomed lawyer called José Luis, the other an engineer, Carlos, a bearded and ramshackle bear of a man who must have weighed three hundred pounds. Most people were amazed to learn that they were, in fact, brothers—perhaps less so that they were passionate Stones fans and were in Israel to catch the first date of the latest and possibly last world tour of the group they called *Los Rollings*. Tomorrow they'd head to Tel Aviv in the almost certainly vain hope of getting tick-ets. And if they didn't, hell, they'd get drunk anyway.

Danny Forbert was one of those natural leaders, whose calm authority meant that decisions were reached with per-fect consensus, with little or no argument beforehand. And so it was under his direction that the six of them flagged down a *sherut* for the couple of stops to Masada.

Tom wished Jack could have seen it. If there were any proof necessary that landscape could be shaped by the hand of man and still look like landscape, this was it. Masada had once been a mountain like any other, but it had been con-verted into a palace and fortress more than two thousand years before, by Herod the Great.

Although now demonized for the Slaughter of the Inno-cents—a tale almost certainly mythical—Herod was unde-servedly less well known for his more concrete accomplish-ments. He'd built a vast sea port at Caesarea that had made Roman Judaea the maritime capital of the Eastern Mediter-ranean. He'd created the amazing cylindrical palace of

Herodium just outside Bethlehem that would have looked *avant-garde* even in the twenty-first century. And most of all, he had created Masada.

Herod's engineers started with a natural hill but had flattened the summit, using the overburden to make the sides almost sheer and impossible to climb, especially if the summit were fortified and manned. But its final days had been wrought in blood. Long after Herod, Masada had been the last redoubt of a caste of Jewish religious zealots, who committed mass-suicide when the fortress was finally stormed by the Roman Tenth Legion, the only force capable of taking it—and even then only after a long siege. The Romans had added to Masada's landscape, by building an immense ramp from the valley floor all the way to the summit. The ramp still existed, now, like the table mountain, just another feature of the Wilderness of Judaea.

Danny was the only one of the six who'd been to Masada before, and he promised them all a 'special treat' when they crested the summit. He led the way to the foot of a dusty and treacherously steep track that switch-backed up the western face of the hill. That they could climb it at all was testament to the effects of two millennia of erosion on Herod's almost unbreachable redoubt, the dry desert winds aided by tens of thousands of eager feet—and the lack of military resistance.

When they finally stormed the hilltop they were sweaty, dusty, seared by the still-strong evening sunshine and fit to drop. All except army-hardened Danny, and, surprisingly, Carlos, who thundered over the ridge like a bright-eyed Visigoth on the rampage, adrenalin trumping exhaustion, and ready for anything.

Flushed with achievement, they started to look around the low, grey stone walls—all that was left of the ancient fortress—and looked up at the stars. Tom had been a latecomer to stars, but when he'd first seen them as a child he was entranced, fascinated. He always exulted in nights of stars, with no Moon or streetlights to spoil them. How could nights be so dark and so dazzlingly bright at the same time? And for all the many nights he'd spent in the garden of the farmhouse, gazing upwards, he'd never seen stars like *this*. The stars he saw from Masada were the best stars he had ever seen, pinpoint perfect from one horizon to the other in the dry desert air, with no moon to spoil their radiance, and no nearby cities to wash the sky with dirty orange fog. The Milky Way was an unbroken bridge above his head. For the first time in his life he could understand what the stars must have meant to the ancients, before the press of human illumination forced them into the background, to be viewed only in planetaria or on screens. Until, that is, a bright green distress flare broke this celestial peace, and the harsh sound of voices.

Advancing twenty yards or so further in and peering over a wall, the huddle of tourists saw what looked like an entire legion of the Israeli army all set up for a party. There were tables laden with produce, a barbecue and a detachment of soldiers setting off fireworks. A small disturbance at the edge of the crowd showed that despite their silence and relatively hidden state, the tourists' presence had been noticed. A single soldier in full battle dress came over. He exchanged a few words with Danny in Hebrew — Tom hoped they were friendly, as indeed it proved, when the soldier turned to the rest of them.

"We saw you here," said the soldier. "I the only one speak shit good English, so Commander she say I make talk you. We fire guns, yes? Bang bang? So you can stay here, but you stay here behind this wall, good? When we say yes, you come join in, yes? We have shit good party, yes?"

Danny confirmed that this indeed had been the treat he had promised, as he had undergone it himself. Newly recruited Israeli soldiers marked the end of basic training with a sixty-kilometer desert route march in full gear, the final flourish being an ascent of Masada using the eastern ramp constructed by the Romans. And when they reached the top, they'd get medals and have a party. Tom, Shoshana and the others watched the ceremony, with each new graduate greeted with a crackling salvo of automatic fire. Tom felt Shoshana grasp his arm, and turned to see the fireworks reflected in the intensity of her eyes. On the surface, she seemed as involved in the froth of the party as he'd expected. Partying really was her element. But there was something else, too, that he hadn't seen before—a dark brooding depth. It unnerved him. With an effort he turned back to the spectacle.

The party ended as abruptly as it had begun. The Army left as silently as their presence had been noisy. By midnight the last jeep had hummed off into the night, and Masada belonged to the tourists and the stars. Danny told them stories of his own experiences, picking up on the general mood of finality that seemed to have infected everything.

"Yeah," he drawled. "They told me that too. This could be the last new detachment they can train for a while. Everyone will be on active duty very soon. Including me." Suddenly, his dark eyes seemed to focus on something far away. "Friends, be thankful that I'm not allowed to tell you half the things I know, for they would scare you *shitless*."

It was then that the sandy-haired Englishman spoke.

"In the absence of such intelligence from Danny," he said, "I have some news which we should all know," he said, fingering his earbud. "It's just coming through on the news—the Pope collapsed at the end of his Mass at Ramat

Gan. Oh no…" The man furrowed his brow in concentration: the conversation around him stalled to an anticipatory hush.

"Oh, sweet Christ," he said. "They say he's… he's… *died*."

Tom and Shoshana looked at each other and thought of Domingo. José Luis and Carlos crossed themselves and talked to each other in Spanish too fast for anyone else to catch. They bade Tom, Shoshana and the others a hasty good-night and retreated behind a low wall a few meters off. Tom heard the two of them talking anxiously and low for some time afterwards.

"Maybe we should all get such sleep as we can," Danny said. "We have to rise early and get off this rock—by seven a.m. the Sun is too scorching to tolerate. Then, maybe we can learn about the Pope. Anyway, I'm beat. *Layla Tov!*"

He and the Englishman each wandered to small private nooks in the deep shadows amid the maze of low walls.

That left just Tom and Shoshana, who found a sheltered corner, unrolled their compact sleeping bags, which they zipped together, and climbed in. The desert night cooled rapidly, and they were glad to have each other's warmth. Exhaustion claimed them, and the only sounds left on Masada were titanic snores from Carlos, punctuated by curses from José Luis.

But Tom couldn't sleep: he was still on a rush, a high after the strenuous climb. After a while he unfurled himself from Shoshana's embrace and set off for a stroll among the stars. As he sought a tolerably comfortable perch for a solitary stargaze, he saw a figure, a dark form against the night. It was the Englishman. Apart from his shocking news about the Pope, he'd said next to nothing during the entire trip, and Tom didn't even know his name. The Englishman spared him any further agony.

"Hi there," he said, silhouetted, a man-shaped hole in the riot of stars. "I'm sorry, we haven't been introduced. Vicar, Anglican tendency, subspecies *cantabridgiensis*, yet to be frocked."

It hit Tom then—he'd seen the man around Cambridge, where he'd plainly been studying at one of the several seminaries that clustered round the university colleges. Tom smiled.

"Tom Corstorphine, archaeologist, *tendence palaeolithique*, same subspecies, same stage of development."

They shook hands with the warmth of those whom shared past experience and present perplexity have thrown together.

"Fearon Brimstone," said the man. "Good to meet you." Tom couldn't help but laugh. "Unbelievable, I know," said Fearon, quite unembarrassed. "Parents, eh? It's as if I was driven to my vocation to make up for it. But you—you're a Corstorphine? Not by any chance related to Jack Corstorphine? Jadis Markham? The Jadis Markham of Souris Saint-Michel and all that?" Tom said that he was. Brimstone seemed suitably impressed and affected doffing an imaginary hat. "I am in the presence of *royalty*," he said. "And we are, in a sense, related."

"We are?"

"Academically, at any rate. My grandfather was Roger MacLennane, who would have been your Mum and Dad's ex-Professor. He always used to chuckle about how he introduced them to each other." Tom was open-mouthed with amazement, at the coincidences that brought him and Brimstone together on this desert mountain top in the middle of the night. After which, they fell into easy conversation.

Like Tom, Brimstone had come out to look at the stars. "Not often you see stars like this," he said. Tom wondered if Brimstone was going to say something about being closer to

God, and had he done so, he wouldn't have been surprised. What Brimstone said did have God in it, but was something far, far stranger.

"Did you ever read a story called 'The Nine Billion Names of God'?" he asked.

Tom was about to confess that he hadn't, when he remembered a battered anthology of science fiction stories that Avi Malkeinu had passed on to him when he was about twelve. Avi had been a fan of science fiction, ever since his father had read him H. G. Wells (although Tom suspected that this particular anthology had been passed down from Domingo). And so Tom recalled for Brimstone what he remembered of the very brief tale, about a lamasery in Tibet where the monks are working out the nine billion names of God, and having got a computer to help them, complete their task thousands of years ahead of schedule. Who'd written it? Someone in the early twentieth century.

"Arthur C. Clarke?" said Tom. "But I forgot how it ends. Why do you mention it?"

"Well, you know," said Brimstone, "it turned out that the enunciation of God's names was the final and culminating purpose of Creation. When the technicians, who had installed the computer, leave the lamasery—on a bright, starry night just like this one, they notice the stars slowly going out."

The chill fell between them like a frozen shroud.

"It's… creepy," Tom said, more to break the silence than anything else. Brimstone turned towards Tom, and looked up at the stars once more.

"Creepy?" he said. "Yes, I suppose it is. But just imagine it, if it were really true. You know, we could be those two technicians, high on a hill in the wilderness, looking up at the stars and wondering that very same thing."

"What makes you say that?" said Tom, nervously.

"Well, it's a funny thing," said Brimstone. "You know, at college, we study a lot of theology, homiletics, ancient Hebrew, Latin, the usual stuff. But we're also encouraged to do as much science as we're able, especially evolution, and cosmology."

"To keep one step ahead of the unbelievers?" Tom's head was still whizzing with Shoshana's shared thoughts. Poor Shoshana seemed so weighed down with religion as he was relatively free of such things. But perhaps, here, in Israel, everyone you met had a view about religion. And then he thought of Domingo, and his mind started to make some connections of its own.

"Ah! No, not a bit of it," Brimstone answered. "All that creationist piffle is past, and in any case, most honest theologians didn't give it the time of day anyway. Dismal theology. Worse science. A no-brainer, really. We study these things to do what scientists of the past did—the greats, you know, Einstein, Newton—to magnify the name of the Creator, and to better understand what the Old Chap was on about. Especially as he seems to have given up appearing as pillars of cloud or burning bushes. So there we are, looking at modified brane theory, loop quantum gravity, nucleosynthesis, developmental macronomics, all that stuff. It's good honest work. I like it."

Tom nodded, thinking that this was probably the best course to take.

"So there I was in my final tutorial before the summer vacation," Brimstone went on, "before I came here—and my tutor, a sweet old darling—not really a scientist, more at home writing tomes on Perpendicular church furniture…" Tom pictured oak pews standing on end, like totem poles. "He took a few of us aside and told us some disturbing news about the fate of the stars. He couldn't make much of it, and wanted our opinions, more than anything. You know,

maybe you could shed some light on it? I'm grateful for anything, because I'm puzzled. And worried.'"

Tom confessed his ignorance of astronomy: but then he
saw what Brimstone was getting at. Jack and Jadis were the
best-known scientists of the Merlin Technologies Institute
for Historical Geomorphology, but Ruxton Carr had also
endowed a sister Institute in Cambridge. Tom remembered
Domingo talking about this, when Jadis was puzzling over
the Sigil. The brief of this other Institute was to map the positions and movements of the stars in the Solar neighbour-
hood. Brimstone, with his family connection to Roger
MacLennane, would certainly have been aware of this. But
apart from that, Tom was genuinely in the dark, and said so.
He did not yet articulate a faint unease at where (he thought)
this might all be leading.

"No matter," Brimstone shrugged. "Perhaps it'll take a
casual bystander — no offense — to see what this is really
about. No, really, I'd like your views." So he told Tom about
a tiny, obscure paper that had been deposited in a tiny, obscure physics archive by a tiny, obscure group of astronomers in New Zealand, some of whom had been funded by
the Merlin Technologies Astrometry Institute. The press
hadn't picked up on it, and Tom had not heard of it.

"Not surprising really," Brimstone continued, "negative
results don't often get noticed. But this was *more* than negative. You see, these astronomers were doing some recent
curation of wide-field plates to assess the proper motions of
nearby stars." Tom looked blank. Brimstone sighed.

"That's basically what the Astrometry Institute funds,"
said Brimstone. "Cataloguing proper motion. You know, the
stars we see aren't fixed, like they're stuck on the inside of a
black velvet bowl. They move around. Some towards us,
some away from us, some from side to side. All stars do this,
but the ones closer to us seem to do it more because — well,

they're closer. The movement is appreciable and measurable over years and decades." Tom look surprised. Brimstone laughed—a warm, musical sound after these chilly intellectual magnitudes. "You know, not everything in astronomy is… er—"

"… Astronomical?"

"Exactly! Anyway, the astronomers take pictures of the sky every so often, compare the pictures with older pictures, work out these movements, so they can update star maps and so forth. But what they noticed seemed very odd. Sure, some of the stars had moved, but a few—two or three out of thousands—weren't there at all."

"Like, they'd vanished? No débris? Rocks? Gas—radiation—whatever?"

"That's just it. Vanished. Rubbed out. *Pouff*!" He waved his hands, like a deity casually swatting the fates of billions. "And yes, before you mention it, they'd checked that they'd taken the proper exposures, and that the stars hadn't moved so fast that they turned up on other plates, and so on and so forth. And they got another lot of astronomers in Chile to check the findings. No, these stars had vamoosed down the back of the celestial sofa. And there was one more thing. The stars that vanished weren't randomly distributed. They were all clustered close to the celestial South Pole—which is a particularly boring patch of sky, so it's no wonder that nobody had noticed anything odd before. And they were all tiny, dim red dwarfs, and all between fifteen and seventeen light years away from us. Now *that's* the real strangeness. The non-randomness of it all."

Tom would have been convinced that Brimstone was spinning a yarn, or trying to tell some obscure theological joke, but if so, this would hardly explain the hairs standing up on the back of his neck, and his sudden recollection of Domingo's strange, expression—knowing, and yet almost terrified—when he and Shoshana had hypothesized that the Sigil had been a warning, a totem to ward off eclipses.

A scourge of stars.

Perhaps they'd been far closer to the truth than they'd realized. Tom felt suddenly as if he'd sobered up.

"Non-randomness implies that it's almost as if there's a purpose to it all," Tom heard himself say, and, to his own horror, he continued, "as if it were meant to happen. But if that's true, it's a purpose quite different from the Clarke story, which gives the impression that the stars were going out more or less randomly, *non*? And Clarke's stars were big ones, that the technicians could just casually see as they were walking along. They didn't have to go looking for them."

"The astronomers in New Zealand didn't say anything like that, of course," said Brimstone, "they just documented the absences. But you know what I think? I think that there's someone or something out there that's trying to creep up on us and bite us on the bum."

Tom felt that his heart had stopped, and that he was covered all over in a blanket of clogging, wet fear.

"Yes, I know," said Brimstone into the silence. "Monumentally paranoid. But what else is there? And even if this whatever-it-is isn't Out To Get Us in particular, something definitely is happening. And whatever-it-is caused my tutor some theological heart-searching. Me too. Has God decided to come out of hiding? If this the twenty-first century equivalent of burning bushes? Is it a test of faith, in the guise of science? Frankly, I don't know what to make of it."

When Tom awoke the next morning, folded around Shoshana's peaceful warmth, all thoughts of cosmic disturbance had vanished from his mind—for apocalypse had arrived.

Chapter 11. Pilot

The Wilderness of Judaea, Earth, August, 2054

Blood and destruction shall be so in use
And dreadful objects so familiar
That mothers shall but smile when they behold
Their infants quarter'd with the hands of war.
William Shakespeare — *Julius Caesar*

The pilot once had a name but he had forgotten it. It had been drilled out of him in a dozen training camps across the Khalifa. But he was content to have submitted himself to a greater mission, a greater conquest. For the final moment had come, when the Khalifa would regain Holy *Al-Quds* and drive the Zionists into the sea at last. Secure in the cockpit of his strike jet, he was wired so thoroughly into its computer, its avionics and weapons systems, that he could control them all with a flicker of thought. He and his aircraft were one, and yet just one barb of one vane of one feather in the ten thousand wings of the Prophet.

With his remaining spark of individuality, he was proud to have been selected for this, the very first wave, to demonstrate that the Khalifa had the resolution to sweep all opposition away, and not (for shame) talk so vividly of blood and skulls and death and yet run screaming like children at the faintest hint of opposition. Those times were over. His task now was not destruction, but terror: to fly beneath the Zionist radar too fast for their missile systems to follow, buzz the rooftops of Tel Aviv, circle over the sea and return. After that, the batteries of missiles would pound the cities into dust, and waves of ground troops would do the rest.

Not that the passage of an aircraft flying at Mach 7 less than a hundred meters over the city wouldn't be destructive in itself. The turbulence of its wake would be as a white-hot airquake, piercing eardrums, shattering windows, ripping any unprotected object smaller than a laden truck off the ground with the demonic rage of a twister. Buildings immediately beneath its path would have the air sucked out of them and implode, and anything organic within fifty meters would burst into flames. The effect on any exposed human being in this range would not be far short of that of a nuclear strike.

The pilot mused on such things with satisfaction as he arrowed across the Jordanian Desert, the currents of his thoughts exalting as his craft danced and wheeled to his direction through the canyons, tracing the contours of the grey and yellow mountains on the wings of dawn, generating a roaring cloud of dust in its train. This was true exhilaration—to have achieved the dreams of centuries, to be as free as a dove, as a raven, even though on an errand of war.

That his senses were occasionally clouded with spots of blackness he attributed to the lurching shifts in acceleration as the plane altered its course constantly under his direction. His own human body, wired into the system, was physically immobile: and so at first he ignored the visuals that warned of increasing damage to his peripheral nervous system, and that his skin conductivity and heart rate now deviated markedly from mission-optimum levels. A message intruded from the outside world, relayed by satellite from Strike Mission Control in Tabriz. The message said:

TELEMETRY ERROR: ABORT MISSION

And, of course, he would have obeyed this command instantly and without question. But he found that he could not. The aircraft was guided, moment by moment, in the only way feasible for a machine that could travel at such speeds, so close to the ground: by the thought of a human pilot directly interfaced with the aircraft's systems. And yet to broadcast such overriding imperatives to his avionics, he would need to underline the point by sub-vocalization. First, to ensure that the commands were clear, and, second, to convince the conjoined, near-sentient machine that his thoughts were significantly beyond the normal variation expected of the merely human. Even though the pilot would not actually need to move his mouth to do this, only to enact the movement in his mind, he found that his jaw muscles were locked in tetany.

Terror rose to the surface as he felt his body squirming helplessly within the shock-gel that lined his flight suit, itself slotted into the cockpit with no room to move. Subdermal proprioceptors registered extensive bruising as his body convulsed within its artificial shell. Motion detectors in his bones traced sharp, jagged movements consistent with un-controlled muscular spasms. His heart muscle had begun to fibrillate. Chemosensory channels in his kidneys and intestines reported rapid spikes in ionic concentrations, indicative of unwitting evacuation into recycling and life-support.

The black spots that he had attributed to rapid accelera-tion were now permanently hovering before his eyes, until they completely obscured his vision. So he would not have seen the sudden rash of heads-up displays, each competing for attention and burning scarlet, recording that his organs were liquefying from within, and that his bones were im-ploding like popcorn crushed in an armored fist.

No longer directed by its human component, the mind of the jet had to improvise. It could not respond directly to Mission Control, whose designers had decreed that the hu-man pilot must always have the override, unless it could be demonstrated that the pilot had died. But although teleme-try from the strike craft indicated the signs of an extraordi-nary transformation, they did not reveal unequivocal signs of death. The brain waves were unprecedented in shape and utterly obscure in meaning, but they were brain waves none-theless.

The aircraft did its best to keep to the planned course, but without the constant corrections of its human partner—who had drifted off into some unrecognized brain-wave cycle, deeper than the merely subconscious, which it could have done something about—the course deviated every nanosec-ond from that which its pilot would otherwise have chosen, until it came on a sudden upon a landscape that was passing it too quickly for it to be able to process the topography into its dead-reckoning system. Somewhere in the Wilderness of Judaea, perhaps inevitably, it met a mountain it did not rec-ognize quickly enough.

The mountain rushed up to meet the aircraft at almost five thousand miles an hour.

Not that the Duty Lead Controller in Tabriz was aware of this incident in particular, as he had his own problems. Of the fifty strike jets in the first wave, sixteen had reported similar pilot-interface problems, of which eleven had disap-peared altogether. Clearly, something was desperately wrong, and, frantically, he recalled as many of the aircraft as he could before things got any worse. But try as he might, screen after screen turned from green to amber to red and, finally, black. Two of the Junior Mission Controllers had suddenly gone off sick, grey and sweating. The Lead Con-troller assumed, at first, that they couldn't stand the pace. But when his own bladder was full to bursting and he'd had to go to the washrooms, he found his absent colleagues. Or, that is to say, he found their *clothes*, alongside what looked like two black bowling balls. He could not account for this. Had they abandoned their posts, on this day of days, to go bowling? In the nude? What was going on?

The day had started with so much promise. He had woken up, looking forward to his shift, on what heralded a great day for the Khalifa. They were, finally, going to expunge this blot of shame from the heartland, he told his admiring wife and three fine sons as he set off for Mission Control. But now it was a nightmare, from end to end.

The Lead Controller felt that he had to take responsibility for his abject failure, and reconciled himself to a harsh and possibly lethal sentence. He hoped that the General would treat his family kindly. But when he had reported to his own superior, the secretary would say only that the General had been 'indisposed'. The secretary had dropped her gaze from his, which was very proper, but then she collapsed on her desk, all decorum gone, looking at him directly with wide, desperate eyes. "I *saw* it, Major," she said. "I saw the General turn into a monster, a black… *thing*! It was horrible, *horrible*!"

From its shock value alone, the mission had actually been a great success, for the eleven missing jets had become ballistic missiles of terrible power. To be sure, six had plunged into the Mediterranean sea, and a seventh had smashed into the Great Pyramid at Gizeh, transforming the First Wonder of the Ancient World into a very large pile of barbecue briquettes. But an eighth had scored a direct hit on a condo in Tel Aviv, demolishing most of a city block and killing at least fifteen hundred people. Alina Jacobs had not stood a chance. Her last thought before being atomized was whether she should tell David that she'd booked a one-way ticket to London.

A ninth had dropped like a meteor onto the Hadassah hospital, vaporizing Dr Mohamed Al Hajj, Resident, along with all his staff and several hundred patients. Dr Al Hajj had been examining a number of cases of the same affliction that had destroyed the Pope, whose remains—if that's what they were—had been removed by an ashen-faced Cardinal Sanchopanza. From what Dr Al Hajj could discover, by darting all over a hospital that was cycling into in a state of rising panic, to see each case for himself as it ran its terrifying, unstoppable course, the patients had been *transformed*, but had not actually died. Even though no equipment at the hospital that he could lay his hands on at short notice could penetrate the matt-black shells of the… er… 'patients,' not even the most powerful X-ray machine, he was still convinced they were alive, even though he could not have said why: and because of this, he had hesitated to commission anything more invasive.

Working late into that same night, Dr Al Hajj drafted a small note to a 3-Web medical bulletin describing the condition. He noted that its incidence seemed too patchy and indiscriminate to be consistent with any kind of contagion. And he also had the honor of naming it: he called it Postembryonic Oolithic Petrosis, or POP for short. Like all conscientious medical men, Dr Al Hajj felt that once a disease had a name, one was at least half way to curing it. He was musing on life and death in this fashion as dawn broke through the window of his tiny carrel of an office, when he sent the note to the server and, a split instant later, his own angel arrived.

The scientists in the Khalifa, being more technically advanced than anyone had suspected or even thought possible, had far more powerful equipment than that available to Dr Al Hajj, and were less squeamish about its use. The first cases of the affliction had come to light in the Khalifa several days earlier, but had been kept secret. Families and colleagues of 'patients' tended to disappear themselves not long after reporting a case—until the pestilence, plague, or whatever it was, became too widespread for this lockdown policy to be feasible. But discerning what had happened to the patients proved impossible. Boiling them in oil, toluene, caustic soda, nitric acid or molten tungsten; dropping them into nuclear reactors; applying the kinds of pressures typical of stellar interiors—none had any effect at all. They didn't

even warm up. They remained similarly refractory to parti-
cle-beam weapons or X-lasers developed for space warfare,
even at close range and in high vacuum.

The last straw came when a few patients had been exposed to the two-million-degree plasma in the experimental
fusion torus at Rawalpindi, but the trial had to stop when
the plasma threatened to break out of its magnetic confine-
ment. The patients were completely unharmed. In the end
the scientists gave up. The black spheres that had once been
people kept their undead secrets to themselves.

The tenth rogue jet dove nose-first into the middle of
Ramat Gan stadium, replacing it with a crater sixty meters
deep and full of molten rock. Casualties, thankfully, had
been relatively light: apart from the Stones' road crew, lighting riggers, sundry maintenance staff and 'Mr Micawber' — a
1950s blonde Fender Telecaster reputed to be Keith Richards' favorite — the stadium had been empty. But the concert
would have to be cancelled.

The eleventh struck the eastern face of Masada about a
hundred meters short of the summit.

In the early hours of the morning, when unfamiliar stars
wheeled just before the rising Sun, Shoshana stirred in her
sleep and, half-waking, stretched, smiled, and curled up
again beneath Tom's chin.

Tom awoke then, his first sight the top of her head, her
glossy curls glinting in the Sun's first rays. Something
caught his eye, just above the low, eastern wall of ruined
building in which they had slept. He thought he saw a column of dust in the dawn, the flash of something silvery, and
then heard a sonic boom from a great distance, eastwards.

He raised himself up to peer over the wall, and his world
went instantly, searingly white, a flash accompanied by a
roar of inhuman volume. The ground shook, buckled and
liquefied beneath him. He ducked down in the utter agony

of his eyes, his mind cast back to a sun-baked front yard far away when he was chasing leaves with Fairbanks and the world of light had cascaded in on him like two comets drilling into his terrified skull. But now the sky really was falling, and the ground beneath him heaving upwards to meet it. Their bivouac which a moment before had been a quiet haven had become the uncertain centre of a crashing, sliding maelstrom of overwhelming noise and a rain of boulders. Tom—blinded and almost deafened—threw himself over Shoshana and put his hands over his head. The sleeping bag that contained them both took off like a wayward surfboard in a tubular breaker. He thought he heard Shoshana screaming, two inches away from his ear and at the top of her voice, but he could only just hear it. The world wavered unsteadily before his ruined senses, fluttered for a moment, and died.

What seemed like hours later—it was, in fact, about twenty seconds—the storm of dust and rocks ceased. Shoshana was now fully awake, uninjured but in shock. That she'd had her eyes closed and her face close to Tom saved her sight, but she was dazed and at first had no idea where she was, or why. The world was dark, partly because of Tom's spasmodic embrace, but also because they had been half-buried in rubble.

She did not know it, but all their companions had perished. José Luis and Carlos, the Mexican Stones fans, had been asphyxiated by a pyroclastic flow of white-hot dust and buried beyond all hope of recovery. Danny Forbert, sleeping closest to the impact, was vaporized in a dead flat picosecond by the exploding plasma fireball. But Fearon Brimstone had expired several hours earlier—quietly, all alone and in unspeakable pain—from Postembryonic Oolithic Petrosis.

The surface of Masada had changed completely. The maze of buildings from the evening before was now an unrecognizable slush of broken scoria. As the Sun began to climb, its rays penetrating the ubiquitous yellow, choking murk and the thicker columns of dust and smoke that fumed all around, Shoshana knew that she and Tom had to get off the ruined mountain as soon as they could. She pulled herself out of the sleeping bag and, slipping and sliding in the rubble, struggled unsteadily to her feet. She realized that she'd been hurt—her left ankle was twisted. Putting any weight on it sent red-hot needles of pain up her leg, making her gasp for breath. She was aware of the silence of the world, as if her ears had been stuffed with cotton wool. She looked down at Tom, curled up like a fetus in the rags of the sleeping bag. Blood ran from his ears and from a myriad small wounds in his scalp and arms. And where he wasn't red, he was yellow, caked in filth and grit. His iShades were gone. His fists were pushed hard into his naked eyes. Awkwardly, she knelt down next to him in the smoking scree.

"Tom, we have to go," she said. "Somehow—but we have to." Her voice sounded adenoidal in her own ears, and very quiet. Tom said nothing. Lightheaded and groggily uncertain of the extent of Tom's injuries, she felt he'd probably come round eventually if left to himself.

So, with the mindless optimism of all refugees and blast victims, she pecked around the rubble for their possessions. Their rucksacks, almost buried in rubble, had been ripped from the foot of the sleeping bag where they'd stowed them, and were torn beyond repair. She pulled out their money and ID-tags and, buried right at the bottom of her rucksack and mercifully in one piece, she found her ancient phone.

God, a phone.

Tom never used one, and she had long since got out of the phone habit that afflicts all teenagers. When had she last used it? When she'd phoned Alina to see if they could doss at her flat. She murmured Alina's name at the handset. No signal. Or perhaps there was, but she just couldn't hear it.

She didn't have a contact for Avi and didn't know how to search for him. She felt she couldn't be bothered to dict a message, and her fingers felt too much like numb sausages to write anything. Oh well, they'd simply have to walk out of here.

Slowly, Tom came to his senses. To be completely blind again after all this time was a blow. To be sure, he felt that he could probably function without sight as he always could, and who knows, maybe it would come back again, but now that he'd been shown the color and vibrancy of the world, to lose it now was almost more than he could bear. And to lose the sight of Shoshana, her hair, her skin the color of pale honey, the freckles on her shoulders, the way her nose wrinkled when she smiled, her strange, purple eyes — he might never again see something and know that it was 'purple'.

He got up, quite easily avoiding every obstacle, and apart from the blood caking his scalp and running like scabby rivers from both ears, what seemed like a thousand painful scratches, especially on his hands and arms, and enough bruises to make him feel like he'd been hit by a train — he didn't seem to have suffered major physical injury. He took his hands away from his eyes and — nothing. He sensed Shoshana close, her early-morning smell clouded by dust and blood and pain.

"Shoshana," he gasped.

"I'm here, Tom — I'm here." And she was there, in his arms. "Tom, open your eyes," she said. Her voice seemed to come from an immense distance. He opened his eyes against what seemed like a tide of sharp grit, and, having done so — saw a darkness deeper than space..

"I can't see a thing," he said. "Nothing at all. But really, I'll be fine, you know that. I was blind until I was six, and then I could see. Now I can't. But I'm sure I'll... get used to it. But Shoshana, I wanted to tell you something last night, but you had fallen asleep."

They both paused. The Sun climbed further. Tom could feel its pressure on his eyelids.

"It's — well, now is not a good time, maybe. But it's just that — well, I love you. Like nothing else. I only wished I could have told you that when I could have seen your face, your beautiful face. You know, it was only when I took my iShades off that I knew... so if I can never see you, I don't know if…"

His hands reached out towards her, navigating her body from her shoulders, to her neck, to the rounded surfaces of her cheeks and lips, and to her lashes, and her eyes, which were filled with tears.

"Oh, Tom," she said, "my own, poor, sweet Tom." She reached up and gently stroked his lashes, his flickering eyelids, the streaks of tears and blood and dirt that striped his cheeks.

"Come on," she said, "let's go home."

How they found themselves in Ben Gurion airport, neither of them could recall. There must have been a bus, or a *sherut*, or a police car, or something — it was all too foggy. They were still too deep in shock for anything much to register on their battered minds. But somewhere along the line they must have run into someone helpful, for they'd been cleaned up and Shoshana had a splint for her ankle. So now, here they were, in what she thought was the international check-in except the signs didn't really mean anything to her and which was full of a sea of anxious people screaming children people bandaged and whimpering trying to get a seat on whatever flight they could out of wherever it was they were. Were *they* checked in on a flight? If so, where were they going? They no longer had any idea. Eventually,

Shoshana felt just too tired to care any more. She would have sat there forever in numb stupefaction.

The constant news bulletins on the screens above their heads reported the two Khalifa suicide jet attacks on Tel Aviv, the destruction of the Hadassah hospital. Masada might have got a mention and there were reports of movements of ground troops into the Galilee and then there was this strange disease. It was all too hard to tell. Tom said he couldn't see anything anyway and they were both still partially deaf and the noise all around them of swirling shouting people was distracting and got confused in her mind with the news reports really her mind might as well have turned to her Grandma Sadie's lockshen pudding.

This strange disease was called Pop! Pop! Pop! and didn't seem to have any pattern said the doctor at the Hadassah who had died. The Khalifa was on the march but hey! Pop! Pop! Pop! Their planes had fallen from the sky which had fallen on them both and she knew she loved Tom so much even though he was blind and buried in rocks and there was something about a pillar of fire and a pillar of salt and loneliness and pain and Jadis—it *was* Jadis—who reached out to her and said she'd always be there for her just like Jack had told her he would and then there was Bob who was also her Dad her wonderful Dad who looked down at her, no, *up* at her, and said *avinu malkeinu aseh imanu tzedakah v'chesed v'hoshiyainu* and so without thinking about it, a well of silence within the crowds, Shoshana took her battered old phone and dicted a text to a number she really should have thought of much earlier, a message that read

jadis jack we're here here safe alive we don't know what to do please treat us with charity and kindness help us

Jadis had returned home from her morning round of the village. She had learned many things on her journey, but none of them added up, and she had exhausted all possible means of progress. And so, by way of displacement activity, she was busily trying to focus her mind on the July accounts for the gargantuan sprawl of a project that Souris Saint-Michel had become. Not that she really needed to, given that the vast project had accreted its own accounts staff at the Institute, which could manage quite well on its own. As Jack had explained, patiently, they'd come a long way since the first days at Saint-Rogatien, when Jadis had been project leader, personnel manager and accounts department all rolled into one. Sure, he'd said, some habits are hard to break, but there wasn't really any need for her to send quite so many exasperated notes to the Institute's Accounts Department, given the pressure it was under. But organization had always been her way of averting and diverting stress. She felt, instinctively, that if you could only arrange your own life, then the increasing disorder all around you would matter less, or in any case seem less disorganized, and anyway, even if it didn't, that at least you were doing something rather than just climbing the walls. If there was one thing she hated, it was being in the position of having too little information on which she could make a decision.

But life's like that, she sighed — and science was a microcosm of life, requiring the ability to make educated guesses, shots in the dark. Jack was always so much better than her at guessing games.

Her hair, ever a mark of her mood, now surrounded her like a swarm of angry bees that some rash interloper had stirred with a stick — as if, in its disorder, it had been acting as a reservoir for the entropic increase she'd banished from her frantic quest to arrange her own thoughts.

Metaphorically, at least.

Whatever else it was, the halo of hair was an efficient heat trap, which worsened her frustration, which made her hair frizz and billow out even more, trapping more heat: a classic positive-feedback loop. A part of her said that she should do something about her hair and break the cycle, but she had always drawn back. It was a part of who she was: were she to tie it back, as some people at the Institute had sometimes suggested (all those, Jack said, who didn't know her any better) she'd be tying back her brain. And cut it off for the summer? Unthinkable. She'd be a different person altogether.

So she sloughed off her sandals instead, placing her bare feet squarely on the cool flags beneath the table, a sink for the heat from her body. The sensation calmed her, the feeling of being rooted to the solid earth. She took time to stop what she was doing, to breathe deeply, in and out, and to listen to the sounds of the house-timbers creaking and stretching in the mid-day heat, the chirp of crickets in the garden.

She felt better.

She could now think things through in a asymptote to equanimity, almost, if not quite, reaching it.

The first fruit of her meditation was the decision to put the accounts aside. In any case, she had reached a point where she was going round in circles and the figures were flying off in all directions.

First the mysteries of the village. She'd run into a wall.

Now the accounts. Nothing more than a fervid, futile cycle.

Surely, she thought, no obstacle could fall beneath her feet if she tried something as simple as get a few things together for lunch? But when she'd looked around for bread she remembered that she hadn't managed to buy any, a result of the inexplicable, unprecedented closure of the boulangerie. It was too late to start baking; and anyway, if she had, the heat in the kitchen would have become intolerable. But it was summer, so there were always tomatoes and cucumbers and lettuces in the garden, waiting to be harvested, so she thought she might make a salad instead. She put her sandals back on again, collected her sunhat and basket and headed through the *arrière-cuisine* to the back door.

August had always been a low month at the farmhouse. Apart from a few forays to the *potager*, where she now collected the warm, ripening tomatoes, it had almost always been far too hot to work outside for much of the day. Although work at SSM took place underground, most of the staff at the Institute usually took the whole month off, so everything went into a kind of sleep mode anyway. The weather of the past few years had emphasized this: from the end of July to early September, noon temperatures climbed into the upper forties, and everyone was reduced to a helpless torpor. The birds were too exhausted to sing, let alone fly. Butterflies and lizards basked on the farmhouse walls with impunity, *Les Horribles* too vitiated to give chase. Only the crickets and grasshoppers chirped gamely on, stalked by the frogs, which could always retreat to their pond to cool off. So, whatever else one might have felt, and however the world outside did its best to buffet her off course, August was a good time for quiet, deliberate housekeeping.

And so it had been, she thought, stooping with her clasp knife to cut some cucumbers from a vine that now sprawled exuberantly over the baked and crusted ground. Except for the worries that Jack had started to bring home from the Institute about ten days earlier, that people who'd gone away on vacation had failed to return; that an extraordinary number of staff had phoned in sick and were not heard from again; and that everyone in the Institute seemed to be doing three jobs to cover for people who could not be contacted. The Accounts Department had been especially badly hit, he explained, which is why nobody was answering her emails (this last made Jadis feel a little ashamed of herself for having pestered them).

And, most disturbing of all, that three people returning from vacation had died, because the three separate aircraft on which they had been travelling had fallen out of the sky.

It was then that Jadis recalled thinking, on her round only that morning, that the village had been more muted than usual, even for *La France Profonde* in its summer torpor. That the Mairie had been shut for the month was no surprise; that the boulangerie had been not just shut, but locked and boarded up without notice, definitely was. The boulangerie was open every single day of the year and had been so for as long as she could remember. To find it closed, without even a notice on the door, seemed like an affront to the laws of the Universe.

Nonplussed, she had gone next door to *Le Sanglier D'Or*. Over coffee under the awning on the terrace—a favourite stop, where she and Jack had breakfasted on their honeymoon—she'd asked Sandrine Pasquier, the burly, matter-of-fact former farmer's wife who'd run *Le Sanglier D'Or* for the past fifteen years, if she knew why the baker had done a bunk. Although Sandrine had never been renowned for cosy chats, she had been more than usually communicative, as if she'd had troubles to share. She even broke her own formerly inflexible commandment and joined a customer at a table, as she now did with Jadis.

She'd been to a lot of funerals lately, Sandrine had said, sometimes for people who'd died for no good reason and were in fact in the peak of health, leaving families and children. If that weren't tragic enough, these enforced absences made it very hard for her to run a business—especially when usually reliable staff kept vanishing with no good excuses and didn't come back, and when the brewery, usually so punctual, could hardly be bothered to send supplies as regularly as it promised. And so, Dr Jadis, if she didn't mind, she would love to talk, but she had a hotel and a *café* to run, and although not too many people came into the bar lately, those that did were always thirsty. Sandrine stood up and disappeared into the darkness at the back of the bar, pretending to busy herself with glasses. Jadis noticed that the bar was currently completely empty, the tables shining in expectation of custom that might never arrive.

So Jadis had once more braved the Sun's relentless photonic assault and picked her way across the scalding cobbles of the Place Etienne Geoffroy Saint-Hilaire, taking refuge in the nave of the church. It smelled of cool stone and beeswax: shafts of hot light blasted through the high windows, picking out motes of chaff and dust. It was utterly silent. Despite her almost total lack of religious conviction, she felt that ordering her thoughts here in the cool dark would be as effective as anywhere else, so she tried to piece things together. And here, in the church, she had always felt the reassuring even if mostly absent shade of her old friend, Domingo. She felt he'd approve of the line of thought she felt she should now undertake.

She found a pew near the front of the church and looked towards the altar, but her searching, brown gaze was now cool, and directed to yet further distances, with the same intense intelligence that many, over the years, had found both enthralling and frightening.

Absences without leave. From the Institute, from the boulangerie, from the *Sanglier D'Or*. And from what Sandrine had said, not just *absences,* but *deaths.* The two concepts became conflated in her mind: given that there had been so much unexplained absence, so much inexplicable death, the two just had to be connected. But she had, as yet, too little information to go much further than that. So the scientist in her did what it had always done best, breaking down the problem into its fundamentals, trying hypotheses on what scant information she could assemble.

Even though it was August and people were absent anyway, the numbers of deaths she knew about seemed anomalously high. To be fair, people did tend to die more often in this pitiless heat, but the victims were the traditionally vulnerable — the sick, the elderly, the very young. But Sandrine Pasquier said that she'd mourned people carried off in their prime.

Chalk one up to the anomalies.

Jack had implied the same, with his tally of absent and possibly deceased working-age staff at the Institute.

Therefore, add another.

And August was not a time when the traditional complaints were in circulation — the colds, the influenza, the hypothermia of their now typically Siberian winters. It was too hot, and people were dispersed, not huddled up in small spaces breathing one another's exhalations.

So, add a third.

The anomalies were stacking up towards statistical significance.

But all of this was local. Could this be something that had struck Gascony in particular? Contamination of the groundwater? An unrecognized contagion spread in truffles or *confits de canard?* Unlikely. Such things had happened, of course. Every few years there was some scare or other that constrained farmers to keep their flocks of ducks and geese indoors, or force people to watch the water they drank, or the food they ate. Bird 'flu' in 2027 and again in 2033; anserine spongiform encephalopathy in 2041; or — as had happened only last year — an epidemic of botulism traced to a local cannery. But if such a pestilence had been unleashed, she thought she'd have heard about it by now, from market-trader gossip. Yet there had been not a word of anything, and market traders being what they are, there would be no possibility of a cover-up. In any case, the scientist in her had no time for conspiracy theories.

Ah, but it *wasn't* local, was it? There had been those air crashes. The ones that had carried off three Institute staff. In her mind she carefully reviewed the cases that Jack had told her about. There had been three *separate* aircraft, but the cause of the crashes was always the *same* — the pilot had died during the flight. Now, what were the chances of three air-craft crashing from the same cause in such a short interval? Infinitesimal.

Chalk up another.

Details, details. The aircraft were all small, with no co-pilots or much in the way of backup systems. But the key fact, she thought, was that the flights had all started in widely dispersed locations. One from Bucharest; another from Stavanger in Norway; the third from an aerodrome just outside the charmingly but improbably named village of Little Snoring, in Norfolk.

More mysteriously, she could find no mention of any specific *cause* of death — no mention of heart attacks, or stroke, or anything else. Such absence was, she felt, suspi-cious. An unknown cause, and, given the tight cluster, pos-sibly the *same* unknown cause.

Corroboration.

Newsfeeds trickling into to her airtab over the past few days had thrown up other instances from locations as far-flung as Western Australia (a mining transport), Denver (a commuter shuttle) and Ukraine (a crop sprayer). Again, she could find no mention of any specific cause of death. *Why?*

Pull back.

Given that she had no clue about precise causes of death, neither in the cases of the crashed aircraft, nor — she sud-denly realized — in the swelling mortuaries closer to home, she had no reason to link any of them. Except one: Occam's Razor, the age-old germ of the scientific method that said that when faced with a choice of disparate causes to explain a set of events, one should always consider the simplest option first. In this case, that all the deaths had a single cause.

It was then, in the cool peace of the church, that her mind transcended the obstacle: the precise cause did not matter, but that there *was* a common cause there could be no doubt at all. Why? Because the newsfeeds that told her all about the air accidents all pointed to a remarkable hike in accidents of all kinds, all over the world—whether in cars, trucks, trains or just generally, together with an unprecedented level of workplace absenteeism.

Pull back.

Correlation is not the same thing as causation. Had she had been right, then, to have equated absence with death? People were absent for all kinds of reasons, especially in the summer; and whereas all living people are much the same, each one dies in his or her own peculiar way. But no—even taking all of this into account, the fact was that everything had happened now, *together*. The sharp-edged gears of the analytic engine inside her head meshed smoothly and illuminated deep ruby lanterns of statistical significance. Something was, definitely, going on.

But what?

For that, as yet, she had no answer.

So she picked up her empty shopping bag, put on her hat, and walked out into the blinding sunshine like a Hollywood star leaving a cinema into a wall of flashbulbs.

Later, her basket now full of new potatoes, chives and salad vegetables, Jadis walked back across the scorched lawn and into the welcoming cool of the *arrière-cuisine*. She took off her hat and washed her face and hands at the tap at the Belfast sink. The water came from their well, but it was running low: it was murky, dark and tasted of soil. She wondered if it would last until the crackling thunderstorms that inevitably blew in during the second week of September. Last year, it had been a close thing, and they'd got by on fruit juice and raids to the wine cellar. Jack had unearthed a lovely bottle of Cahors, and they'd taken it to the Spinney to watch the last sunset of August together.

How long ago it seemed — Tom hadn't yet gone to Cambridge, then, and Shoshana hadn't arrived in their lives. She wondered what they were up to now, and with all these thoughts about death and air accidents circling like vultures inside her skull, she had become anxious about them in a way that she hadn't before. Yesterday she'd read a newsfile reporting mass cancellation of flights, airlines going broke, airships being mobbed, general panic in the travelling public. So even if Tom and Shoshana were safe, how on Earth were they going to get home?

Thinking of Tom and Shoshana and wondering what they were up to, she took the basket of vegetables through to the kitchen. Her airtab still displayed a snarl of figures from the July accounts, but a flashing icon betrayed the arrival of three new emails. One was from Jack — he was on his way home for lunch, be home in twenty, looking forward to a siesta. But there was no word from Tom or Shoshana. To be sure, Tom was so laidback as to be practically horizontal, and was completely hopeless about keeping in touch. There had been just two emails from Shoshana for the whole time they'd been away. The first was a chatty note to say that they'd arrived in Israel safely but after a hell of a journey, and that Avi had met them at the airport and sent his love.

What a funny man he is,

Shoshana had written:

> So much like Tom, together they look like two puppies
> playing a game.

Jadis thought back fondly to Avi in Cambridge when they were all so young, and Tom as a boy, and to Fairbanks. Where had all the years gone?

The second was very much terser and scattier, and had been sent when Shoshana was, evidently drunk. It was after they had cut short their time with Avi and were going to stay with a friend of Shoshana's in Tel Aviv, if her friend 'would only answer her goddamn phone'. At that, Jadis had sent a stern email to Avi demanding to know what happened.

His reply — at least three days overdue, she thought, censoriously — was the second email now winking at her. She'd expected it to be full of his usual mischievous and rather patronizing macho bombast, saying that he always thought her a babe, or sex-on-a-stick, or whatever, all of which had once been faintly amusing but now seemed rather silly and more than a little tired. The email she read, however, was quite unnervingly different. Subdued and cryptic, it had troubled her.

> I have shown Tom and Shoshana the Battle Cave I
> told you about yesterday and the revelation disturbed
> them

he had written. Jadis could understand why. Avi's descriptive email and his hypothesis to explain the cave, an over-the-top yarn of blood and death and conquest, was quite lurid enough to have given anyone sleepless nights. To have seen the cave itself must have been overwhelmingly horrible: but even so, she thought, it was not at all like Avi to have come over all *gothick*, like that lurid old pulp fiction

Jack liked to read when he thought she wasn't looking. Avi's latest note continued:

> However do not worry. T and S are fine but it is clear that they need a break. In any case I might be called away on urgent matters elsewhere.

But it was the last part that had haunted her. It sounded like a valediction.

> I have encouraged T and S to enjoy themselves, to see as much of my beloved homeland as they can, while they can. There is no more time to waste. I am not sure when I shall be able to write again.

Her eyes had begun to sting in anticipation of what came next, its finality.

> You and Jack have always been to me like a mother and a father and always an inspiration. When I needed it, you were always there with your kindness and your help. Shalom, Avi.

She sat back, motionless and unmanned, staring at the cursor blinking at the end of Avi's signoff. Not quite knowing how to reply, or even if she should, she dicted a command that opened her newsfeeder and discovered the startling news that the Pope had collapsed during his open-air mass in Israel, and that he *might* have died.

Death?

Absence?

Which was it?

Either someone had died or they hadn't. Why couldn't people just *make up their minds?* Jadis thought back to the vagueness over causes of death in all those air accidents; the gears in her mind whirred into renewed life. The significance level notched higher.

The third message, as if on cue, had come from that other Titan of her Dream Team. She dicted back to the mail segment. That Avi should have been in any way cryptic was surprising; Domingo, however, was full of complex allusions she was sure she'd missed. This example, however, was the very pinnacle of obscurity.

> My dear Jadis—the trip to the Holy Land has not gone entirely according to plan. I have some news you should know but it must wait until I can see you in person. I shall have business in Rome but will get to you as soon as possible thereafter. Suffice it to say that Mr Richards can no longer play with Mr Micawber. You and Jack are ever in my prayers as always—D.

Just who the hell were Richards and Micawber? Actors? Estate Agents? *Undertakers?* She wished people would take the time to say what they meant. Even Domingo.

No, *especially* Domingo.

In a state of exasperation now close to fury, she pushed aside the airtab without even bothering to dict a hibernation command; rose; set a pan of water on the hob; cleaned the dirt from a handful of potatoes, and threw them into the water as if they were hand grenades. Then she started to chop the rest of the vegetables with such expedition—and mental distraction—that she was lucky not to have cut herself.

The airtab, disregarded, and just intelligent enough to realize that its owner was not interacting with it, wiped its display from the air molecules that were giving it shape. Jadis, therefore, failed to notice the arrival of another message. Neither did she notice that Jack had arrived until she felt his steadying arms now around her waist, his breath on her cheek, reassuring. Every particle of the suppressed rage that had been surging through her body disappeared into the ground in an instant, like the guilty shadows that flee into the corners of a darkened room when a door is opened from an illuminated hallway. She closed her eyes as he kissed her neck.

"Dearest Jack…"

Jack was quiet, increasingly beaten down by the pressures of mundane administration, with less and less time for roaming the wilds. She turned in his arms and rested her hands on his shoulders. Her eyes seemed slightly troubled, downcast.

"What's up?" he said.

"Lunch! Lunch is up!" she said, shaking herself free and briskly setting the table, sweeping the airtab aside, burying it beneath the crisping printouts of the July accounts; a shopping list scrawled on an envelope; a recipe torn from the local newspaper.

She explained her worries to Jack, as they ate: her unnerving trip to the village, and her feeling that things didn't make sense — unless there were a single cause for the general tide of disappearance and death. She waved her hands as she ate, as if she were conducting an orchestra. Her color rose when she talked Jack though the uncharacteristically odd emails from Avi and Domingo, pulling the airtab out from beneath the clutter and dicting it into life. The display materialized in the air before them, so they could both see it. Jack's eyes darkened with the apparent finality of Avi's somber message, but he made no comment.

"Who are Richards and Micawber?" Jadis asked him. "Any idea?"

"Ah, yes!" Jack laughed. "Mr Micawber is Keith Richards' name for his favorite guitar. A vintage Fender Telecaster, I think."

"How…? Did you…?" she gasped, in wonderment.

"Oh, you know, just one of Domingo's little jokes," he replied. "You never listened much to the music he and Avi used to play at *Le Dig*, did you? I think they always turned it off when they saw you coming. 'Brown Sugar' was one of Domingo's favourites."

"And all this time, I never knew! Amazing…"

"But I can state an unfair advantage. I believe that the Stones were due to kick off a world tour in Israel, at Tel Aviv… er… about now, actually, given the time difference…" Jack suddenly froze, his face ashy white.

"Jack, are you…?"

Jack got to his feet. "Oh, shit—Holy fucking Christ on a bike," he said. "Why had I never thought of it? *That's* what I meant to tell you but it flew out of my mind. We've got to get in touch with Tom and Shoshana, because the war has started—I just heard it on the car radio—suicide jet attacks on Tel Aviv…"

Jadis would have been startled almost into witless terror by this news, except that it was now her turn to calm Jack, rising to her feet to pull him down. So he told her what he'd heard. Early that morning—the morning after the Pope's 'indisposition' ('that's how they put it on the news') several Khalifa jets had struck Israel. One had hit Masada in the Judaean desert, but two had struck Tel Aviv, one scoring a direct hit on the Ramat Gan stadium on the day the Stones were due to play.

"Now I can see what Domingo was on about," said Jack. "But none of this registered at the time, because the lead headline was how one of the jets demolished the Great Pyramid. Demolished. I mean, what harm had it ever done to *them?*" Jack's eyes were full of the vengeance of archaeologists. "After what they did to Petra. If I could ever catch one of these bigots, I'd… I'd…"

"Jack, what about Tom and Shoshana?" Jadis pulled him back. "I'm worried. They could be anywhere. How are they going to get home? What with the airlines in such a mess? The newsfeeds…"

"Jadis—have you tried to phone them?" Jack was stern.

"Why, no, I…"

Jadis tore her eyes away from his, ashamed that she hadn't even thought of it. She looked at the airtab display before them, and, finding an unopened mail, dicted it open.

"Oh, Jack, look…"

They read the text together. "I think she's hurt," said Jadis. "Or concussed. All that stuff about 'charity' and 'kindness'." She turned towards Jack. Her voice was edgy: "What shall we do? What *can* we do?"

His answer was thoughtful and deliberate, as if he re-membered something that he'd put away in a safe place long ago, and only now recalled where it was, and what he could use it for.

"The header code will give the exact location of Sho-shana's phone," he said, "and when she sent this mes-sage…" He looked more closely at the message, his eyes fly-ing over the display, dicting icons, gesturing down menus. "Ah yes, there it is… and she sent it, what, less than twenty minutes ago."

Jadis, now desperate: "But what's the use of knowing where and when, if we can't get to them?" Her conscience reeled, her shame at her own laxity. Tom could always look after himself, but in her mind she'd thought that In Israel Tom would depend on Shoshana—and she, Jadis, had prom-ised to help Shoshana in any way she could. To fail her now would be insupportable.

Jack looked slowly up.

"Jadis, I think we can. Or *somebody* can. Ruxton Carr's people." Jack recalled his sole visit to their benefactor almost twenty years before; of a kind and mildly eccentric man with novelty dinosaur braces; unflinching faith in their abilities; a bottomless pocket that had supported them ever since—and a very fast private jet. And as he explained all this to Jadis, the great thing about the jet was that it was a drone, and so would not fall from the sky. Ruxton Carr had died some years before, but he'd made it clear that his hyperjet would always be at the disposal of anyone at his Institutes who needed it.

Jack pulled out his phone, dicted at it with a strangely intense gaze which, Jadis thought, he reserved only for the most intractable problems. As if it were a number he'd keyed in once, long ago, and had never used.

And so it was that Shoshana's phone bleeped with a message from Jack that said:

> Message received. Do not move from where you sent it from. Magic Carpet is being sent for. We love you both—J&J.

Jack turned to Jadis. "It is all set. Tom and Shoshana are at Ben Gurion. Merlin Tech will send a hyperjet to pick them up. They should be arriving in Toulouse tomorrow, at dawn."

Jack pointed out that there was nothing that either of them could do now but wait, and suggested that she join him for his siesta, noting that one wasn't obliged to spend it fast asleep. Not all of it, anyway.

"We'll have a long wait until morning," he said. "We shouldn't spend it each alone."

At sunrise, Tom and Shoshana were greeted by Jack and Jadis and a brand new day free from pain. Jadis could see that they were both suffering from profound shock. Tom, cut and bruised everywhere and evidently dazed, fell mutely into the arms of his mother as if he were a small child. A limping Shoshana just cried and cried despite her best efforts to stop.

Jack and Jadis maneuvered them into the back of the jeep, swaddled them in blankets, and drove off as silently and stealthily as their magic carpet had been, if only a tiny fraction as fast. When they arrived at the farmhouse, the passengers were asleep in each other's arms.

Chapter 12. Apparition

Central North Africa, Earth, *c.* 6,355,000 years ago

Lo, in yon brilliant window-niche
 How statue-like I see thee stand,
 The agate lamp within thy hand
Ah! Psyche, from the regions which
 Are holy land!
Edgar Allan Poe—*To Helen*

SURRENDER OR DIE.

The voice boomed over the burgeoning city. The noise of the slogan was itself an assault. So shrill that it made the eardrums bleed of all those who heard it; so powerful that it winded anyone within range; so rumbling that it made the ground shake and half-grown towers topple onto the terrified crowds below. And yet the Eldest Elder of the Annakhnu was glad. For this was the sign for which he had waited all the years of his life. The storm, and after that, the calm of peace—such would surely arrive.

SURRENDER OR DIE.

The voice came from above, from the roiling clouds, in their own language, if in a mode so laughably ancient that only he—perhaps alone of all the Annakhnu—was capable of understanding it as it was meant to be understood. The long-staid language of their nomad years had changed rapidly since the Annakhnu had settled here on the heights, so that the heavenly imprecation would have sounded more, to the City-bred modern ear, like:

HAVE AN INCOMPARABLE ORGASM

And that, reasoned the Eldest Elder, was proof enough that they just had to live through this temporary (if devastating) interruption for the peace that would come after.

Proof also, if the prophecies were right—the prophecies of *Ha'Shekhna*, seasoned with the ages of millennia piled upon millennia beyond count; the prophecies as given by the Goddess herself to *Ani'kh'a'av*, the All Father, on sun-graven tablets of meteoric iron, in the earliest days of the Annakhnu when they lived far to the East. The prophecy that she would soon come and smite their enemies, deliver them from evil.

Which all meant, reasoned the Eldest Elder to himself (for he was too much deafened and dumbstruck and cast down to the ground bleeding and fractured to be able to discuss the matter with anyone else, even had anyone else survived to listen), that salvation was hours—even minutes—away, and the long-desired City could be allowed to take shape. No matter how bad things looked, they had nothing to fear.

Propped up, bruised and whimpering, on the balcony of the temple, looking westwards over the Grand Plaza and the Gates and onto the plains, he saw the sky boil. Everything went blinding white before his eyes and he felt the stones crack and crumble beneath his feet.

SURRENDER OR DIE.

Oh, go compare your *own* orgasm. The Eldest Elder closed his eyes and rested for a spell. After what seemed like only a few minutes, but it might have been more like hours or even days, he awoke to find himself buried under an uncountable mass of rubble. Pinned though he was, he found he could breathe: fortune, *b'r'k h'ten Ha'Shekhna*, had seen fit to bury him beneath an arrangement of spars that had once supported the conical roof of the topmost spire of the temple. The sturdy, interlaced timbers had taken the weight of the masonry that had fallen above him, interring him, uncrushed, in a kind of cave. Immediately after registering this amazement and proffering his thanks, he was seized by wracking coughs as his lungs sought to eject masses of mud-brick- and plaster dust. He lay there then, wretched; his chest heaving in pain; his eyes sore almost to distraction; his throat feeling as if he had been marinated in mud, turning slicker with his own sweat and the chill dampness of his own condensing breath.

Slowly, with the patience of ages, he calmed himself, corralled his panic; brought his breathing and heart rate down to a level that would allow conscious thought. Reason, he had always said; reason is the conqueror of all things. Not love, not even piety, but reason. He was grateful for the iron discipline with which he had always conducted himself. He knew that, one day, it might save his life.

The victory of reason meant that after a few minutes he found that he could move his arms and legs—so nothing broken—and, seeing a glimmer of light close to his face, scraped, with sore fingers and chipped and blackened nails, a tiny spy-hole onto a most intriguing vista. Before him, spread out, was the Grand Plaza of the City, by the great gates, and he could see the whole thing from perhaps a foot or two above ground level, from near the bottom of one of seemingly several large piles of rubble.

Ah, me, he mused. The Grand Plaza had once been a fine thing—the walls with the great gates, and the principal buildings all around, the temple among them, and before all a bustling marketplace, thronged with herdsmen and their families, wearing their brightest robes for the great trip to the City, their droves of pigs and keryx before them; merchants and farmers, rich, their proud harems jangling with jewellery, parading their finery for all to admire; troopers on great rhinos, garlanded with flowers in this time of peace, the beasts accepting gifts of fruit from laughing children, tiny before the beasts' imposing bulk; stalls with bright awnings selling all manner of wares from around the ever-expanding Annakhnu realm. And all around music, and noise, and chatter, and shouting, and laughter, and more noise, noise, always noise. The Eldest Elder appreciated — demanded — quiet in all things, but was wise enough to know that quiet is not such unless counterpointed with noise: and that sound, free, untrammelled, is a sign of life. And life, *b'r'k h'ten Ha'Shekhna*, is what it's all about.

His view now, though, showed him only the serenity of death. All was waste. All was levelled. The rubble piles smoked in silence but for the primeval crack of burned, cooling rock. The great stones of the Plaza were littered with charred masses of what could only have been bodies, once. Instead of the walls, their immense stones chiselled into precise positions by masons of cunning craft, he could see only the bald western horizon, bisecting a huge red sun lying as if cursed, dog-like, beneath oppressive bars of crimson cloud, the disc bloated by the refraction of rising smoke.

The Eldest Elder, bringing his reason once again to bear, had been buried for at least six hours, then, for the Sun had been riding high when the terrible voice warning of either instant death or unmatched ecstasy had first sounded from the sky, and what looked like bright shining Moons, each reflecting the Sun's glare, had landed on the plains around the City, disgorging legions of tiny silver troops, each one with a deadly satanic fire at its command.

The Eldest Elder saw those troops now, in ordered files, their marching feet in step ringing louder as they approached. Before them a ragged mass of people, wretched women sobbing as they clutched at children; men, bowed, defeated. Every now and then a trooper, silvered from head to foot, would wrench a child away from its mother, and, with a ray of perfect, white light issuing from its fingers, blast its head off. Screams of horror or agony were silenced in a similar fashion. Had the Eldest Elder wanted to cry out—had reason let him do such a rash thing—the cry would have been stopped in his throat at the sight.

The Eldest Elder hoped that many, or even most of the citizens had escaped into the fields, or through the network of tunnels that he and the other Elders had long prepared in case of siege. After all, the prophecy could not be fulfilled if there existed a City, desolate, but without the people to give it life. The people corralled before him, then, must have been the unlucky ones, those too slow to have seen the signs; those for whom some delay, a search for a missing babe, a toy, a precious object, would now cost them their lives. But perhaps not. Reason told the Eldest Elder that troopers like these, these silvered creatures riding moons from some remote quarter of heaven, would be nothing if not ruthlessly efficient, and that the people before him were all those who were left, the remnants of the entire Annakhnu people, from the City itself and the fields and townlands round about. The people on whom the words of the prophecy hung.

The last of the Sun sank below the horizon, casting a spar of light to bathe the clouds above in livid red before it disappeared. The troopers had herded the mass of cowering people into a circle in the middle of the ruined plaza. The Eldest Elder, in his cramped hiding place, could smell the stench of fear. The troopers, encircling the prisoners, stretched out their arms inwards, to deliver their captives from life in a final frenzy of incandescence.

It was then that the Eldest Elder realized that the moment of truth had come, the moment for which he had waited all his life. He thanked the Goddess again for allowing him to witness the impending miracle, and uttered a final imprecation, very quietly, the whispered sound hardly even stirring on his parched lips.

Z'manh z'dakh'aa v'khe'sed v'hosh'khn'uu. Goddess, show us charity, show us kindness—help us.

And the troopers, as if on one command—just as they were about to blast the Annakhnu race to extinction—shrunk in on themselves. It took hardly more than an eye-blink, but if he were asked to describe it, the Eldest Elder would have said that the troopers had each been somehow turned inside out while being compressed to tiny points—that, or appearing to recede, each one, to the end of its own infinitely long corridor until, when they reached their own vanishing points, disappearing into nothingness.

The captives stood there in their circle, stunned, hardly daring to break out. Over the next few seconds, some realized that they had been delivered, in the nick of time. Mothers, crying with relief, comforted their shrieking children, and others who had lost their own brood. Men, crying and shouting and sobbing all at once, sank to their knees, some to lie prostrate on the ground, in prayer. They had been saved.

The Eldest Elder closed his eyes, content to rest in his unplanned tomb. He was sure that his body would soon be discovered by the citizens, the guardians of the Annakhnu Revenged, builders of an ever greater and more glorious City on the Heights. Whether he'd be alive or dead, well, that was a somewhat nice point he'd debate with himself while he waited. But if death was now his destiny, he would be happy, now that his life's dream had been fulfilled to the last.

The clouds burst, the pent-up rain of weeks and months landing on the parched land like a deluge, scouring it clean.

The Eldest Elder felt the first drops of rain soothe his crusted eyes and was content.

-=0=-

SURRENDER OR DIE

The voice boomed over the roof of the chapel, now packed with the Brethren and their guests. The noise shook dust from the rafters. Some of the older Brethren fainted on the spot. Others covered their ears and cowered in the many nooks and corners of sandstone pews worn smooth over millennia by the bodies of so many supplicants. Leila and Lilit, though, started to giggle: perhaps it was simply nerves, or fear, the Abbot wondered, the kind of threat that can inculcate nothing but laughter in those who have lost all hope. But Alfred looked to the vaulted roof, the bright green intelligence of his eyes fully awake.

Alfred looked down then, locking eyes on the statue of the Goddess at the far end, in her niche, the sandstone drapes of her robes chipped and eroded with time, the scarlet paint long worn away; the agate lantern in her outstretched left hand bearing one, dim candle; the drapes falling from her right hand revealing a forearm almost as soft and smooth and yellow-pink as that of a young and living girl; her face worn almost featureless, eye-sockets hollowed, only her smile remaining in reasonable shape, and that smile a teasing enigma, slashed across her face.

The Abbot followed Alfred's gaze, likewise in wonderment. They had gathered here for the Apparition—at a time when such a thing would be of greatest value, that is, at a time of direst need. The Abbot had now seen the moon-ships falling to the plains for himself, and they were just as Alfred had described, and the columns of silvered troopers they disgorged.

He had seen them set fire to the farmsteads and stockades and villages of the Annakhnu on the shores of the Great Lake, and knew that they would be marching on the City. But the House of Shinaar would not be safe from their predations. If the Goddess did not appear, they would all be dead within the hour.

SURRENDER OR DIE

A blast like the sound of gigantic bronze doors slamming shut in hell rent the air above them and the earth below, and, before they were even aware of its happening, they were caught up in a sleet of splintered wood and stone as the roof caved in. The chapel was now open to the sky, darkening as the sun set. The Brethren and their guests shrunk further between the pews, some clasping themselves to make sure they were still alive, others reaching out, blindly in the shrapnel, for another living body. The Abbot saw Alfred felled, like an ancient forest tree, by a block of masonry that landed on his head, splitting it open. As he watched, appalled, he too was struck by a chunk of wood that hit him in the chest, winding him. He sank below his pew's seat, doubled in pain. A small, furry body scurried towards him and snuggled up in his arms, whimpering. It was the pithek, Mandergast, his faithful retainer of twenty years. The Abbot was strangely grateful, and put his arms round the small, shuddering form. The Abbot felt a sensation of wetness around his lower body, and caught an acrid, ammoniac odor. He realized that Mandergast had peed himself with fright. Or perhaps it was himself. He hugged the trembling creature closer to his breast.

He heard, then, rather than felt, the great ironwood doors to the chapel burst inwards, breaking up into microscopic shards that surged through the air at several times the speed of sound. Had anyone dared to stand up just then, or put their head above pew level, they would have been shredded to atoms. No-one did. But then there was silence, and the Abbot opened his eyes to find the light had changed. It was not black and crimson, dark and full of smoke, but even, and calm, and deeply golden, like the sunset that promises a fine spring morning. He weighed up the evidence and decided, not without swallowing his fear, to raise his head above the pew. Mandergast squeaked his fright and grabbed on to the Abbot's legs. What the Abbot saw filled him with such reassurance as he had never felt, nor was likely to feel again.

"It's all right, Mandergast," he said. "No harm will come to you now. Why don't you come and see?" The little pithek raised his hairy head above the pew, too, and gasped, and the Abbot and his companion clambered over bodies frozen in stasis and into the debris-strewn aisle. There before them stood the Goddess, her statue now glowing with an inner light. The Abbot looked around him—there was no sign of the silver troopers, not even any sense that they had ever been present. The great doors of the Chapel were gone, their iron hinges creaking in the smoke-laden evening breeze. The remaining walls of the chapel looked several shades lighter than usual, as if they had been scrubbed clean. The rest of the congregation, though—everyone who had not been killed by the falling masonry—had been frozen in mid-gasp, mid-cry. The Abbot and his pithek were the only people free from this constraint. The Abbot was too stupefied by the turn of events to find this in any way curious.

He was not too surprised, therefore, when the statue of the Goddess moved, climbed down from her niche, and stood before him as a young woman in a billowing scarlet robe, with long, black hair and the grin of a young girl. But the fatigue of thousands of millennia could be seen in her owlish black eyes. As she approached the Abbot and Mandergast, she put down her agate lamp at the end of a pew and subsided into the Abbot's arms. The Abbot steered her to the nearest pew, dusted the splinters and chips of stone from the seat, and invited her to sit. Once again he did not find it curious to find himself seated in the front pew of a ruined chapel, with a terrified pithek clinging to his left arm, and the divine object of his most pious contemplation resting her cheek on his right shoulder, sobbing quietly into his vestments. The job of an Abbot is to provide comfort at need, he thought to himself — to anyone who needs it.

He put his arms round both of them.

After many long moments, the Goddess sat up, wiped her eyes with a corner of her robe, and spoke.

"Evolution has no foresight, no memory," she said. "It is a contingency of the eternal present. To force it, to direct it — that's a contradiction in terms. Why the hell didn't you tell me? *They* tell me? Evolution like that can be nothing more than a rampant growth forever teetering on the edge of becoming a cancerous mass, poised on a critical wave, like a stylus being made to balance on its point while riding a ship tossed in a storm — for millions upon millions of years. And I'm so *tired*."

She looked up into the Abbot's face: red-eyed, yet smiling. The warmth of the expression in her wide mouth, dimpling her cheeks, counterpointed the unnerving hardness of her dark-eyed stare. "I'm not making much sense, am I?" she said.

The Abbot was too stunned to answer the question. Nothing in his training had prepared him for suitable things he might say to a Goddess in the line of ordinary conversation, outside the usual round of devotional offerings, such discourse being of necessity entirely one-way. What do you say to a deity who answers back? Do you say anything? Do you dare? He compromised by offering the briefest of nods in acknowledgement. She didn't seem to take offense, for she continued, this time along a tangent that was, if anything, even more mystifying.

"The problem, I now think, is too much *choice*," she said. "I mean, you know what it's like, you go into a store and all you want is a pint of milk. You know what a pint of milk should look like, because in your head you carry a picture of a bottle, or maybe a carton, with a blue-and-white painted jug on it, or a jolly milkmaid, or a cow or two in a green field. But when you get to the store you can't just buy 'a-pint-of-milk'. It's got to be full milk, or semi-skimmed, or skimmed, or with added calcium, or vitamin D, or long-life heat-treated, or organic, or several of these things in combination, or none at all. So what should have been the easiest thing in the world is made stressful, derailed by choice.

"And so it is here. There is so much scope for evolution among the prosimian and anthropoid primates all around us. So many promising lineages—but which one do you choose? Even with the gift of a certain amount of foresight, it's hard to see—when you're down here, digging in the dirt, so to speak—how it's all going to look when the building is finished the way you want it.

"So in the end you have to hedge your bets. The Annak-hnu, I admit, they've been a good try, but they're not 'it'. And I'm sure there'll be other nearly-men, not yet a twinkle in my eye, who might offer something, but they won't be 'it,' either. There is still time. Thankfully, there is still time."

The Abbot found his voice, then. "Holy One—what did you do—to the silver warriors from the sky?"

She turned to him, her strangely round eyes now wide, and brimming once again with tears. She sank back in her seat again, put her face in her hands and wept aloud.

"I'm so sorry. So *sorry*. That's me all over. I try my best, I really do. But somehow I can't do the job without leaving a huge mess behind for others to clear up." The Abbot put his arms round her again, pulling her to his chest, where her hair spread over his robe. The little pithek joined in, stroking her hair and making small, soothing sounds rather like a dove, cooing.

"Look, it's like this," she said, looking up at him, "and I apologise in advance if this is all too much information. The fact is, Abbot, you and your Brethren are among the last of an ancient prosimian race that conquered the Earth and just about all the stars you can see in the night sky. It was the greatest Empire that this Galaxy has ever seen, save two.

"But that was fifty million years ago, and the Empire went the way that all Empires do. All species. Inevitably. But before it died, it split, with each fragment going its own evolutionary way. I've had a good old meddle with some of those fragments, too, just to see if… if…" She sighed. The Abbot felt the warm breath of her exhalation. For a Goddess, she felt very warm, and alive, and human.

"Holy One?"

"Well, those 'silver warriors,' as you put it, were the results of some of my meddling. I had to intervene. To put a stop to it all. Just in the nick of time, it seems. I wonder… perhaps I saw it all coming, even then? Who knows? Anyway, I hope I've made things right. Please forgive me. I couldn't stand it if you didn't."

"Forgive *you*? Holy One, it's we who should beg for forgiveness, we mortal sinners, we…"

The Goddess looked up and put a single finger to the Abbot's lips. "Pish and tosh, Abbot. You, more than anyone, have kept the faith, as indeed should I. There was no need for me to have hedged my bets any further afield than sweet planet Earth. For you, Abbot—yes, you—have been waiting all these long years, and it is through your efforts—yes, yours—that success might be achieved."

"Me? Mine?" The Abbot's mind was assaulted by a barrage of images from without, of places he'd never seen, of gigantic spaceships, and tropical beaches, and a silver skein that stretched endlessly into the sky, and a girl who looked very much like the one standing before him. He felt his lips shape a word he was sure he'd never spoken, but now breathed silently onto the air.

"Xalomé?"

But the Goddess was once again distracted. "Ah, the Earth. Well, you probably won't know this—how could you, really?—but the first Galactic Empire happened more than eleven billion years ago, when the Universe was young, the Earth was a twinkle still five billion years in the future, and even this Galaxy didn't really exist as it does... well, *now*. But that Empire was... *destroyed*."

The Goddess looked up. The abbot could see a glint of determined hatred cross her eyes, her face turn, fleetingly, into a snarl. She looked directly at him, then. He concentrated hard on her words, strange though they were, in case he fell headlong into the incandescent lakes of her eyes.

"I know little more about this Empire than the fact of its destruction," she continued, "and of the warning it left us. The second Galactic Empire was much more recent, around a billion years ago, give or take, and probably *much* more glorious. It extended its reach throughout this Galaxy, all its satellites, and brought the Andromedans under its hegemony. For a brief while it ruled the entire Local Group, and was making a good stab at the Virgo Cluster when..." She paused. She sighed.

"What… happened?"

"What happened? It died, too, of course. The Emperor decided that all was vanity and ceded all his dominions until just the home planet was left. That would have been fine except that without the Empire, the planet became very crowded and the economy collapsed. I'm afraid that the Empire's final knell was probably of its own making — catastrophic climate change that covered the whole planet in ice for a hundred million years."

"Where was it? This planet?"

"It was here, of course. The Earth. I don't know why, but there's something about this part of the Galaxy that's fresher, more *alive*, than anywhere else. That's what attracts *them*, I suppose. If the Earth, and the Universe, too, is to be saved from these… these… *destroyers*… then the solution will come from here. I'm sure of it." She untangled herself from his arms and stood before him, glowing.

"You're doing a great job, Abbot. Keep it up! I bless you now, as I always have, and as I always will. I shall try to do my part, as well as I can. It's not perfect, I know…" She bent over and kissed the top of his head. "But please be assured that I'm doing the best I can."

She took a step backwards. The Abbot knew that the enigmatic interview would soon be at an end. He rose to his feet, panic surging through him.

"Most Blessed One!" he cried: "Don't leave us! What are your instructions? Were should I go? What should I do?"

She smiled again. "Oh, Abbot, *really*. What kind of a question is that? I'm tempted to say 'Frankly, my dear, I don't *give* a damn.'" She stretched her arms out wide, from side to side. Small, yellow flames arose in her fingers and coursed along her arms. Within seconds she was wreathed in flames.

"But… but… Holy One…" The Abbot was on his feet, but didn't dare approach the flaming figure.

"I'm sorry—didn't I tell you?" the Goddess said, her face now hidden from view. "Look after the pitheks. I think they're 'it,' or will be, one day. Saviours of the Universe. In fact, I'd put money on it."

There was a rush of heat and light, a flash of sudden flame, and the Goddess was gone, leaving the Abbot standing in the deserted nave. He heard the sounds of people stirring, rising from their seats, coming back to life. He looked round to see Mandergast, next to him. He didn't recognise him for a second, because the pithek was standing straight and tall, a quite different posture from his usual slouch, and was looking straight at him with an expression he could not quite fathom.

Chapter 13: The Last Battle

Earth, August/September, 2054

The cry is still, "They come!"
William Shakespeare—*Macbeth*

For Avi, the Last Battle started when the army Jeep squirled and wheeled to a right-angled stop on the hot tarmac in front of the Technion, temporarily pitching up on the nearside wheels against the kerb before bouncing back to a halt.

"Get in. Now. *Do it*." yelled Rivka, from the driving seat. Avi climbed in beside her.

Or perhaps the Last Battle—the first skirmish, anyway—had come a few days earlier. Oh yes, that was it. In their kitchen, the evening before he'd seen Tom and Shoshana off to Tel Aviv, when Rivka had told him of the latest intelligence intercept—that when the Khalifa invaded Israel, they'd head first for Mount Carmel.

"But why?" asked Avi. "Unless there's some strategic importance, I guess..."

"Oh, for sure, Big Boy," said Rivka, lighting an Alia and resting her broad backside up against the worktop. God, he loved those hips. But why did she have to smoke that Jordanian shitweed? When he'd tried one he felt like his scalp had rotated ninety degrees with respect to the rest of his head and he'd wanted to fall over. "But what they want is *you*."

"*Moi*?" Avi smiled and pointed to himself theatrically, but as he opened his mouth to speak again, his face darkened.

"Aha! The penny dropped!" cackled Rivka, exhaling two streams of pungent smoke through her nostrils. "Professor Schlong doesn't *just* think with his balls, no?"

"No. Perhaps not," he replied. He moved towards her, putting his arms around her, steadying his nerves by earthing himself to the ground through her curvaceous warmth and the magnetic luster of her hair, but his mind was far away. The Buddhas of Bamiyan. The statues at Petra. If there was one thing on which the Khalifa refused to compromise, it was the continued existence of—or even any memorial to—any religion that antedated its own. And there was nothing more ancient than the religion of the Neanderthals.

"For sure, they didn't mention anything too specific to begin with," Rivka continued. "I mean, it was all the usual boring shit about 'paving the road to Damascus with the skulls of Jewish children.'" The old ones were the best, thought Avi. They'd been saying things like that since at least the 1967 war. "But buried in all that dismal crap— believe me, baby, I had to listen to hour after dreary hour of it—the words *Malkeinu* and *Muhraka* did come up rather often." Muhraka was the Arabic name for the part of the Carmel massif that stood above the Battle Cave. God, he'd thought that the Battle Cave was a closely guarded secret. This was *precisely* what he'd been afraid of.

Then came that fearful morning of the suicide jet-bomb attacks on Tel Aviv and Masada. But the direct hit on the Great Pyramid was the one that stuck most in Avi's mind as he'd arrived at the Technion, the shocking news still on his car radio. He supposed classes would now be cancelled. Later, when she'd picked him up in the jeep, Rivka tried to reassure him that the suicide attacks were, ironically, far from deliberate. She had known this, because the technoids in her department had hacked the telemetry. Okay, sure, they might have *looked* like suicide attacks, but the crashes had resulted from some kind of pilot error, possibly connected, she said, with this strange new disease called POP, but she hadn't been sure about it. That one of the jets had hit the Pyramid was an utter fluke.

"Accident or not, they'll milk it for all it's worth," insisted Avi, as they bounced along towards Mount Carmel. "They'll say was a deliberate part of their Year-Zero policy, and no pre-Islamic artifact, however ancient or treasured, will stand in its way."

Rivka turned to him. "My thoughts exactly, Big Boy. Exactly," she said. Her coal-black eyes blazed with furious excitement.

The truck was full of equipment and supplies for a last turn round the Battle Cave, an emergency mothballing operation: to seal it against assault in the hope of reopening it later. The idea was to blow up the back end of the SSM-lite, filling the ravine that led downwards to that bone-choked tartarus. They had infra-red night goggles, plastic explosive and all the trimmings, and—just in case—a load of hand-grenades, a bunch of standard issue uzis with plenty of magazines, a few nano-uzi machine pistols and even a couple of RPGs.

"I got thermobaric heads," said Rivka. "Fuel-air explosives. Ka-fucking-*boom*! Never know when you might need 'em, so I signed out as much as I could. If the bastards scored a direct hit on us now, we'd be absolutely, completely, gloriously *fucked!*"

"But Rivka..." Avi gasped. "*Fuel-Air Explosives*? In a *cave*? Full of *bones*?" The noise and shrapnel would be unimaginable.

"Oh poor baby!" she mocked. "If you like I'll go back for face masks and ear defenders! And a change of diapers in case you shit yourself!" And then, more seriously. "But we have no more time. We have to hurry. I didn't tell you when we got up, because what you had *done* to me in *bed* had made me *lose my mind*." Avi knew that Rivka had always found the prospect of warfare and imminent death a huge turn-on. Hence the orgasmic prospect of using FAE-loaded rockets in what was, even in the loosest sense, a confined space. "And also because I heard just now"—she tapped her earbud—"that the Khalifa Tenth Legion has crossed into Israel. Just south of Deganya."

"What?"

"You heard, Big Boy. I know. Crazy. No air superiority. Thirty per cent down because of this POP thing. And our jets will probably pick off a lot more. But I told you what they'd got lined up in the desert. There are so fucking *many* of them—wave after wave—that it probably won't matter. So the plan is for us to dynamite your cave before they do, and get the hell out, yes? We'll go to my office, see what the Boss wants, and take it from there." Avi was too stunned to argue.

The jeep shuddered to a halt between the two prefabs, outside the steel shutter that led to the cave. Avi and Rivka jumped out of the cab. She ran round to the back, jumped under the canvas and busied herself with the equipment. Avi looked around nervously, expecting to see a platoon of Khalifa troops cresting the hillside as he watched. Catching his breath, he realized they'd have forty-five minutes, tops, before they'd have to get back down the mountain and into Haifa. He got a couple of headlights from the machine shop. They'd need them, at least to begin with: he hadn't turned on any of the cave illumination systems.

"Who the fuck keeps filling this vehicle with watermelons?" came Rivka's muffled voice from inside the truck. Moments late she jumped out and handed out kit.

They each had night-vision goggles, a pair of uzis and magazines in easy reach, a rocket launcher and rocket rounds. They tucked nano-uzis into belts or boot tops where they could find spaces. Feeling rather like a walking arms dump, Avi picked a kit bag full of the explosives they'd need to blow up the cave—Rivka took another bag, this one containing hand grenades. Finally, they strapped on their headlights and Avi rolled up the shutter.

Just before crossing the threshold, they paused, and Rivka turned to him. She was wearing an expression of tenderness, of softness, that even he saw only in their most private moments. She reached up to him and kissed him very slowly on the lips. Pulling back, her eyes burned as she said, "this will be a close call, soldier. Let's hope we can get away before the cockroaches arrive.

"And if they catch us in there while we're at it—well, we won't be able to hear ourselves think, so I'll say it now. I love you, Big Boy. And I always will. You're amazing. No… no… no…. don't fucking cry on me, you *schmuck*!" But Avi's tears ran full into the long, glossy hair of his wife of twenty years, this difficult, irascible, foul-mouthed, chain-smoking, argumentative, violent—and yes, he had to admit, very sexy woman. Jadis had started it, but she'd only ever be on a pedestal, a guiding star, like the Statue of Liberty. But it was Rivka who'd been woman enough to make him into a man.

"And I love you," he said—"and let's *go*." So turning on their headlights, they took each other's free hand and stepped forward to their doom.

A few minutes later they had reached the ravine at the back of the upper cave. Placing the charges was more difficult than they expected. They'd had to use step-ladders to place them on the roof. Avi knew that there were at least two or three long ladders hanging around in the excavation, but finding them took precious minutes. Even then, it was sometimes hard to find a crevice in which a wedge of the putty-like material could stick. Rivka wished she could have got hold of some of the new nanostructural explosive that moved and flowed like quasi-intelligent amoebae, covalently bonding itself into place. However, the explosive they had would be good enough. It had been radio-tuned to detonate by remote control, hopefully when she and Avi were in the jeep and flying back down the mountainside.

It was not to be. Marching feet were already in earshot. Retreat was no longer an option: Avi scrambled down the ladder, doused his headlight and flashed up his night visor. Rivka did the same and, picking up their weapons, they scrambled as quietly as they could down the ravine path and into the Battle Cave.

It was totally dark. At first, his night visor gave Avi nothing to go on, but a process of intelligent adaptation had picked up just enough photons to steer by. As fast as he could, he jogged down the main pathway until, about a thousand yards out, he started to pant and sweat from the weight of the weaponry. Rivka was always one step ahead, fighting fit and hardly breaking sweat despite her forty-a-day *Alia* habit.

What a woman!

Rivka led him along a kind of dodge, a small path that diverged from the main way, between two mounds of shattered bones. Avi followed her as they clambered up the mound so that they faced back the way they'd come. It was hard doing this in the dark, but thankfully some of the bones had been glued together with a thin coat of stalagmite and didn't crumble and clatter as they'd tried to climb them.

Once at the top, they lay flat on their stomachs, laying out their weapons. It was then that Avi realized their mistake. They wouldn't be able to shoot from a single location as they'd be picked off instantly, especially if they used their rockets — the flares would be a dead giveaway. They'd have to dodge and weave. Fire and move, fire and move, hoping to create enough noise and confusion that they'd be able to slip behind enemy lines and escape. Yeah, right, Avi thought — right past dozens, perhaps hundreds of soldiers in a cave mouth not ten feet wide without getting noticed. Like that's really going to happen.

Rivka must have been thinking along these lines. "Are you sure there's no back door to this place?" she whispered.

"We've looked and looked," he replied, "and we've never found anything more than dead ends."

"No way out?" She asked.

"No, none."

"Just making sure." She clasped his hand once more, just as they heard shots ring out. "Fuck it," she said (this time in Arabic). "They must have picked us up. But we can at least take some of the bastards with us." She groped in a pocket for the radio detonator, armed it and pressed the stud. There was a terrific, rolling boom, a flash and a blast wave that almost buried them in fragments of bone and rock. Avi found himself spitting out shards of cannibal Neanderthal and brained human children, forty-odd thousand years dead.

Rivka's detonation had pinched off all but the first few Khalifa troops, successfully sealing the cave against further assault — and all but the remotest chance of their own escape.

He couldn't see her face, but Avi was convinced that his wife was stoked to bursting on adrenaline. He could smell her musky sweat — this gave him a huge hard-on, and he laughed out loud. Her voice became sharp and imperative.

"Fire at will, soldier."

His last words to her were "Yo, *baby*! What a way to *go*!"

The red blobs now popping up in his night visor told of about twenty or thirty Khalifa troops converging on their position. The first shots winged and whizzed past his ears as they each loaded thermobaric rockets into their shoulder launchers. Avi fired first, into a group of soldiers scaling the mound towards them. His view exploded into white-out, a rank smell of petrol and charred flesh. Wow, he thought, good for Rivka: anti-tank weaponry on exposed infantry at close range. Nothing exceeds like excess. Another blast came when Rivka aimed hers at another pair advancing up at them from the other side. He barely heard her demoniac shouts above the racket. More machine-gun rounds pinged at their feet, raising dust and bones from a battle that had raged here more than four hundred centuries before. The Neanderthals would have loved fuel-air explosives, he thought, as a bullet lodged into his shin, fracturing it. He gasped with the pain and sank to his knees, not without let-ting another rocket whoosh towards his assailant. It skimmed just inches over the cluttered surface of the ground before exploding in a star of white edged with red, dismem-bering three or four Khalifa troops as he watched. In his night visor he could see their flat red images disaggregate, flying off in all directions, cooling. He had to admit it, his mind groggy, the Khalifa infantry were crap at guerrilla warfare. Perhaps they could afford to waste human lives.

He lobbed a hand grenade down the slope, just to make sure, and then pulled out two uzis and started firing. The more he fired, the slower the firing rate seemed, as if the bul-lets were moving in slow-mo, like in the movies. He had just managed to eject their spent magazines and reload when another two bullets slammed into his chest, lifting him clear and dropping him down onto his back, into a bed of bones right by Rivka's feet. The bones danced as more bullets found him. He thought that she hadn't been hit yet, by some miracle.

What a woman!

His last sight before his eyes closed forever was of his wife, blasting away with an uzi in each hand, and a post-coital smile on her face, hair flying.

What a woman!

Lets her uzi do the talking!

Three times a night! *Matinée* on Shabbat!

My Rivka.

Rivka…

Faye. Primrose… Domingo (Domingo always and forever!)…

Jack.

Hair flying. Jadis, behind her hair.

A sharp pain between his eyes and his head was thrown back, breaking his neck. Really, it had always been Jadis.

Shema Israel, Adonai…

And then nothing.

-=O=-

What became known as the War of the Last Days was intense, destructive and short. The suicide air strikes that had hit Tel Aviv, Masada and the Great Pyramid were soon revealed to have been mistakes in an opening salvo that had gone badly wrong. But the Khalifa pressed on with a massive ground invasion, supported sporadically by long-range artillery and missile bombardments. Now wary about using piloted aircraft, Khalifa commanders launched conventional ballistic missiles from silos in Kazakhstan, Dagestan in the North Caucasus and what had once been called Chinese Turkestan.

The temptation to use their more-than-respectable stock of nuclear warheads was restrained by the Imams, who reminded the commanders that the Holy Places would be useless if reduced to radioactive rubble. As for Israel's civilian population, however, they did not care: although given the smallness of Israel, and the proximity of most of it to Holy *Al-Quds*, the commanders were advised to limit the mega-tonnage. For their part, Israel's commanders knew that to unleash hell from its silos at Dimona would have been to write a suicide note—and that moment had not yet been reached.

And so, on the day that Avi and Rivka fought their last battle, Haifa and Tel Aviv were reduced to smoking ruins that glowed only mildly in the dark. Total countrywide destruction was averted by Israel's own strike forces, which holed several Khalifa warships in the Mediterranean and Red Seas, and by retaliatory missile strikes on Damascus, Amman and Baghdad, capital of the Khalifa.

But the most immediate worry was the wave after wave of hardened Khalifa tanks and ground troops that swarmed into Israel from all sides, destroying everything in their path. They rained by parachute down from Ha-Golan, poured in from Lebanon and Egypt and crossed the Jordan by amphibian into Galilee; they established footholds in despised Palestine—seen as a cowed client of the Zionist Entity, and thus worthy of more thorough despoliation—and they pushed into the coastal plain, and towards Beersheva and the Negev. They absorbed the terrific loss from IDF low-level bombing, to tankbusters armed with depleted uranium shells, and even the mysterious plague, by sheer weight of numbers. They threatened to overwhelm Israel within two days, but the weight of the plague picked up, and from the increasing disorder of Khalifa operations, it became clear that the pestilence had sunk its teeth into its military command structure.

The desire to crush the Zionist Entity, great as it was, had been overtaken by even more pressing problems closer to home. Within weeks, almost sixty per cent of the population of the mighty Khalifa—from Morocco in the west to Indonesia in the east, from Kazakhstan and Bosnia in the North to Sudan and Zanzibar in the south—had succumbed to Postembryonic Oolithic Petrosis.

Not that anyone had any idea of this appalling statistic as the green and black tide broke on heavily defended Jerusalem like a storm surge, before falling back and fading into the dust. News pictures of the scene showed a relentless firestorm, pillars of cloud and of smoke, the only centre of peace and clarity the Mosque of Omar, the Dome on the Rock where Mohammed had ascended to heaven, and arguably the most heart-breakingly beautiful building on the planet. Not a few people compared the scene with the famous photograph of Saint Paul's Cathedral in London, defiant amid the blitzkrieg.

And then everything stopped, as suddenly as it had begun.

Israel pulled itself out of the wreckage, nominally the victor, but in reality, broken and almost inviable. Almost three million people in Israel and Palestine had fallen to the Khalifa: even without this, around forty per cent of the population would have been wiped out by POP in any case. Jerusalem itself, sacred to so many, held its golden head high above the carnage and ashes.

The survivors, including Prime Minister Seamus O'Shaughnessy, did their best to pick up the reins where they'd left off: but within a few weeks it was clear that Israel had been blown back to the days when it had been Palestine under the decadent, unraveling Ottoman Empire: a picturesque and largely unpopulated backwater in which the Holy Places were maintained, as much as possible, by small and largely inoffensive religious groups.

Eight months after the War, O'Shaughnessy was only too pleased to welcome the embassy of the newly crowned

Khalif of Baghdad, suing for peace and friendship and access
to the Holy Places. The young ruler did not arrive by plane,
or even airship, but in a camel caravan that had taken two
weeks to traverse the desert.

The luxury hotels atop the Mount of Olives always had
the best views of Holy Jerusalem, but they were now
bombed-out shells. Instead, the Khalif and his court pitched
their tents in the Garden of Gethsemane, letting their camels
graze amid the groves of trees so ancient that some could
have spoken of Jesus and his disciples. As if from a scene
straight from the Old Testament, O'Shaughnessy had come
to the Khalif's tent for the ritual pleasantries, in which both
parties decided to end one of the longest and cruellest enmi-
ties in the history of the human race.

And so, amid the general economic collapse as a once-
modern state regressed to the near-medieval, the Rabbis of
Safed picked themselves up, dusted themselves off and continued to debate the more obscure passages of the Talmud,
much as they had for centuries. The Druzes of Carmel, although depleted, came out of hiding. Monasteries of a wide
variety of Holy Orders renewed and resumed their contemplation of the infinite, and many new Houses were founded.
The inter-denominational bickering over space in the Church
of the Holy Sepulcher continued as much as it always had.
And Moslems continued to worship at the *Al-Aqsa* Mosque
and within the eternal loveliness of the Mosque of Omar.

Traders in the *suq* sold freshly-pressed orange juice and
halal meat, carpets and coffee, leatherwork and silver, much
as they had done for years beyond count. That fewer sold
mass-produced tat to gullible tourists was a testament both
to the shortage both of mass-produced tat and of tourists. In
short, Levantine life went on much as it had before the twentieth century had arrived to interrupt things, a disorderly
conglomerate of religions in one Holy City.

But with one difference. Only a minority of the monks, worshippers and traders would have identified themselves as *Homo sapiens*.

Not that much of this would have been evident to the residents of the farmhouse at Saint-Rogatien in mid-September, 2054, as autumn broke in sheeting thunder-storms. The house, in a spume of constant rain, was a haven of befuddled peace for some of its tenants, and anxiety for others.

The loss of staff at the Institute had been so severe that Jack found it impossible to continue, and he decided to mothball it, laying off most of the remaining staff — many of whom seemed relieved to go. Souris Saint-Michel was also shut up, indefinitely: an inevitable decision given the sudden plunge in tourist visitors. The last act was the removal of the Sigil. This was mounted on a small plinth, sealed in hard vacuum within a transparent cylinder of some acrylic polymer, packed into a crate, and made its way to the barn of the farmhouse, where it now rested under a tarpaulin, wedged between two hay bales.

No administrator likes to be the last to turn off the lights, but Jack faced the additional problem that contacting Merlin Tech's office in New York to discuss the Institute's new financial arrangements was proving impossible. There was as yet no answer from New York, and after the favor he'd asked in August — to rescue Tom and Shoshana — he was reluctant to impose.

But Jack always had a way of putting his own wryly positive spin on things, and as the September rain continued to cascade down the study windows from broken and overloaded guttering, he looked up at Jadis over the pile of teetering paperwork, and reminded her that the absence of new discoveries in the foreseeable future might give her the chance address the formidable backlog of findings yet to be described.

"Think of it as a sabbatical," he'd said, putting his feet up on the desk, his arms behind his head.

Jadis looked up from some mending—she'd given up trying to wrestle with the increasingly erratic cybersphere—and smiled over the rims of her reading glasses. She had now taken to wearing them for close-up work, and they made her eyes look even larger and more owlish. "Now you've *finally* got up to date on the accounts…" Jack continued. She threw a book at him and laughed as he fought off the assault. Unperturbed, he went on: "you might start that big general monograph you've always talked about."

Her expression clouded. "Oh, you're right, as always," she said. "But I've a feeling that whatever I write will be slanted one way or another by the Sigil. So, I need to describe that first—and I daren't. Not yet."

"What's stopping you?" he replied. "The world has many more things on its mind right now. Amid the general brouhaha, some bizarre, possibly alien and definitely indecipherable message written before humanity evolved would hardly register."

Jadis tried not to rise to Jack's gentle taunts, other than to flash a stern glance at him, magnified by her glasses. Hamming it up, he pretended to have been pierced through the heart, but he overdid it and fell backwards off his chair, disappearing below the level of his desk. She climbed out of her own chair and helped him to his feet. There followed the routine succession of near-telepathic reassurances and pleasantries that couples of a certain age always exchange when one suffers some trifling injury. These over, they paused and looked at each other for a long moment, both knowing that before they could publish the Sigil she felt she needed Domingo's approval, though she could not really explain why. Domingo had advised her to keep quiet for the moment, and so quiet she had kept.

Jadis wondered when or if she might hear from Domingo again. The weird message about Micawber and Richards had been the last. As for Avi, she'd given up sending messages and given the short but brutal war, she now feared the worst. The newsfeeds collected by her patient airtab had been increasingly patchy and out-of-date, even on those treasured occasions when she could get a connection, and when there weren't power outages.

However, all sources had all been quite clear that a plague of unknown origin had swept through the Middle-east. There had been speculation that this was the same disease that had carried off the Pope—but without Domingo's input, she was unable to corroborate these suspicions. It did occur to her, though, that the plague that seemed to have brought the War of the Last Days to an abrupt and merciful close might have been the same thing that had afflicted so many of her neighbors. Occam's Razor said that it might, but as always she had as yet too little actual evidence to go on.

Whatever its cause, the plague was slowly forcing her, with everyone else in and around Saint-Rogatien, to fall back on a more restricted, ancient and homely existence. Getting to market was becoming difficult, partly because supplies of fuel were sporadic, and also because the markets themselves were thin. If the traders hadn't disappeared or died, they, like her, had been marooned for lack of fuel. She became more reliant on her own efforts on the *potager* and in the kitchen, and aware that she needed to store or preserve excess produce, or trade some with her neighbors. They'd kept chickens and ducks for as long as they'd been at Saint-Rogatien. Jadis started to advertise eggs for barter at the farmhouse gate. They were beginning to run out of things they could get no other way—things like soap, and salt. Milk was almost impossible to obtain. She decided to get a goat, if she could. Maybe two. And a cow.

Jack, like Jadis, was also thinking ahead, to the coming winter. He had a hunch that the already unreliable electricity supply would get no better, and might even cease altogether. So he commissioned their old electrician friend Laurent Gaspard to upgrade the ageing solar panels on the farmhouse and barn roof, and cram in a few more, if he could. They asked him to install a wind turbine on the western elevation of the house, to catch the prevailing winds. And—oh yes—to wire their jeeps to run on batteries.

Gaspard said that trade in such items was booming and presented Jack with a huge bill—which Jack honored with a credit transfer drawn on the Institute account. He thought it wise to spend as much as he could on capital investment before the world banking system froze permanently for the winter, along with the pond, in (he estimated) early November.

As it turned out, he was only a little too optimistic. The world's banks collapsed on Hallowe'en, from chronic lack of staff to maintain its electronic systems. It picked up again the following spring, but only after incalculable damage, riots, mass looting and millions more lives lost in cities all over the world. But by then, Jadis and Jack had electric vehicles, re-supplied by their own generating system, and could at least keep a refrigerator, deep freeze, computers and a few electric lights.

Jack asked Gaspard what would happen when the world supply of light bulbs ran out. Gaspard gave that most expressive of gestures—the Gallic Shrug—before revealing that he was buying up as many candles and matches as he could lay his hands on. Jack made arrangements then and there for a year's supply, managing to talk Gaspard down to a reasonably favorable discount.

That the world of the farmhouse was beginning to contract around them meant a great deal more domesticity for Jadis, who consequently did not make her customary rounds of the village every single day, breaking a habit of more than a quarter of a century.

When she did, she found that the Mairie had failed to reopen after the summer. The boulangerie remained closed (she reminded herself to locate a source of flour), and was soon followed by the *Sanglier D'Or* as Sandrine Pasquier gave up the struggle and left with no forwarding address. The church went through several temporary priests as each succumbed in turn to the plague, and it was eventually abandoned: people had to conduct funerals without clerical supervision, as well as digging the graves for their loved ones. Many fields were left unharvested, many houses abandoned. That so few had burned down or had been looted spoke to a rain that fell as hard on the just as on the unjust.

The nature of the plague itself was still elusive. Families of the victims were dead-eyed with horror and grief so that Jadis felt she could hardly inquire. However, she began to amass scraps of gossip about how victims were locked in tetany and were literally *eaten up* by a wave of blackness that spread across their bodies. The rumors about what happened next were even more unbelievable. But Jadis had noticed that the coffins in the frequent funerals marching to the swelling graveyard at the top of the hill were rather small, even for the corpses of children.

The reason why details were so hard to obtain was, simply, fear. Initially, the houses of victims were as shunned as medieval pest-houses, in case the disease could be contracted by close contact. As a precaution this seemed wise, as nobody knew how the disease was transmitted. But from what Jadis knew of epidemiology, it seemed sporadic, striking everywhere at once, with no sign of any particular pattern of spread. However, it did seem to occur most often within families, and its effects varied enormously from place to place. Even though it had exacted an enormous toll in their corner of the world, Gascony seemed to have emerged from the plague relatively unscarred, at least when compared with many other parts of southern France. She'd heard that the coast in particular had been badly hit, and that Marseilles and Montpellier and many other towns were all but deserted. Toulouse had been much less stricken, and a few places such as Carcassonne had been hardly affected at all. Jadis was at a loss to explain why.

Nevertheless, she thanked whoever-it-was who might be flying around above the clouds that the Angel of Death had yet to point his skeletal finger at the farmhouse itself. But with no clear understanding of its rhyme or reason, the worry was always there, at the back of her mind.

Jack and Jadis had the additional worry of Tom and Shoshana, both of whom remained dazed with shock. In the absence of an easily available physician, Jadis had managed to bandage Shoshana's wounded ankle, and was thankful that there seemed no obvious physical injuries that would have called for hospital treatment. Doctor Makeba was almost never available, and Jadis wondered when her longtime physician would perish from overwork, if not from the plague.

Not that the injuries weren't serious enough. Tom, lacerated and bruised all over, had evidently lost his sight. So much was clear from what Jack and Jadis could infer, because Tom himself had hardly said a word since his arrival. He wandered around the house and garden as sure-footed as ever, but seemingly without comprehension, and was often found curled up like a baby in odd places. Jadis wondered whether she should keep him indoors in case he wandered off and got lost. She hesitated, because whatever part of his mind Tom had lost, he seemed to know that this was his home. He refused to sleep alone, and would either curl up in Shoshana's embrace, or attempt to climb into bed with Jadis and Jack.

Shoshana was neither blind nor mute, and at times appeared quite happy and even chatty, but her mood would lurch without warning into black depression. She'd be with Jack and Jadis before the fire, Tom asleep in her lap, burbling amiably away, but would stop in mid-sentence, eyes staring straight forward, blank and dull.

Jadis was almost beside herself for the first week, until Jack calmed her: Tom and Shoshana were suffering, quite understandably, from some kind of post-traumatic stress reaction, and they would presumably get better, in time. In any case, Jack said, they ought to contact Cambridge to tell them that one student might not be returning for his final year, and another might not be arriving for her first. Getting through to Cambridge was as difficult as it had been to anyone else, and after a while they gave up trying.

Eventually, in the second week of October, when the air was growing chill, they received two postcards from the University—one for Tom, the other for Shoshana—to say that 'owing to circumstances beyond its control' it would be closed until further notice, but that all courses would be resumed when such notice might be given. The postcards had no signatories; were scuffed and battered; and, from the evidence of the postmarks, had taken several weeks to arrive.

Jack and Jadis had no way of knowing that the ancient University city that had brought them together, in which they had first loved and courted, was now almost completely devoid of human inhabitants.

As autumn advanced, Tom and Shoshana slowly began to emerge from beneath their personal rain-clouds. By the beginning of October Tom began to speak complete, intelligible sentences, and confessed — to Jadis' evident delight — that he could see again, though his eyes were playing tricks on him. He'd be happier, he said, if he'd be either blind or sighted, but this kind of in-between state was driving him demented.

Tom struggled to describe what he was seeing, even to himself. His best attempt (so he said) was that his vision was a hybrid between regular, normal vision — though heightened in some way he couldn't begin to address — and the kind of geometrical, kaleidoscopic patterns you see when you close your eyes and rub them. And this was just it: normal objects in the everyday world were accompanied, more or less, by a train of dancing, psychedelic after-images. Jadis could hardly begin to conceive what this might be like, except that it must be like seeing the world through one of Domingo's shirts. In any case, whatever Tom's new conception of the world might be, Jadis felt it orthogonal to her own, and hoped for his sake that Tom would learn to live with it.

What Tom kept to himself — partly, though not wholly through his inability to describe it — was with his new eyes, Shoshana looked even more fascinating than she had before. Every person he saw now seemed to be surrounded by a coruscating, electric aurora, and he soon worked out that this was not some objective view, but deeply conditioned by his own feelings. Jack glowed with green reassurance; Jadis with maternal love, a sparking, purple corona edged with ferocity and possession. But Shoshana's aura blazed brightly enough to eclipse and consume all else, in colors beyond the range of normal human vision. And there was more: he could now sense the flow and pulse of blood beneath her pale skin, alert to every nuance of her mood, arousal or depression. He hardly knew how to begin describing this to

Shoshana, so he did what he always had, which was to re-place words with demonstrative action. In perfect tune with every beat of her body, he could make love to her in ways that left her gasping for breath. He hardly needed to touch her, let alone penetrate her: it seemed like he only had to wave his hands around her, like a conductor with his baton, describing some pattern in the air, and she would be brought to a state of saffron orgasm that would last for hours.

Not that she did not want him to emphasize his skill more physically, for she loved to be caressed and kissed as much as ever, and the yeasty-buttery texture of her skin, the allspice-cinnamon smell he raised from it when he ran his fingers across it, were powerfully arousing for him. He gloried in the smell and texture and sight and *beyond*-sight of her curves, her aura an excited yellow-bronze around her full hips and golden thighs: he was always amazed by the softness of her neck, her shoulders and her hair, and the richness of her breasts, streaked with rose; and the hugeness of her indigo-velvety nipples. When she climaxed the room was filled with pink and violet streaks of joyful self-annihilation. But he noticed that when he came inside her, her aura darkened to deepest ruby edged with black and lined with lightning bolts. He had no idea what this could mean.

And, just once, her body and the air all around it radiating a playful fur-edged magenta, she insisted that he stop pussyfooting around and penetrate her firmly from behind. He tried to be gentle, but she pushed herself backwards onto him, parting her buttocks so that he was as fully inside her as possible. Kneeling behind her, he dusted his hands lightly across her shoulders, around her breasts and hips. Without his moving inside her at all, she came in glorious waves of deep crimson rapture. Her insides squeezed against him in exhilarated response, forcing him to come. But the instant he did so, she stifled a scream and her aura *switched off*, like a light—just for an instant, before resuming its glow, a subdued, funereal amethyst.

Afterwards, when she was lying in his arms, beads of sweat like bright maroon blood on her brow, her salty hair in disorder, a powerful smell of panic-edged musk from between her legs and her aura more or less recovered, he'd asked her what was wrong. She did not reply, except to kiss him.

No, he'd insisted—there was something *wrong*, he could feel it, he could *see* it.

Don't be so sensitive, she'd responded, perhaps rather too tartly. They'd both been through a hell of a lot together, hadn't they? Perhaps she'd been bruised or something in the explosion, maybe?

C'est possible, he'd said. After all, the effects of the explosion on his own sensory system had been both drastic and alarming. Some as-yet-undetected internal bruising might be expected.

But he remained unconvinced. He wished that she could get herself checked out by a doctor. He didn't say this, however, as even the most basic doctoring was currently very hard to come by.

Shoshana knew more. Since they'd been in Israel—even before the Masada incident—she had been troubled by nonspecific, internal pain. At first it went away with a few analgesics, but it was now a constant, nagging, metallic ache. Her periods had never worried her greatly, but now they were titanic in intensity and volume, as if someone had poked a garden hoe up inside her and had been stirring vigorously—and the blood was always very dark. Then came the day that her blood turned black. There were spots of blood in her urine, too. They were black, too, and soon her urine itself was black, like oil from sump.

It was then that she realised what was happening. She had the plague, but instead of consuming her in a single episode of overmounting horror, it was eating her, slowly, slyly, from the inside out.

She dared say nothing to Tom. After all, what *could* she say? But as the weeks passed, she noticed that he became worried, too, fretting in silence at her insistence—which she swore she'd maintain to the end—that it was nothing to worry about.

Chapter 14. Ascension

Gascony, France, Earth, December, 2054

I lingered round them, under that benign sky: watched the
moths fluttering among the heath and hare-bells; listened to the
soft wind breathing through the grass; and wondered how any one
could ever imagine unquiet slumbers for the sleepers in that quiet
earth.

Emily Brontë—*Wuthering Heights*

Winter came earlier and was far harsher than it had ever
been, ravaging a countryside already weighed down with
shortages, tragedy, disorder and death. The residents of the
farmhouse were as well prepared as they could be for the
blizzards that they knew would strike by the end of November, working hard to lay in as much winter store as possible.

For Tom, working with his hands had proved excellent
therapy: he and Jack were out from dawn until dusk, shor-
ing up the roof and filling cracks, stripping down and main-
taining the generators, mending frozen pipes and hauling
firewood. Shoshana joined Jadis in the domestic department—preserving and bottling, drying and blanching, making and mending. But it was clear to Jadis that the relentless
work did not have quite the restorative effect on Shoshana
that it evidently had on Tom.

First, Shoshana had lost weight. She was not the round
and rosy girl who had first jumped so confidently from the
jeep that April, so enchanting Tom. Her cheeks had hollowed, making two great fiery saucers of her eyes, and if
Jadis hadn't known better, she could have sworn that Shoshana had aged ten years in as many weeks. Although she
tried to hide it—and the effort had been heroic—her pert
sassiness had been traded for something mournful, almost

spectral. If Jadis had to summarize it in a phrase, as she did to Jack one candlelit evening in the second week of December, when the weeks-long snow storm had subsided leaving a starry, dead-white calm — it was as if the Shoshana had had all the stuffing knocked out of her.

What was so infuriating, Jadis said, was the fact that Shoshana never complained but soldiered on regardless, brushing away any inquiry, spurning any offer of help, wearing a smile and not counting the cost. Jack responded that he recalled another brave and defiantly self-reliant young woman he'd once known who'd been through similarly life-changing events, insisting that nobody should bear the burden but she herself, regardless of her actual capability.

"It's just like you to worry," he said, "but you shouldn't. Shoshana has been through a lot lately, as have we all. She's resilient. She'll get over it, in time."

"But Tom's bounced back," replied Jadis, "so why hasn't she? I do wish she'd talk more. She knows I'm always here. You know, to talk."

"Don't hold it against her," advised Jack. "We all have our ways of coping. And remember, we *know* Tom. Shoshana could be a new person every day, and we'd never know which one was for real."

Jadis made a noise signifying total lack of conviction as she turned once more to her mending, and noticed, as if for the first time, that the saggy old sofa seemed rather a long way from the hearth, and that she missed a hearthrug beneath her feet.

"You know what?" she said. "We could do with another dog."

Jack laughed. "I see — in addition to the menagerie we have already acquired."

Over the past month and a half, Jack and Tom had converted the old field lab in the barn into accommodation for two cows, three goats and a horse, all of which now grazed, weather permitting, in three otherwise abandoned fields close to the house. An outbuilding was full of chickens, and the ducks and geese that now roamed the garden often fought running skirmishes with the Horribles, and, more often than not, winning. The ragged gang of piratical cats soon learned to keep well away from the geese, with their sharp beaks and long, roaming necks that gave them a quite extraordinary reach.

In the absence of anything like silage, locating fodder and bedding for this expanding ark had occupied many scarce daylight hours—though the several abandoned farms round about provided rich stores of maize that could be made into animal feed. Jack thought that one of the fields he was now 'minding' would have to be sown with maize next spring, assuming they could find seed.

"Oh, Jack, I know," she said. "But I still miss Fairbanks. I once thought that to replace him would have been sacrilege, but perhaps ten years might be thought a decent interval."

Jack smiled again. "I get the picture—Fairbanks was therapy for you, so a Mark II version might cheer up Shoshana?"

Jadis pointedly ignored his taunts.

"It's a good idea, though," he said. "For other reasons. A guard dog would be good. A gun dog. Not to mention a gun."

Security was a problem that had loomed large in both their minds of late. The general lack of people had meant the woods were full of boar and deer, which would be useful, if only one could shoot them. But if local gossip were anything to go by, there were also wolves. And there were worse things that Jack had seen for himself.

There had been some odd types roaming around lately—mostly sad and sorry refugees from the cities, trying to sell scavenged items. But some, they was sure, were also looking for places to plunder, to take by force. And a few of these people were very odd indeed: people with long, white, shaggy coats, hammering on the door at all hours and making all sorts of eccentric demands and showing very long teeth if refused.

The clock ticked away a few more seconds, and then, as if on cue, the kitchen door succumbed to a thunderous battering. They both stood up with a start and raced into the kitchen.

"Who is it?" Jadis shouted, lighting a candle on the kitchen table and reaching into the drawer for a long knife.

"A very old friend!" replied a muffled but instantly recognizable voice. Jadis sighed with relief and Jack threw open the door to what looked like a giant snowman. Domingo, unkempt, snow-maned and heavily bearded, swept into the kitchen, sloughing, in one single movement of surprising grace—a vast ankle-length woollen greatcoat, moleskin waistcoat, mittens, scarf, broad-brimmed hat, balaclava and a rucksack the size of a Shetland pony.

Underneath it all was the big, toothy smile that always brought the sunshine—and a Hawai'ian shirt, if rather faded and torn in places, worn over thick corduroy trousers and a pair of boots, each one the size of an amphibious landing craft.

"My dearest friends," he said, shaking a small drift of snow from his beard, "I apologise for the… er… *smell*," (he did indeed smell rather strongly) "but would you mind if I stayed for a night or two?"

Jadis thought Domingo, with his abundance of long, white hair and beard, looked a cross between Santa and a character from *Easy Rider*. Jack asked the visitor if he'd like a glass of whisky, and without waiting for an answer, disappeared into the cellar. Jadis smiled as if she were a little girl and this was the best Christmas present ever.

"Oh, you silly man," she said, "we've missed you like *anything*" — they had had no contact with him since his email from Israel that August — "and you know you can stay here as long as you like." As if willing him to stay forever, she hugged him like a small limpet hugs a vast, black, barnacled boulder. The top of her head hardly managed to brush his chin, and her slim arms wouldn't quite meet round his substantial girth. "Middle-aged spread," he admitted. "Not that you and Jack have been so afflicted."

She looked up at him with shining eyes, which darkened and sharpened as she remembered something. "I've been meaning to ask you, Domingo…. What's all this about 'Mr Micawber'?"

He paused as if he'd suddenly remembered something, reached into his abandoned overcoat and pulled out two objects. One was a sawn-off shotgun wrapped in oilcloth, concerning which Domingo made no comment. The other was bulkier and floppier. Wrapped in sheepskin and fast asleep was a golden retriever puppy, perhaps three months old.

"Jadis, meet Micawber," he said. "Micawber, meet Jadis. Happy Christmas. I rescued him from a house that was abandoned. I'm afraid his mother and littermates had died. He followed me unbidden, walking all this way with me until he tired, so I stowed him in my pack with my socks, until he got cold. Or perhaps the smell revolted him. So I… uh… translated him to my overcoat pocket with my… er… armoury. He is a *gun* dog, after all."

"Domingo… How could you have known? We were only just talking about it…"

"Ah, well, sometimes one... ah... just knows. Goes with the... er... calling. Now, where are the young people? Are they here?"

Jadis explained that Tom and Shoshana were asleep, and, when Jack had returned and had also been introduced to Micawber, for whom accommodation was swiftly found in an old cardboard carton by the kitchen stove, they made tea and filled glasses with whisky. While they drank, Jadis had given a brief account of Tom and Shoshana, their traumatic experiences, dramatic escape and subsequent troubles. Domingo's eyes darkened when he heard that Shoshana had not been well and seemed to be worsening.

"I expect I'll see them in the morning, then," he said.

Jadis suddenly remembered that Domingo would probably be very hungry, but before she could do anything further, the big man shambled over to his up-ended rucksack and (as if it were a sackful of toys) pulled out another parcel, roughly folded in a red-checked tablecloth of summer-picnic *cliché*. He unwrapped it to reveal a vast pork pie; a round of local farmhouse cheese as big as a car tire; and two large loaves.

"Tolerably fresh, relatively unsquashed" he admitted, "and only *slightly* nibbled." Jadis was awed and stunned. She chastised herself for having gotten out of the habit of having Domingo in her life. Domingo took the pause to be of a more active variety. "*Benedic, Domine*," he said, "*nos et haec tua dona quae de tua largitate sumus sumpturi, per Christum Dominum nostrum. Amen*," before fetching plates and refreshing the teapot. Jadis was cast back to their very first meeting when this titan (black-haired, then, rather than snowy grey) had barged into her kitchen and had made her lunch before she'd even known who he was.

It wasn't long before Domingo started to flag. His surprise arrival was, he said, the much-wished culmination of a long journey, which he'd be pleased to tell them all about, but only in daylight. "Some of my tale is rather… uh… grim," he said, yawning widely. So Jadis rushed around in a fluster after towels and soap and bedding and warming pans and showed Domingo to a room that had once been his very own quarters, long ago. There was a wash-stand and even the unvarnished oak *prie-dieu* that he'd bought in an antiques market at Seissan—in another world, it seemed. He was asleep and snoring not ten minutes later.

It took Jadis rather longer to find sleep, given the unexpected arrival of their old friend after such a long absence, and not only that, but a friend who had brought Fairbanks resurrected, just as they had been talking about him, and wasn't that a strange coincidence? She tossed and fidgeted next to Jack, who, lying supine, said "well, he did *say* he'd come as soon as he could.

"And given that he presumably had other things to do… and the journey must have been difficult… and it *is* Christmas…" his voice faded, and he yawned, as if in sympathy with Domingo. But she was stirred, jumpy, and wouldn't be quietened so easily. She turned towards him, and nibbled his earlobe. Without a word he responded—not mechanically, nor habitually, but simply because he knew the moods of his wife's body better than he knew his own. Her legs, he reflected, as she wrapped them around him, were as lovely and long and slender and smooth as they had always been, since she had been a young girl, he thought, half in dreams of dells and bluebells.

Across the hall, Tom stirred to find Shoshana's aura blazing in decadent sickly orange splendor. She woke, paused, kissed him with violent intensity, her aura now a migraine fractal swirl of deep orange and magenta, surrounding the bright ultraviolet of her open eyes. She pulled away from him, sighed and looked at him. "I love you, Tom," she said, after a long moment, "and don't you forget it." Her voice was filled with resolution—and also with a keening and regret which spoke to Tom of some imminent, eternal parting.

He lay down again, pulling her next to him. "*Sois gentil*," he said, "we are young. We have all the time in the world." But her body thrummed with suppressed urgency, as if the very opposite was true, that the world might end at any second.

Tom pulled the covers over them both and cradled her in his arms. As she subsided into sleep, her aura dulled to a filthy orange-brown haze, like street lights seen through an icy smog. Tom stayed awake for a very long time.

The next day, after the family had returned home from their various morning chores, Jadis convened what she called a lunchtime 'house meeting'. Unusually, this was to take place in the sitting room, rather than the kitchen that had traditionally been the venue for all such convocations.

But Domingo had wanted to tell a story, the implication being that it would be a long one, so she wanted everyone to be comfortable. And this is how she saw it as she stepped into the wan, gray shafts of light through the two tall windows that overlooked the snowbound front yard. She bore a tray laden with tea (an increasingly scarce and special treat), new bread, and wedges of Domingo's cheese.

Jack had cleaned and stoked up the fire: Micawber, instantly at home, had settled on the hearth as close to the embers as he dared, imperiously displacing two Horribles, who scowled at him from behind the curtains.

Domingo sat at one end of the sofa, in trademark aloha shirt, his long, graying hair combed and tied at the back with what looked like bailer twine. Jadis thought Domingo looked more than ever like an ageing rock star. She half expected to see a Harley parked outside.

Shoshana rose to help Jadis with the overloaded tray, but she seemed ungainly, awkward, and looked absolutely terrible: her skin was grayish and blotchy, the rose in her cheeks shrunken to two carmine spots beneath her heavy eyelids.

"Shoshana, are you…?"

"Oh, don't worry about *me*, I'm fine," said Shoshana. "Just didn't sleep too well, that's all." She smiled at Jadis but only for an instant, as if she could hardly afford any greater effort: and then, turning her face away, making a great fuss and business of sorting out plates and slices of bread, before sitting — subsiding — on the sofa next to Domingo.

Domingo's much greater size and weight meant that Shoshana couldn't help but collapse on top of him, but his proximity seemed to have an energising effect, so that she now smiled more broadly.

Tom rushed in, late, having caught up with what Jack had self-deprecatingly called 'seeing to the stock'. He murmured an apology and sat down next to Shoshana. Jadis warmed to the infinite and minute concern that her son had for the girl, but it was a pleasure mixed with worry.

As they finished their bread and cheese and topped up their tea mugs, Domingo started his story.

"What I have to tell you will seem somewhat… ah… startling," he began, "but I can make no apologies for that. For I think you should know. And, if I am honest, *I* should know, too."

Domingo paused, as if he were about to launch some great manifesto. "My good friends, we live in a world that has changed. We can no longer hang on to the past. And despite all our discoveries here which, in some ways, have caused people to change their views about things, I had not realized this until fate dealt me a rude blow in Israel this summer. As you know, I was by way of personal assistant to

His Holiness, Linus the Second. I say *was*, because His Holiness has now been gathered in. Or so I believe, at least, for all practical purposes."

It was true then, Jadis thought to herself. Or, at least, the ambiguity of the news wires told no more than the truth.

"And, as I suspect you know," Domingo went on, "His Holiness was to give an open-air mass at a large sports stadium near Tel Aviv. The Rolling Stones were going to give a concert there the following night, and I had been hoping to attend, but—ah, well" His eyes misted over in memory of what Jadis now knew was a mildly disreputable folly of his youth.

"His Holiness gave a creditable account of himself, though he had been overtaxed and overtired, or so I thought. I was watching from offstage, but to my shame, I had got so... er... *carried away* by the proceedings that I did not immediately notice that he had collapsed. Or perhaps my eyes refused to believe what they had seen. Until, that is, a stretcher was wheeled straight past me towards the loading dock. I gave chase and accompanied him in the ambulance to the hospital. His Holiness was alive and barely conscious, but just got grayer and grayer, despite all the heroic efforts of the ambulance crew. Nothing they could do had any effect, and as the body of His Holiness became ever stiller, the crew whirled around him in what seemed like a blur of panic..." Domingo paused to catch his breath, then. "And so it was that without any idea of the precise... er... *nature* of the ills that had befallen my superior, he was placed in an isolation cubicle. I was, I regret, not permitted to administer any last rites, a circumstance which I deeply regret—and which caused me, I have to say, considerable distress—although I can understand why it had to happen."

Domingo now began to choose his words carefully. A dark cloud draped itself over the pale sun, casting the room into drear monochromatic shadow in which all its inhabitants became indistinct blurs.

"The body of His Holiness was at first quite still. But then he started shaking uncontrollably and quite… ah… *violently*, waving his arms all about, so that he had to be restrained with manacles. Then, it appeared as if his muscles contracted into a kind of tetany…"

Jadis started, as if in recognition.

"… throwing his jaw open wide and locking it in place. The isolation cubicle was soundproofed, so I could not hear if he was making any sound, although it looked—I was watching on a TV monitor—like he was screaming. But then—oh, *then*—his body shook with such power, as if he was possessed, that his arms ripped free of the manacles… severing both his hands."

Jadis gasped and paled, her own hands flying to her mouth. Jack embraced her from behind. Tom put his arms round Shoshana who looked up at Domingo, her expression unfathomable until her brow creased minutely, as if she were reacting to some inner pain.

"It was then that the final, awful, transformation started. A small patch of black appeared at his throat. This spread quickly to envelop his whole body in a black shroud, but that was not the last of it. The shroud was active, *alive*. It contracted around him, more and more, until by the time it had stopped, His Holiness was nothing more than a sphere, quite black, of about this size." Domingo brought his hands forward, indicating a sphere about the size of a human head.

The sun now peered from behind the bank of ragged clouds that had obscured it. Although it was late morning, it hung low in the sky, a shaft now piercing the window-glass to illuminate Domingo's hands, as if they were the only things in the room.

"After that, things moved rather… ah… *quickly*," he continued. "The plan was that His Holiness would stay in Israel for two days as a guest of the Prime Minister, an old friend of his. I was going to get time off and perhaps see Avi. Sadly, that was not to be." He stopped, as if looking in the middle distance, and then turned to Jadis, pre-empting her next question: "my dear Jadis, I have no news to report. Our old *confrère* has not answered any messages, and what with the destruction of Haifa and the millions who died in the conflagration, I can only fear for him—*pray* for him." He left unsaid the possibility that Avi, like the Pope, might have succumbed to this dreadful new disease.

How fate has a habit of laying one low, Jadis thought. She recalled how her Dream Team had gathered on the sunny back porch in 2031, twenty-three years before. Of the eight guests at her dinner table, six were now dead. Roger MacLennane, aged seventy, was driving, when he suffered a massive stroke and drove into the back of a petrol tanker, which exploded. Marjorie, unable to live without him, much as she tried, found a bottle of barbiturates and swallowed the lot. Primrose and Faye in Tibet. Avi, almost certainly, in Israel. And Mathilde had once told Jadis how, one day, she had woken up in a bed soaked and dripping with the blood pumping out of her poor Eric's every orifice, the first—and last—symptom of the Naivasha-6 virus. Which left Mathilde herself who, as far as Jadis knew, was still in Cambridge, in a University that had shut down until further notice. And Jadis knew then that she'd had the temerity to have wished them all well, if only in her mind, as if granting such fortune were in her power: the horrible irony being that she and Jack had sailed on regardless, unscathed, apparently unchanged, forced to live with the consequences.

"I had to make several decisions rather quickly," Domingo went on. "I gathered the last remains of His Holiness, including his hands, directed that they be put on ice in a sterilized medivac container, and I left, before anyone could stop me. Exit, pursued by a storm: I had swept out of the Holy Land within three hours, on the Papal hyperjet.

"When I arrived in Rome," he continued, "it was no picnic, either. I found that the plague had struck there, too, with some violence, and the city was close to erupting into anarchy. I did the best I could, holed up in Saint Peter's with what was left of the College of Cardinals, a crowd baying outside, people left and right just… uh… *condensing*, right there, in the square. I saw Cardinal Fratellini, a close and dear friend and colleague, collapse—implode—into blackness, before my eyes.

"As for His Holiness, my colleagues (those that remained) and I could not at first decide what to do for the best. Was His Holiness actually dead? None of us was sure, as there has, of course, been no exact precedent. But even were he alive, we were sure that he would be incapable of office, and after many hours of debate we decided to proceed with the deliberations we'd need to… oh dear, am I boring you?" He looked up at Jadis. She now knelt down in front of him, clasping his hands which were still half in the air, still describing the shape of the absent Pope.

"Domingo, please go on," she said. The man had clearly been brooding over his tale for many lonely hours, lost in a blizzard. It was no surprise that he sometimes appeared to be talking to himself.

"Oh, well," he sighed, "I shall be… er… *brief*. My fellow cardinals appeared to look to me for guidance, because, I suppose, I had had the ear of His Holiness. They asked me what we should do."

Jadis' heart sang towards him: the real reason, she guessed, was because Domingo was intelligent and resourceful, and as he had neither a handsome face nor an elegant frame, he had been forced to become a good listener rather than seek any glory for himself. He had been a friend to her and to Jack, to Tom, to Avi, and presumably to many more.

"… and so my advice was clear," he said. "Given the times, that we should all take some time off for reflection, so naturally I wanted to come here. I apologise for my sudden arrival: as you might appreciate, it is now very difficult to… er… phone ahead. And there was another thing I needed to do. Even though the hyperjet could have had me here within an hour, I decided to take the slower road, for I wanted to see for myself how the land lay.

"You will have a good idea of course, that the world is in a state of some… ah… disorder, but this is hard to appreciate for those of us who spend much of our lives cloistered up in St Peter's. In those rooms we Cardinals shuffle to and fro, admiring the Michaelangelo. But, you know, *ars longa*, and… er… *vita brevis*, or words to that effect. I felt a need — a duty — to stay close to the ground. I set off on the twenty-sixth of September, which just happens to be my birthday."

Jadis was bemused by this, and realized that in all the years she'd known Domingo, she had no idea when his birthday fell, or even how old he was. He had always seemed ageless to her, and he was, of course, an expert in avoiding questions that he thought pried too closely into his origins or early life. He'd dropped hints that he came from Spain: but that was it. That he'd vouchsafed the date of his birth was a revelation.

"I have been travelling ever since," Domingo said. "By bus, by train, but mostly on foot, trudging the highways and watching the world fall to bits around my ears. I was nearly robbed three times, hence the… er… gun. Cities are no place to be, and the countryside is full of anxiety and horror. I have slept under hedges, in barns — following the example of the excellent Dr Corstorphine." Domingo's eyes sparkled. Jack, now standing by the fire, bowed low, pretending to doff a non-existent hat, as if he were in a pantomime. But it had been a long time since Jack had roamed the woods and fields alone.

"Domingo," said Jack: "what's your assessment of the spread of this plague? Jadis and I, well, we've thought about it, and it doesn't seem to be anything normal, you know, contagious."

"That's my feeling exactly," replied Domingo, "but it does vary markedly in severity from place to place. Northern Italy has suffered greatly. People were falling like skittles as I left Rome, and by the time I reached Milan it was quite deserted. Turin was a little better, but as I moved westwards, I met refugees from Liguria who said that Genoa was a ghost town and a haunt of demons and werewolves. An exaggeration, I suspect, but one gets the drift.

"Matters were worse still as I continued my westward course. By the time I reached the Côte D'Azur the plague seemed to have passed, leaving absolutely nothing behind. *Nothing*. I remember a week or so at the end of October when I saw not a living soul, during which I visited Nice. There was nobody there at all—except for a few black spheres, which I took to be the last remains of… er… *people*. I was very tired then, and footsore, and hungry, and I needed a holiday. So I checked in at the Hotel Negresco and availed myself of its elegant hospitality as the only guest, and even then, distinctly self-service, may the Lord forgive me. I ate well and enjoyed two or three tolerable nights' sleep: barricading myself in, of course. On the first night there were sounds that woke me in the small hours I should not like to describe, even here, and in daylight. And so the next day I found a supplier for the *chasse*, not entirely looted and… er… armed myself.

"I am glad I did, for I regret that my shotgun has seen use, and at close-range. For as I continued westwards, across the Rhône, there were more people, and that's when some of them tried to relieve me of such small things I possess. But I am happy to say that there are parts of south-western France that seem hardly to have been affected at all. You will be surprised to learn that Gascony has been only mildly stricken, and in parts of the Languedoc and towards the Pyrenées this *peste* is only a rumor.

"But on the whole the picture is terrible. I am sure it will get better, but it will need help. When I return to Rome, or what's left of it, I shall advise my colleagues that whoever assumes the Throne of Peter should spend as little time in it as possible, but go out and about to see what can be done. Without wishing for a soapbox here, I'll make a case that what we need is a new kind of approach, crossing the papacy with the old Friars Mendicant, a sort of Portable Vatican. I do wish Avi were here to keep me up to scratch on my Hebrew, for he had a wonderful phrase that meant 'mending the world,' as if it were our ordained function, that really said it all."

"*Tikkun olam*?" This from Shoshana, who looked straight up at Domingo as if she were a tiny polar-bear cub seeking approval at the feet of its immense father.

"Yes, Shoshana, that's exactly… er… *it*." Domingo looked down at her proprietorially, and Jadis was pleased and relieved to see how the girl's face changed, as if the sun had fallen on it, or that she'd shed a shabby old raincoat to reveal a shimmering ball-gown beneath.

Having now reached the end of his story, Domingo asked whether anyone might mind were he to take a turn round the village? Footsore he might be, but Micawber needed exercise, after all, and he felt he needed to call in at the church. A professional visit, you might say.

"When you get there, you'll find there's a vacancy," said Jack. "'Mending the World' might start rather close to home, if you've a mind to start right here."

"It is as I feared—and, I confess, for shame, secretly hoped," sighed Domingo. "I shall be the Parish Priest at Saint-Rogatien once again. At least for a little while." He thanked them for their attention, rising to help Jadis with the plates and mugs. Tom and Jack had to hurry outside again for another seemingly endless round of farmyard chores.

Jadis always had plenty of other tasks to keep her busy, so it was Shoshana who asked whether she might accompany Domingo on his short trip up the ancient hillside. A little voice inside her told her that this opportunity must not be wasted, for it would never happen again. She asked the little voice how it could be so certain of this, but it gave no reply.

To begin with, she felt a little embarrassed even talking to him, as if she were undressing in public, or something. Not that this ever embarrassed you *before*, a new voice inside her said, replaying a picture of a school-bus bacchanale. She waved it down: that's ancient history, she insisted. I've changed. And with that, her nervousness ceased. But the new voice persisted. What did she think she was doing, a nice Jewish girl, talking over these things with this strange (*very* strange) man she hardly knew, who, in case she hadn't grasped this fact, was a Catholic priest, *noch*? She interjected that it really rather depended on what one meant by *nice*, and, moreover, whether in the context of her own particular early experience, at least, this bland epithet could ever sit next to *Jewish*, until another voice joined the internal conversation. This was the first voice, the one that had told her to hurry.

And then her own thoughts reigned: she had, if she were honest, no qualms whatsoever about baring her soul to this man. *Not* because he occupied a unique position, in the family circle, but not of it, that afforded both knowledge and objectivity; *not* because he was (she had to admit) far more articulate than Jack, or Jadis, and certainly more than Tom (not that she loved him any less for it); and *not* that he was a man trained and used to keeping secrets. But simply because he was a good listener. She recalled what Tom had said to her, on the shores of the Dead Sea, four months and a million light-years ago, about the comfort of Domingo's very presence, to small, lost souls in distress, even small boys who'd lost their dogs.

There was something else, too. That despite everything, their many superficial differences, she felt that she and Domingo shared a community of experience which, for her part, she had never felt entirely happy discussing with anyone else, at least, not fully.

So, sitting together in the front pew of the freezing church, their breath forming damp clouds in front of them, she told Domingo about the trauma of her early life. How the humanity of religion had been sapped by ritual so rigid that one could no longer see God (yes, she—*she*!—talked about *God*). Of how she'd found greater humanity among those who wore their religion more lightly, or even—she meant no offense—not at all.

So there.

She'd told Domingo everything. *Everything*. About her Mum and Dad, and Howie Levinson. About Avi and her trip to Israel. Most of all, she told him about Tom, and her love for him, and of the pain inside that would soon, she was sure, soon sweep her away from him, and all of them; that it was now so great that she felt she could hardly stand. Yet for all that, she still smiled, for she very much did not want to hurt Tom, or put any stain on Jadis' act of charity and help, in that she had been offered a new home, away from all that *stuff*. And there she sat, still, waiting for Domingo's judgement.

Domingo put his arm round her. She looked up into those inscrutable eyes, and saw that they were—or was she imagining it?—glinting with moisture.

"In return for such candor, I should tell you things, Shoshana, that only my Maker knows," he said, his voice almost inaudibly quiet.

"Domingo?"

"Hmm? Oh. Yes. Despite all external appearances, my dear Shoshana, we two have much in common. Perhaps. Well…" He seemed unsure whether to go on. Looking straight ahead, he began a story which, Shoshana was sure, he'd never told a living soul.

"I never knew my own parents, Shoshana," he said. "I was a foundling, discovered, or so I believe, in the gutter of a small mountain village in southern Spain. I was taken in by the Sisters of Mercy who, while they had undoubtedly saved my life, gave me, as a kind of joke, I think, the ridiculously inflated name under which I now labor. Are you aware of my name, in all its baroque, even rococo glory?"

Shoshana said that she wasn't.

"Wait for it—it's Domingo García Vasquez Santéria Sanchopanza de Orellanzana von Hohenzollern und Taxis." Shoshana tried and failed to suppress a giggle. "But my friends just call me 'Pongo'. Yes, I know. As someone once told me, it's quite a handle."

Shoshana pulled closer to the big, warm man, a buttress against any amount of cold the world might throw at her.

"But—where was I?" Domingo said. "Ah, yes. I throve, and grew, and that was the problem. I kept on *growing*, so that the Sisters, while they looked after my material needs, told me that whatever the Lord might think, I was such an *ugly* child. Yes, I have to say that I was spurned, and kicked, and teased in front of the other wretched children who'd found their ways to the Sisters. But I soon forgave them. Especially as I grew to be a lot bigger than they were, and was able to retaliate in kind. After all," he said, turning to Shoshana, "I was only a child. But as I got older I was generally left alone, until the Sisters found the first opportunity they could to pack me off to a monastery.

"It was just as hard learning to be a monk as it had been to learn to be a... uh... a human being. And, I agree, the strictures of religious observance did sometimes make it hard to see God. And this, my dear Shoshana, is how, in spite of all appearances, we two are so much alike.

"As you know, a long time ago, Avi Malkeinu and I were great friends, working with Jadis, here at Saint-Rogatien. Like you, Avi found it hard to see God, and I remember our having a very similar conversation. That ritual gets in the way. I found it hard to put this into a succinct... ah... *sentence* at the time, but Avi helped me out. It was something he was taught long before, by his grandfather, he said. That there was once a famous rabbi, who said that the ritual is neither here nor there. The important thing was *love*, because—what was it? Ah yes—because 'everything else is commentary'. It was a Rabbi Akiva, I think...?"

"It was Hillel," said Shoshana, finding herself smiling, embracing the big man by her side.

"You see! I *knew* you'd know," he said. "And rabbi... er... Hillel was quite right, and so are you."

But, he noted, looking directly at her: that just because the ritual hides God doesn't mean that God isn't there, or that he doesn't *care*. It was because of this knowledge that despite the abuse he'd suffered all his life, he had embraced the Church, finally, with gladness. And it was because of this same knowledge, he said, that he found Judaism so full of contradictions, which he found fascinating.

"How so?" she asked, her eyes closed, nestling up against his warmth.

"Avi asked just the same questions. I see it like this. That there is more to the Jews than having a covenant with God: they are, in truth… ah… *defined* by it. So how is it, then, that Judaism demands every perfection of ritual with no demand made on the supplicant that he has faith? If he has not faith, how can he be a Jew?"

"I used to have a lot of rows with my stepfather about this," said Shoshana. "My goodness, did *we* have *rows*. But I can see now, that he was only trying to do right by the ritual. He'd say that if you walk the walk for long enough, then you'd learn to talk the talk, and then you'd find yourself believing in God without knowing it. You had to have the ritual to *invoke* God, my stepfather said. Of course, being a stroppy teenager, I said that you had to have all the marching up and down just to convince yourself that God existed."

Domingo was silent for a spell. He could see it was logical, he replied, but to him it was logic, inverted. And yet both views—faith before ritual, and ritual before faith—led to the same place.

She continued: if God exists, if God cares, then how can it be that God tolerates such suffering? The suffering that you—we both—have endured? The suffering of everyone in the war, this plague?

Ah, he replied, he *doesn't*. But the fact remains that although God has a plan and a design for the Universe, he has, nevertheless, granted each one of us the gift of free will. And, yes, our actions are indeed free, because without freedom, we cannot fairly be judged; and without freedom, God's ultimate design might not be revealed, for if it were otherwise, he'd have thrown his own game, in which case everyone's lives would have been lived to no purpose. The Universe would be stripped of meaning.

But, she said, I did not *will* this pain. And your Pope did not *will* himself into that dreadful fate.

This is true, he admitted. Some people would have you believe that all is explicable through belief, that God can be second-guessed: that we can know what God wants. But in reality, faith is not so different from science, properly construed. There are many things that we do not, and perhaps cannot understand.

"God is infinite, Shoshana," he said, "and we are infinitesimally tiny. The deeds of God may seem kind to us, or cruel, but they are, in a formal sense, incomprehensible. The most we can do is strive to improve our world, and if our circumstances box us into a corner, we have to… ah… *accept* them."

"I cannot do that," she said, firmly, her insides gripped as if within the teeth of a black steel vice. She shook, and started to sweat, but Domingo's grasp stopped her falling to the floor.

"My poor, sweet child," said Domingo, partly to her, partly to himself—that she should suffer so. "But you must."

"Why?"

"*Because you have no choice.*"

She looked up at him, questioningly.

"It is the tragedy of our human state, Shoshana" he said. "Animals meet their destiny without being aware of it: acceptance does not come into it. But we—we human beings— *know* what's coming, and so, despite free will, there comes a point where we *cannot* avoid our fate. It is at that point that we exercise the last option we are given, as part of the *privilege* of humanity—that we *choose* to accept our fate. Even though no other option is available."

Shoshana pulled herself up, now sitting on Domingo's lap as if she were a small child.

"And if we don't?" she said, "if we don't accept?"

"There are two things that make us human," he replied. "The first is that we can see God. The second is that we can love. I think that the two are one and the same, and they are both related to acceptance. And I see it in you. You are afflicted with something which, it seems, is like the plague, which you feel will soon claim you for its own. And yet, as far as I know, you have not breathed a word of it to Jack, nor Jadis—nor to Tom. And you have kept your secret because you do not wish to distress them. In other words, for love. Truly, you know more about God than I do."

She said no more. So he picked her up in his arms, called for the dog, and tramped slowly through the snow back to the farmhouse.

She sat in the same place a few days later. It was Christmas Eve, and Domingo, dressed in threadbare vestments he'd found in some cupboard somewhere—over which he wore his greatcoat—was performing the ancient rite of the Midnight Mass. Tom sat to her left, Jadis, and then Jack, to her right.

They were not alone. Horses, carts, bicycles and a few electric vehicles jostled in the Place Etienne Geoffroy Saint Hilaire, and the church was full. People for many miles around had heard that Father Domingo had returned, and that even after all their troubles, the horror of the past year, that Midnight Mass would be celebrated in the church on the ancient hill. Father Domingo had done many good works in his tenure at the church, twenty years before, the village elders had said. It was no surprise, a man like that, that he went on to greater things. But he had been missed. And it was only proper that he had come back. It was as if normal service had resumed.

Before the service, people greeted one another, embracing, crying, for all the world as if they had emerged from some collective nightmare, and that the future would be brighter. The church was washed a honey yellow with the glow from dozens of candles. Perhaps there is something to be said for ritual after all, Shoshana thought to herself, as a first step in *tikkun olam*.

Not that she could repair herself, at least not directly. For as soon as she had stopped fighting, she knew two things.

The first was that knew her sickness, its nature, it moods. On the outside, she was fresh and new, uncorrupted. On the inside, her entire body cavity was stained black. Her heart pounded in a black epicardial soup; her lungs strained within a cavity hardening like brittle charcoal.

The second was that she felt no pain. Only joy.

Jadis and Tom had noticed how much better she'd seemed. To Jadis, Shoshana had stopped shuffling around like a penitent, and had rediscovered the spring in her step. The color had returned to her face: her skin glowed the color of soft summer sunshine. To Tom, this glow extended to a renewal of tenderness instead of ferocity, calmness instead of desperation. The evening before, they had made love as if for the very first time: her love had a sweetness that he would remember for the rest of his life. And through it all, she was cloaked in a bright electric mantle of butter-yellow, fringed with the sienna of cinnamon.

Shoshana, however, looked straight ahead at the fluid movements of the priest, and realized that Domingo had unbarred the gates for her, so that she could now see God, radiant. And God was calling to her—'come'.

Credo in unum deum, her soul replied: *Adonai eloheinu, Adonai echad*.

God knew everything, *patrem omnipotentem, melekh ha'olam*, and all we had to do was to trust him when he said that there was a purpose in being, because all the rest was commentary. She did not know why, or to what end, only that her life had meant something. It had not been for nothing, and because she had lived, the world would be different.

Avinu Malkeinu, aseh imanu tzedakah v'chesed v'hoshiyainu, she begged him: *dona nobis pacem*.

And her prayer was answered.

Tom turned round then. He noticed, first, that her face was radiant as if reflecting the last rays of the setting sun, and filled with utmost peace. And second, that she was dead.

-=0=-

To be concluded in RAGE OF STARS, Book Three of The Sigil Trilogy...

ABOUT THE AUTHOR

Author Photo by John Gilbey

Henry Gee was born in London in 1962. He received his B.Sc. in Zoology and Genetics from the University of Leeds, and his Ph.D. in Zoology from the University of Cambridge. Since 1987 he has been on the editorial staff of *Nature*, the international weekly science magazine, where he is now Senior Editor of Biological Sciences, and was the founding editor of *Futures*, *Nature*'s award-winning SF column.

He is the author of several works of nonfiction including *The Science of Middle-earth*, *In Search of Deep Time* and *Jacob's Ladder*, and a novel, *By The Sea*.

He lives in Cromer, Norfolk, England, with his family and numerous pets.

ReAnimus Press

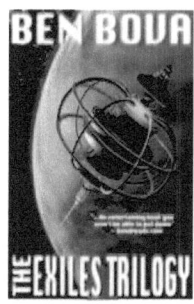

Test of Fire, by Ben Bova

The Kinsman Saga, by Ben Bova

The Craft of Writing Science Fiction that Sells, by Ben Bova

Staying Alive - A Writer's Guide,
by Norman Spinrad

Space Travel — A Guide for Writers,
by Ben Bova

Shadrach in the Furnace,
by Robert Silverberg

The Transcendent Man, by Jerry Sohl

Night Slaves, by Jerry Sohl

Bloom, by Wil McCarthy

Aggressor Six, by Wil McCarthy

Murder in the Solid State,
by Wil McCarthy

Flies from the Amber, by Wil McCarthy

Side Effects, by Harvey Jacobs

American Goliath, by Harvey Jacobs

"An inspired novel" – *TIME Magazine*
"A masterpiece…arguably this year's best novel" – *Kirkus Reviews*